Drop Dead

Robert Imrie

AuthorHouse™
1663 Liberty Drive
Bloomington, IN 47403
www.authorhouse.com
Phone: 1-800-839-8640

First published by AuthorHouse 4/6/2010

ISBN: 978-1-4490-1786-6 (e)
ISBN: 978-1-4490-1784-2 (sc)
ISBN: 978-1-4490-1785-9 (hc)

Printed in the United States of America
Bloomington, Indiana

This book is printed on acid-free paper.

For Reiko:
My flower of beauty fair.

ACKNOWLEDGEMENTS

My sincere thanks to Dan Plumeau, whose patient and diligent devotion to this project made the book better than it ever could have been otherwise; to Pat Cummisky, Bill Patterson, Bobbi Moschkau and Sheila Anderson for gentle yet meticulous proofreading; to my sister, Jean, for always having my back; to the Reference Staff at the Southdale Library in Edina, Minnesota for having answers to every question I asked; and to my wife, Reiko, constant symbol of all that is good and possible.

Characters in this book, MightyMall and the town of Saint Commercia are completely fictional.

CHAPTER 1

On the morning of Thursday, November 15th at just past seven o'clock, 77-year old Greta Turnblad strode purposefully into MightyMall, the world's largest shopping and entertainment complex, located in Saint Commercia, Minnesota.

Outside, the wind blew cold amid a slushy snowstorm. Greta had left home earlier than usual because she knew traffic would be slow going. Thick, wet flakes had been falling since midnight, with several inches expected by noon. Cloud cover kept the morning sunlight to a minimum. The temperature was 28 degrees; the dampness made it feel colder.

Greta stopped just inside the entrance, waiting for the door behind her to close. The difference in air pressure inside the building and outside created a faint moaning sound. A final *stomp! stomp! stomp!* and the remaining snow and salt fell from her boots.

The first floor of MightyMall felt like the inside of a 21st-Century techno-cathedral with its hundred-foot ceiling and galaxy of wall colors blinking like CGI-generated stained glass windows. Space above the store fronts was dominated by endless 30-foot video screens announcing special sales, upcoming celebrity appearances and testimonials by aging actors insisting that they shopped at MightyMall or they shopped nowhere at all. Public service announcements reminded everyone that MightyMall Gift Cards were "the ideal way to show you care."

Some of the video screens periodically flipped open, allowing futuristic robots to jut out above the passing crowds to sing and dance like corporate Hummel figures, spouting the name and web address of their sponsor, before returning silently to the bowels of the mall like high-tech butlers.

Greta enjoyed the shows as much as the next person but felt vaguely guilty: weren't there better things to spend money on than the myriad products they advertised? But then she remembered how much she enjoyed the climate-controlled comfort of MightyMall, or an advertisement she'd seen for something available *only at MightyMall,* erasing the guilt from her mind like an invisible Handi Wipe. *Follow the light, the light!*

Greta's cheeks burned slightly from the sudden warmth after the stinging combination of cold wind and snow outside. She was wearing a long, red, hooded parka with a flannel-lined nylon sweat suit and snow boots. She had a small frame, despite her Scandinavian heritage, barely over five feet and one hundred ten pounds. *These old bones freeze up quicker than they used to,* she thought to herself.

Greta walked over to a wooden bench in front of the Welcome Desk and pulled off the boots she always wore outside during the cold Minnesota winters. She put on a pair of white sneakers she had bought at The Sports Authority on the sixth floor, carefully tying the laces. The pink swoosh on the sides matched perfectly with her pink sweats.

Greta came to MightyMall to meet her best friend, Char Goblirsch, three times a week to walk and chat for an hour or so. They visited more frequently between October and April when it was just too cold and slippery to stroll outside. Lake Harriet, she thought, beautiful as it was to amble around in the summer, sailboats bobbing in the background, was darned unpleasant in the winter. Once the autumn leaves were gone there was nothing to stop the arctic winds that raced down from Winnipeg from rubbing your skin raw.

It never snowed inside MightyMall, was never windy, never too cold nor too warm. Greta never got lost, though the two-mile circumference could be challenging when her arthritis acted up. From a few miles away it looked like a giant, glowing piston; Greta wouldn't want a monstrosity like this in her back yard, but twenty minutes away by car was fine. She and Char used to take their walks at that other Twin Cities mega mall over in Bloomington but got tired of the confusing parking ramps named after states and fruits. Finding her car at MightyMall was a snap since that nice young man at the Welcome Desk had given her a credit-card-sized medallion with a viewing screen and metallic strip to put on her dashboard. It showed the location of her car inside the mall parking ramp and gave her step-by-step instructions to get to it from any point in the mall. No need for one of those confusing mobile phones.

"MightyMall is plenty good enough for walks," she used to tell her husband, Hank, before he succumbed to heart disease four years ago. "As long as you're safe and warm," he would say in return.

Greta liked to start early in the morning while the hallways circling the mall were still relatively people-free. Storekeepers didn't arrive for another couple of hours. Except for the coffee shops, which she never bothered with anyway; coffee gave her the runs. She and Char occasionally completed a once-around in the morning without seeing another soul, especially if they were done by eight o'clock. That was when most of the mall walkers began trickling in. *The storm will probably keep people away until 8:30 or 9 today,* she thought, as she stood up from the bench.

Greta had considered moving to a warmer climate after Hank died. They had no children and most of her friends were living in Florida or Arizona at least part of the year. But Greta liked her old house and so did her two cats. She loved her garden in the spring, and the fall colors, and all the lakes with paved walkways. And Minnesota winters were gosh darned pretty, the blankets of snow making everything look clean, quiet and peaceful. She wondered what she would do in a place like Florida that looked and felt the same year-round and was always getting washed out to sea.

The MightyMall Welcome Desk sat just inside the entrance, next to a bank of coin-operated lockers. Greta had her pick of the lot at this time of day. She walked over to one and set her handbag down on the floor. She chose a locker at eye level-no point straining her back if she didn't have to-and swung the small door open.

Greta removed her parka, carefully folded it and pushed it to the back of locker #501. She inserted her boots, careful to face the heels away from her parka; the parka was new and she didn't want to soil it. Satisfied that she had loaded all nonessential items, Greta took the four quarters she had brought specifically for the locker out of her sweatpants pocket and dropped them into the proper slot and swung the door shut. She turned the orange locker key, heard the lock click and the quarters fall as if in a slot machine, removed the key and dropped it into her pocket.

Still facing the locker, Greta paused to wonder where Char was. Char was always so punctual. Stuck in the storm? Greta began turning around when her foot struck something on the floor below: her handbag. She had forgotten to put her handbag in the locker!

"Uffda," she said. "You forgetful old biddy." She smacked herself lightly on her forehead with the palm of her hand.

Greta wondered if maybe one of those nice MightyMall security officers would open the locker for her. She wasn't trying to cheat anyone—she'd paid her dollar—but if she reopened the locker now she wouldn't be able to close it again without another dollar, which she didn't have. Surely the officer would understand her predicament and be sympathetic.

Greta looked down the great hall, hoping to catch an officer on patrol, or rounds, or whatever they called it. No one in sight.

"Well, there's a phone at the Welcome Desk," Greta said to no one in particular. "I just know there is."

She walked over to the Welcome Desk, intending to push open the wooden gate, and walk behind the counter. "I'll just call the operator and explain things to her." Or him: she had noticed more operators these days were male. The gate was closed.

The Welcome Desk wasn't actually a desk but a ten-foot-long counter flanked by two four-foot-high sides. It served as an information desk for first-time visitors, a dispenser of wheelchairs and a supplier of discount brochures and mall maps. The purpose of the wooden gate on the right side was less about security and more about containing newly arrived guests who were über-eager to get down to the business of shopping till they dropped after twenty-hour motorcoach rides from Kansas City or fifteen-hour flights from Shanghai. Everyone needed their brochures, discount cards and electronic maps now, now *NOW* and didn't want to wait in a stupid old line to get them. The concentration of so many ways to spend money in a single, enclosed building made adults behave like tweens attending a Lady Gaga concert.

Greta had seen staff reach inside the gates when they thought no one was looking and unlock the door from the inside. Standing on her toes, she reached over the gate and slid her hand around trying to find the latch. When she felt nothing latch-like after making several wide passes with her hands, she leaned farther over to get a better look.

"Oh my," Greta said, as she fell forward, ass over tea kettle as the British say, her body coming to rest inside the Welcome Desk.

Greta Turnblad was dead before her body hit the floor.

CHAPTER 2

"This is *it?"* screamed Carolyn Noxon Batch, MightyMall's Senior Vice President. "A dozen raisin cookies and coffee? For a major press conference like this?" She scanned the faces of her junior staff. "Is this a fucking *joke?"*

On a rectangular table against one wall of the Voyageurs Room sat a large imitation stainless steel serving plate adorned with twelve cookies. Two coffee dispensers sat next to the plate. Styrofoam cups were stacked between the dispensers and the serving plate. Four round meeting tables covered in white linen tablecloths sat at the far end of the rectangular room. A portable dais with microphone stood at the very back. A projection screen behind the dais proudly displayed the MightyMall logo.

"They're fresh ..." said Nicole, manager of the MightyMall VIP Premium Voyageurs Room. "I think. I mean ... they're warm. The cookies ..."

"Well, thank *God* for small favors," Carolyn snapped. She picked up a cookie, took a small bite and chewed meditatively. MightyMall's Senior Vice President had joined straight out of college. Her father was

Denny Noxon, owner of *Sell-U-Right*, the Upper Midwest's largest chain of pawnshops and a tenant in MightyMall from the start. Denny had been negotiating with the mall's owners for a space for his latest retail concept, a chain of bait and tackle shops called *Spawn.* MightyMall granted his daughter an internship in the public relations department as a gesture of good will. *Spawn* failed to catch on, but Denny's daughter swam quickly up MightyMall's corporate ladder.

Though Carolyn was only five feet five, she was still a formidable woman. She knew how to project her voice and she switched easily between four letter expletives and multi-syllabic corporate mumbo-jumbo depending on the crowd; her staff was usually on the receiving end of the expletives. For today's press conference later in the morning Carolyn was wearing a black Ann Taylor suit with a skirt that ended above the knee. She'd fretted over which shoes to wear— the Christian Louboutin platforms she preferred in cold weather like this, or the Prada pointed-toe pumps. She went with the Pradas because they were more comfortable; she would need absolute focus when talking to all those nasty reporters.

"Would you like me to call Fantastic?" asked Nicole said. "See if they can bring some more food, maybe?" Fantastic Catering had purchased exclusive rights to provide food and beverages for all MightyMall's public and private events. A representative had dropped off the cookies and coffee earlier in the morning.

"My *God*, yes!" Carolyn said. "I'm about to make the biggest announcement in the history of Minnesota in, what," she glanced at her watch, "two and a half *freekin* hours?"

"I thought it was all about the presentation," Jeff Patter said. "The project? The visuals? The future?" Patter was Carolyn's Director of Marketing. "Aren't they going to be busy watching you and the screen?

They're not really going to care what they're eating, are they?" He knew the answer but enjoyed egging Carolyn on when she got like this.

"They won't notice the food if it's good," Carolyn said, "but they will if we serve them something that looks like I picked it up at a Super America convenience store on the way in. These aren't refreshments," she waved dismissively at the cookies, "they're after-school snacks."

"Those jerks from Fantastic are simply *awful*, aren't they?" Patter said. He made a sympathetic *tsk tsk,* then pursed his lips together. Patter was slim but fit and in his mid forties. He was currently sporting a pencil mustache like the one Brad Pitt had worn recently. Consensus among the women in the office was that the look worked for Brad Pitt but not for Patter; it made him look like an effeminate Hitler.

Patter had suggested days ago that they hire a special chef for the event. If Carolyn wanted to save on costs, as she *always* did, then how about cheese, cut fruit, fresh-baked bread, and wine? Snobbery worked at events like these. Carolyn, however, in her infinite wisdom, had been confident she could bully Fantastic Catering into giving her what she wanted free of charge. *Fine,* Patter thought. *How's that working out for you?*

"It'll be great publicity for them," Carolyn had told Nicole last week, explaining why Fantastic should give them free refreshments for the event. "Tell them that. They'll make it all back in the new clients they'll get."

The Fantastic representative had been less than enthusiastic when talking to Nicole. "What do I care about publicity? I've got a spending budget and I've got sales goals. People listen to a press conference like this and then they leave and go to their next meeting. They don't give a shit what they ate at the press conference."

"But Carolyn said ..."

"Doesn't matter," the rep had said. "I'll send you some cookies and a couple pots of coffee. And that's just because you're a nice kid. But anything more than that and your boss lady is going to have to pony up and spend some real money. Sorry. It's in the contract."

"That's okay," Nicole had said. "Thanks."

"What is *wrong* with them?" Patter maintained a look of concerned consternation on his face.

Carolyn took another contemplative bite of her cookie, careful as always to display the $38,000 Cartier diamond and sapphire ring she wore on her right hand. Her father had bought it for her after her divorce from Luther.

"Is the projector hooked up?" Carolyn said.

"It will be," Nicole said. "Tech person's coming at nine o'clock. I can't remember her name."

"Are the artist renderings all set?"

Nicole snapped her fingers. "Rakhshanda … ?"

"What?"

"Sorry," Nicole said. "I think the techie's name for today's presentation is Rakhshanda. Or something like that." She shrugged. "From India, I think. Or Pakistan?"

Carolyn leveled a withering gaze at Nicole. "You might want to stay focused here, sweetie. You've already fucked up catering arrangements. Let's hope you don't make it any worse." She turned around to stare out the window.

Nicole glared at the back of Carolyn's head. "Sorry," her voice wavered. Her eyes were moist. "They're in the closet," she said. "The renderings, I mean. I'll put them up after we finish setting the tables." She fished a tissue out of her purse and dabbed her eyes, hoping no one noticed.

Patter leaned toward Nicole and spoke softly in her ear. "Honey, don't let her get to you. Everything is *always* someone else's fault. Except when something goes right; then it's all her brilliance and execution. You better learn to accept that or you'll be crying all the time."

"Coffee and twelve fucking cookies?" Carolyn said, still counting the cookie she was eating. "How many media are we expecting today?" She brushed the crumbs from her hands and picked up another cookie.

"We've invited every newspaper and magazine on the Minnesota and Wisconsin public relations list," Patter said. "Plus all the TV and radio stations … except Channel 6, of course. We're still mad at them because their reporter snuck that piece of dynamite into the mall."

"The police should've arrested him, the prick," Carolyn said. "And stop saying dynamite. It was a firecracker with the fuse removed."

"Right." Patter nodded obediently. "A firecracker. But our sniffer dog gave the Channel 6 guy a pass and started barking instead at some guy eating a bratwurst ten feet away. Channel 6's camera caught the whole thing."

"Filming inside our mall, private property, without permission." Carolyn pursed her lips together.

"Right." Patter shrugged. "Not much we could do. It was already done."

"Bastards."

Carolyn became Vice President eleven years after joining the mall, the same day she filed for divorce from her husband, Luther. She had taken the morning off to sign the divorce papers and got back to the mall in time to field calls from the media about her promotion.

Carolyn had suspected her husband of infidelity since she became pregnant with their daughter. She'd hired a private eye who followed Luther one weekend in January to one of the hundreds of secluded lakes in the Voyageurs National Park. Employing state-of-the-art cold-weather scuba diving equipment, the detective slid a pinhole video camera up a hole under the ice fishing house that Carolyn's daddy had given Luther. The video revealed her husband playing Hide the Walleye with his own set of Minnesota twins, Laura and Ashley.

The divorce was quick and painful, for Luther. Their house, a wedding gift from Carolyn's father, was already in her name, as was the cabin near Giant's Ridge and the 50,000 shares of *Sell-U-Right* Daddy had given her when the company went public. The clarity of the ice fishing video also allowed Carolyn to secure Luther's BMW, his prized shotgun collection and his hunting dog, Ruby. Carolyn allowed Luther to keep the ice fishing house.

"Carolyn, could we maybe spare some extra money for a menu upgrade, just this one time?" asked Lucy Evans, Carolyn's Administrative Assistant. "Assuming there's still time to get the additional food here? To make sure everything goes right?"

Carolyn was gazing out the window overlooking Gonzoland, the giant amusement park occupying twenty acres in the center of MightyMall.

"How much did we pay for this anyway?" Patter said. He knew the answer but liked to ask. He thought Carolyn looked like Tammy Faye Bakker. He waited until Carolyn was looking at him before he shook his head, pursed his lips again and hunched his shoulders to convey his disdain for Fantastic Catering.

"They make a mint from our *damn* contract," Carolyn said. "They've got a food service monopoly, for Christ's sake. They can afford to spring for breakfast once in a while. Aren't they required to do these events for free?" She turned toward Patter, who was at that moment thinking about the shoe sale at Bloomingdale's due to start later in the day.

"Hmm?" Patter said. "Um, I don't know."

"Lucy?" Carolyn said.

Lucy Evans kept track of Carolyn's schedule, screened incoming calls, typed reports and was her all-around gofer. She was thirty years old and single with shoulder-length dark blond hair. She kept her bangs long to hide persistent acne on her forehead that had broken out soon after she started working for Carolyn.

"Well, I know the management office is entitled to a twenty percent discount on food and non-alcoholic beverages," Lucy said. "I don't know about free breakfasts, though. Sorry. I'll check the contract when we get back to the office."

"Fine," Carolyn said, starting for the door. "Nicole, call Fantastic *now* and tell them we've got $250 to spend, and that's *it.* I want fresh-baked muffins, fresh-sliced cantaloupe—honeydew and orange—for 20 … no … for 30 people. And I want it here in two hours, or tell them I'm canceling their contract." She picked up another cookie as she headed for the door.

"Yes, Carolyn." Nicole said.

Carolyn looked at her watch. "Eight o'clock. Come on Lucy. It's time for morning rounds."

"Yes, Carolyn."

CHAPTER 3

Security Officer Mike Foreman rushed into the West 1 Entrance of MightyMall, skidding briefly after clearing the mat in front of the door before catching himself. He had punched in late for the previous day's shift after his car wouldn't start. Foreman's next-door neighbor had been nice enough to give him a jump start but he still arrived ten minutes late. Foreman's boss would not look favorably on a repeat performance. He had left thirty minutes earlier than usual this morning because of the snow, but traffic backed up when a tractor-trailer jackknifed near the Fridley exit on Interstate 694. Foreman didn't want to get a reputation as a slacker after just two months on the job. He was hard working and diligent and took his job seriously.

Foreman had brown hair, was fit and, as the women would say, a hunk. He walked with an easy grace seen most often in world-class athletes who are physically and emotionally comfortable with themselves. He had been active his whole life, working for years on his father's farm, and he had also been a swimmer in high school. He kept in shape these days by riding his bicycle as often as he could. He entered the Lifetime Fitness Triathlon each summer.

Something in the corner of his eye caught Foreman's attention. A red handbag on the floor over by the lockers. He looked at his watch. 7:55 A.M. Five minutes until his shift started. He did not want to be late for work again. He looked back out the door he just came in, then down the hall. No one in sight. He looked at the lockers. No one nearby.

Foreman looked back at the handbag. It looked like a woman's bag. He jogged over to the women's room and knocked on the door. "Excuse me. Mall security. Anyone in there?" No response.

He cracked open the door and stuck his head in. "Anyone in here leave a handbag out by the lockers?" Silence.

"Damn." The Lost and Found department was not on the way to security; no way he'd be able to drop it off and punch in on time. He checked his watch again. The digital face of his Timex Ironman Triathlon read seven fifty-seven.

Foreman couldn't assume that the owner would come back and retrieve it before someone stole it. And he couldn't pretend he hadn't seen it. Foreman picked up the bag and sprinted toward security. He would stow the bag in his locker until after morning roll call. There'd be time to bring it to Lost and Found after roll call.

As Foreman reached the basement and rounded the corner for security, he passed Eric Lemke of the maintenance department.

Lemke saw the bag Foreman was carrying and whistled. "I like it. The color brings out the highlights in your hair."

Foreman gave Lemke a good-natured middle finger as he ran by, then stopped suddenly. "Hey, I thought you were off this weekend. Going to Missouri or something, weren't you?"

"Don't fucking ask," Lemke said, as Foreman arrived at security and pushed through the door. "I'll be here all weekend."

CHAPTER 4

"Come on, Lucy," Carolyn said. "We need to finish up rounds early today."

Carolyn began each morning inspecting the interior of MightyMall. She wanted to see the mall from a guest's perspective. Were the facilities clean and well maintained? Did MightyMall have products and services that their bread-and-butter guests—middle class families with two kids—wanted? Were there enough high-end stores for the wealthier guests, empty nesters, and DINKS (Dual Income No Kids), and were they separated sufficiently from the Joe Six-pack shoppers to prevent awkward intersections? Carolyn herself wouldn't be found dead in a Magnet Max, Al's Farm Toys, Sears, or, heaven forbid, a food court, and knew that others in her income bracket and social class felt the same. She had to constantly remind those damn leasing people not to place a Chopper World next to a Williams Sonoma but mistakes happened nonetheless, and she had to be ever vigilant.

The mall's two-mile circumference was too long for Carolyn to circumnavigate on foot. She did her rounds riding in an electric cart she had appropriated from maintenance years ago. The carts, "Cushmans" everyone called them, were capable of doing ten miles per hour—though no one was supposed to drive that fast—which allowed Carolyn to inspect one or two floors each morning without impacting the rest of her workday. She drove while Lucy took notes.

"Tell LeVander these floors look like they're covered in dried piss." Karl LeVander was MightyMall's Managing Director of Operations and made no secret of his desire for Carolyn's position.

"No, cancel that." Carolyn stroked her lip with her index finger. "Let's put it this way. Ask our dear Karl if there's any *possibility* that he could find in his budget enough money to keep the MightyMall floors more *hygienic* so that we can protect Titanic Properties' investment." Carolyn turned the electric cart slightly to the right and headed toward the entrance of Nieman Marcus, one of MightyMall's seven full size department stores.

Floor plans for each of the seven floors looked like perfect circles, which had caused several months of consternation for the developers when it came time for them to provide addresses for each of the mall's 2,000 tenants. Assigning Cole Hahn the address "382" might clue people to the fact that it was located somewhere on the third floor, but not whether it was on the north, south, east or west side. The operations people had wanted to divide the floors into geographical sections, but the building's shape, a circle, didn't provide natural landmarks to serve as the end of the "Northeast" and "Southeast" sections. The owners worried that confused shoppers might lose their way, become frustrated after one visit, and never return. The marketing people finally won the day with their compromise to divide the mall into northern and southern hemispheres. "Northern Lights" would have more interior lighting, more stores themed after products or services associated with the northern climes of the United States and Canada—outdoor sports, nature, Nordstrom, coffee shops, Broadway theaters, and stores selling high tech goods. "Southern Warmth," it was decided, would have hotels, Southern hospitality, aquariums, travel agencies, Tommy Bahama and convenience stores (because of their connection to gas stations and oil.) Signs on each floor would read "Northern Lights 1," "Southern Warmth 6," and so on. The leasing department, miffed that they were not consulted in the planning process, "We're the ones who have to find paying tenants, you know!" went along with the theme regulations for the first year. When storefront spaces became available after that, leasing filled them with whichever store could pay the most rent, regardless of their product category. The mall soon had beachwear stores in Northern Lights and a store selling hockey merchandise in Southern Warmth. Customers didn't care about themes as long as they could find the stores they wanted.

What shoppers didn't like were long, cumbersome entrance and exit names. "Southern Warmth East 4" soon became "South 4" regardless of how hard the mall tried to educate people with TV adds and mall circulars— "Thirty percent off today only on *Southern Warmth East 4!"* The official floor designations remained in name only. Shorthand and expediency had prevailed.

Carolyn gazed briefly inside the Nieman Marcus entrance, beyond the shuttered gates, and headed back onto the main thoroughfare.

"Commend Karl," she continued, "on the great job his team does sweeping and mopping, but mention that the volume of dried chewing gum and unidentifiable sticky fluids on the floors concerns me. Tell him that perhaps the cleaning solvents his team is using, particularly in light of recent increased outbreaks of the H1N1 flu, influenza and SARS—"

"Wasn't SARS several years ago?" Lucy said.

Carolyn glared at Lucy. She didn't like to be interrupted. "Fine, leave that out," she said, dismissing the triviality of details with a wave of her hand. "But in light of those other things, tell Karl that I *am* concerned that an outbreak of a serious illness here at the mall would reflect badly on the owners, and isn't there perhaps a stronger solvent his people could use? Or maybe better and additional training?"

Lucy scribbled dutifully.

"Write that up and send me a draft. I'll edit and get it back to you before I leave for the day."

"Do you want me to email it to Karl and put a hard copy in his mail box?"

"Yes." The corners of Carolyn's mouth curled up slightly in a smile that, while not as frightening as Jack Nicholson's Joker, was absent both sincerity and warmth. "Yes!" she said, with the same tone of voice one might use in response to the question, *Shall we go have ice cream?* "Yes. And why don't we copy Phil at headquarters this time for good measure." Carolyn meant Phil Kahn, President of Titanic Properties, the mall's owners. "I'm sure he'd like to know how well Karl is, or is *not*, taking care of the building."

"Got it."

Carolyn smiled brightly and stopped the cart momentarily. "Now. Let's go check the collateral displays at one of the Welcome Desks. They're always a mess." Carolyn punched the accelerator pedal and launched the Cushman back on its way.

"Christ, look at that." Carolyn pointed as she stopped in front of the West 1 Entrance Welcome Desk. "Those brochure racks are a freekin mess."

Carolyn pulled out her iPhone and snapped off a few photos. Karl always pooh-poohed her complaints about poor appearance and service at the Welcome Desks. Carolyn thought the primary mission of Welcome Desks should be to create positive first impressions of the mall. She wanted to see smiling, helpful desk clerks eager to hand out mall maps and brochures, committed to ensuring a satisfactory mall experience, dedicated to generating revenue for Titanic Properties by selling coupon books, gift cards and souvenir shopping bags to visitors who may not have realized they even needed them. She overheard Karl say once that mall visitors were like in-laws he took care of because he had to.

"Wait a sec," Carolyn said. "Let's see if last night's closing staff cleaned and locked all the cabinets."

Carolyn walked around the side of the Welcome Desk and leaned inside to flip the door latch and inhaled sharply.

"Oh, my fucking God," she said.

"What?" Lucy was still sitting in the Cushman, writing down Carolyn's last salvo of notes.

"Oh, my fucking Jesus Christ."

Lucy got up from the Cushman and walked over to stand next to Carolyn.

"Oh my God," Lucy squealed. "Jesus God Almighty." She placed both hands over her mouth and nose and started backing away. She whimpered like a small dog that needs to go outside.

Carolyn ran over to Lucy and grabbed her arm. "Hold on there, sister." She looked around, relieved that no one else was in sight.

"It's okay," Carolyn said. "Shh shh. It's okay." She put her arm around Lucy's waist and started walking her back to the Welcome Desk.

"No. No. No," Lucy repeated over and over. "I can't. No. No. No."

"It's all right," Carolyn said in her best imitation of a soothing tone. "Just get over by the gate," and with a final heave, Carolyn pushed Lucy back to the side of the Welcome Desk.

Lucy stood motionless, looking down intently at her shoes. She was breathing heavily.

Carolyn stepped back to the Welcome Desk counter and looked down at the twisted body on the floor.

She surprised herself by how unafraid she was. She had never seen a dead body before. The only funeral she'd attended had been that of her grandmother years ago. Carolyn had been four at the time. Everyone wore black, like in church. She remembered holding Mother's hand as they walked to the front of the room and sat in a reserved seat.

Carolyn had noticed a large wooden box surrounded by pretty flowers. A black and white photo of her grandmother stood on an easel behind the box. She leaned forward and looked down the rows of chairs to the left and right, then behind her, searching for her grandmother. She found Daddy, who sat staring straight ahead, and Peggy the maid, who looked like she was crying, and some of Mommy and Daddy's friends. And there was Grandpa sitting closer to the big box.

"Where's Grammy?" Carolyn had asked. "Is she up there?" She pointed toward the casket. "Is she in there?"

"Hush down, Carolyn," her mother had whispered.

"Is she sleeping? Is Grammy sleeping up there?"

"We talked about this earlier, *didn't* we, Carolyn?" her mother had said. "You must be quiet today."

"But why?" Carolyn had sensed that something was wrong but didn't know what. No one had smiled back when she smiled and waved at people as they walked in. "Where's Grammy?"

"Be *quiet!*" her mother had said. "You're upsetting all the nice guests with this childishness." Carolyn saw Daddy turn and look at her mother with an expression she had seen when they used to quarrel sometimes before he moved away. He looked down at Carolyn for a moment and smiled like he used to do when she fell down or bumped her head.

Carolyn's mother noticed her ex-husband and daughter looking at each other and slapped Carolyn on her left thigh. Carolyn yelped in pain and started to cry. Her mother rubbed the red spot on Carolyn's leg and said, "Look what you made me do. Now be a good girl."

Carolyn was brought back to the present when Lucy took in a large breath, pursed her lips and let the air out slowly, creating a faint whistle.

The sound startled Carolyn. She noticed, in a clinical way, that the dead woman didn't look at all like her grandmother, who had been almost six feet tall and big boned. The woman lying inside the Welcome Desk was short and thin. She looked more like old Aunt Dora, who wasn't really an aunt at all but had been a fixture at family holiday gatherings until Carolyn went off to college. She heard from one of her friends back home—she couldn't remember who—that Dora had died of congestive heart failure. Carolyn never liked Dora much—she smelled like old cooking oil.

Dead Dora—not knowing this dead woman's actual name, Carolyn had unconsciously attached that moniker to the body—lay with eyes wide open, as if she had been surprised before dying. Carolyn wondered what the woman had been surprised about. Maybe everyone was surprised to die. The body lay unnaturally, legs and arms folded in a way that wouldn't happen to someone who had just dropped dead and crumpled to the ground. Had someone attacked the woman? Carolyn looked around her reflexively.

"What?" Lucy said, startled.

"Nothing," Carolyn said, distractedly. Could someone have attacked Dead Dora here in the mall? That would not be good. A death from natural causes—the lady *was* old after all—could be managed with good public relations. Maybe she had a heart attack. Too bad, that's life, buy the old bag's family some flowers, no more press coverage in a day or two, end of story. But a murder? Here? Now? Carolyn shook her head sharply as if warding off a nightmare.

"What?" said Lucy, staring at her boss, now more exasperated than afraid.

Carolyn turned away from Lucy, waiving her hand distractedly, as if shooing away a gnat. Could someone have killed Dead Dora and brought her here? Maybe hired by a competing mall or attraction? She looked again at the entrance and down the hall to confirm that she and Lucy were still alone, then down at Dead Dora. Carolyn guessed the woman was probably in her late 70s. The sweat suit suggested that she was a mall walker. Carolyn hated mall walkers; the biggest bunch of complainers she had ever seen, and they never spent any money in the mall. Just walked around and gabbed, bitching if the heat was too low in the winter or too high in the summer. Bunch of leeches.

Carolyn noticed a gash over Dead Dora's left eye and a small amount of dried blood on her face and the floor underneath. This was no natural accident.

"Lucy, you stay here while I see if she's still alive." Carolyn already knew the woman was dead—no one would lay on the floor in that position with eyes open if they were alive—but she needed to make sure. It wouldn't do to have the woman make a miraculous recovery and tell the jury that MightyMall's Senior Vice President had left her there to suffer in agony; and please award me $50 million dollars in stocks or bonds for unusual pain and suffering.

Lucy was silent.

Carolyn unlatched the gate but it wouldn't open. Dead Dora was wedged against it. Carolyn shoved again and was gratified that the body slid slightly. She planted her feet on the floor behind her for leverage and pushed again. After four tries, Dead Dora had slid over enough to allow the gate to open about six inches, enough for Carolyn to shimmy her way in. She put one foot near Dora's head, held onto the gate for balance, and stepped over Dead Dora's body. She let the gate close behind her and knelt down.

She touched Dead Dora's neck, gingerly, searching for a pulse. Carolyn wasn't sure where to touch. She pressed her index finger into the underside of the woman's jaw. Nothing.

Carolyn thought of something and yanked her arm away.

"What?" Lucy said. She was beginning to worry about Carolyn's twitches and ticks and talking to herself. Was her boss going crazy?

"Nothing," Carolyn said. "I just ... never mind." It had occurred to Carolyn that by touching the woman's body she might be leaving small amounts of DNA that could later be traced back to her and construed by some asshole DA as evidence of her guilt. She had been an avid fan of CSI and its progeny for years.

Carolyn relaxed when it occurred to her that she hadn't done anything wrong. But she thought it best to have a back up story, just to be safe. *Officer, I tried to save the poor woman, I truly did. Alas, I failed.*

She touched her own neck until she found a pulse. She touched the woman's neck in the same place. No pulse.

"She's dead."

Carolyn stood up and smoothed out her skirt. She scanned the area again, confirming no one was in the vicinity. That would soon change. She pulled her left earlobe with the index finger and thumb of her left hand, something she did unconsciously when nervous. Dead Dora was going to be a problem. Two dozen TV, radio and newspaper journalists were on their way to MightyMall to attend a press conference later in the morning. TV crews might already be setting up and testing equipment. If any of them found out that a little old lady had died in MightyMall this very morning, they would be down here faster than a pack of dogs on a three-legged cat. They would skip her press conference altogether.

"Lucy," Carolyn said. "We can't let this happen."

"Lucy!" Lucy had drifted away from the Welcome Desk. "Get the fuck over here!"

Lucy resumed studying her shoes.

Carolyn stepped over the body, exited the Welcome Desk, walked over to Lucy and grabbed her arms. "Lucy?" She shook her assistant slightly. "Anybody home?"

"Can we call the police now?" Lucy said. "I don't feel very well."

"Lucy, I need you to listen to me." Carolyn put her arm around Lucy's shoulder and guided her back to the Welcome Desk. "We are not going to call the police."

Lucy looked up for the first time. "Not call the police? You're not serious. We can't just leave a dead body here."

"Lucy, you don't seem to understand how important today is. The press conference at eleven o'clock? The press conference I have been planning for two months? The press conference where I get to announce the launch of MightyMall 2?"

"I know, but ... geez." Lucy shook her head as if waking from a dream. "That poor woman is dead. Don't we have to tell someone?"

"It'll be a zoo." Carolyn sounded like a mother explaining to her child why they couldn't go to Disneyland on the Fourth of July. "The reporters, the cameras? Think how the owners will feel if today's top news story is about a dead old lady dumped at MightyMall. How will that make us look?"

"I know, but ..." Lucy said. "But it's ... the body ... it's already *here*. And what do you mean dumped? You think somebody killed this lady and brought her body here?"

"You tell me," Carolyn said. "She's inside the Welcome Desk area—an area that's been locked since last night. She's dressed in sweats, meaning she had to have come in here this morning. She's got a gash on her head, which you don't get from having a heart attack. You tell me how she got in there."

"Well ..."

"One thing is for sure, it wasn't a natural death. Which means someone killed her and dumped her body here. Do we want that kind of publicity? Can we *afford* that kind of publicity? Am I getting *through* to you?" Carolyn didn't appreciate having to explain herself.

"But what other choice do we have?" Lucy said. "Are you saying we should, what, move it somewhere else? Hide it? Like a cover up?"

"Not cover it up." Carolyn moved her head closer to Lucy's and whispered in her ear, as if sharing a secret. "Transfer it."

"Transfer it?" Lucy shook her head slightly.

"Maybe," Carolyn said, "just maybe, we can turn this into a positive."

Lucy stared at Carolyn. "How can a dead old lady be a positive?"

"For the mall," Carolyn said. "For the mall." Her voice became more soothing. "Bear with me for a second. Who in Minnesota is not going to be excited by our expansion plans?"

"Who isn't ... huh?"

Carolyn now spoke to Lucy as if she were a dimwitted child. "What organizations ... who will not be happy to see MightyMall more than double in size?"

"Oh," Lucy said, struggling to follow Carolyn's logic. "Um. People living nearby? Nature lovers? Tax payers who don't want to subsidize the construction?"

"No, no, no!" Carolyn took a deep breath to calm herself. "What businesses?"

"Oh, I know that." Lucy was disappointed she hadn't gotten the answer on the first try. "Other shopping malls and amusement parks."

"Exactly! The same people who would love nothing better than to see the mall roasted in the press for a suspicious death," Carolyn said. "You see where I'm going with this?"

"I, um … no."

Carolyn pinched the bridge of her nose and took another deep breath, then opened her eyes and smiled brilliantly at Lucy. "Lucy, we need to do unto our enemies before they do unto us. We can't afford a body being found here, so…."

"You're not saying…."

"Yes," Carolyn said. "We're going to move the body. We're going to give this problem to one of the other shopping malls. I just don't know yet which one."

"You're not serious," Lucy said. "That's like … that would be … that's not legal."

"Maybe not," Carolyn said, clapping her hands together, ready to get down to business. "But that's what we've got to do. For you, for me, for everyone at MightyMall."

"I just don't know if I'm comfortable with this," Lucy said. "I mean … couldn't we get into a lot of trouble? I don't want to go to jail."

"No one's going to jail," Carolyn said. "Besides, and completely unrelated to this, I've been thinking about the great work you've done for me these past few years."

Sure you have, thought Lucy. *That's why you keep giving me those two percent annual raises.*

"I've always wanted to do more for you, of course, but there's just never enough in the budget to pay you what you deserve."

But enough for your six figure bonuses, though, isn't there? I end up with a gift certificate to one of the restaurants in the mall—which you get for free—and flowers on Administrative Assistant's Day.

"So I've been thinking of how I can properly show you how much your hard work and professionalism mean to me."

This oughta be good, Lucy thought.

"How would you like to use my vacation home up in Lutsen for your next vacation? You and a friend. My niece, Emily, is the only one who ever uses it, and she hasn't been there since she started medical school at Selby University."

That's it? Your bribe to keep my mouth shot about finding a dead body is one week's use of your precious cabin? If you want my silence then you're gonna have to do better than that!

Something at that moment broke inside Lucy, like a rubber band pulled too tight, or a painful cramp releasing after prolonged agony. Lucy's head cleared. She felt calmer now, more collected, than she had in years. Her fear of seeing a corpse and the potential legal problems for helping Carolyn with her crazy plan were fading against the anger she felt at the paltry size of the bribe. *Do you think so little of me that you believe you can shut me up by giving me something that costs you nothing?*

Lucy nodded once, as if giving Carolyn's offer careful consideration, then looked her straight in the eye. "Gosh, Carolyn," she said, with all the enthusiasm of someone visiting their proctologist, "a week at your vacation home. Gosh. I don't know what to say."

"It's the least I can do," Carolyn said, oblivious to sarcasm from subordinates.

"But, you know," Lucy said, as she screwed her mouth up in an expression she hoped conveyed concern. "And I don't want you to think I don't appreciate the offer, because I do. Really. But my big problem right now is my car."

"You're having car problems?" Carolyn said, eager to accommodate. "Well, you don't have to use the vacation home now. You can wait till your car is fixed and use it anytime—"

"No, and I'm sorry to interrupt," Lucy said. "What I mean is, my car is a piece of crap. I could never afford to buy a new one, and the one I have now already had seventy five thousand miles on it when I bought it three years ago."

"I don't think I know what you mean," Carolyn said. But she did. Lucy could see by the look on Carolyn's face that she knew exactly what Lucy meant. This made Lucy happy.

"I love working for you," Lucy said, lying, knowing that Carolyn knew that she was lying. "I hope to work for you for many, *many* more years. But my salary is too low for me to afford a decent car. It's all I can do just to keep it running."

Carolyn's face hardened. She was trying to smile, but the muscles in her face seemed to have stopped working. "I suppose we could discuss a larger raise."

"A raise would be great," Lucy said. "Ten percent a year would keep me ahead of inflation."

"Lucy, I don't know about—"

"But, you see, my immediate need is a car. A *new* car." Lucy's smile radiated with warmth and excitement, happy to offer an equitable solution. "I'd prefer a Toyota Prius because it's so environmentally friendly and all. But if they are out of stock I'd be fine with a Camry."

The pseudo-smile was gone from Carolyn's face. No more pretenses. "You want me to buy you a new car?"

"Wow, that would be great," Lucy said. "Thank you! And that raise would be great too."

Lucy's annual performance appraisals had always been adequate, but not exceptional. Carolyn had written the previous year that Lucy was competent but lacked passion for her work, that she was more reactive than proactive, that she said, "Okay, I'll do that" more often than she said, "How can I help you?"

Coincidentally, Lucy felt increasingly passionate about the direction this conversation was heading.

Lucy had noticed that Carolyn loved telling people about her divorce. About how certain compromising photographs of her ex-husband and two women in an ice fishing hut had allowed her to take him to the cleaners in divorce court. Lucy often heard Carolyn telling the story over the phone and to senior female colleagues in the office. When she told the story to Lucy—every six months or so—she told it as an allegory. *Learn from this experience*, Carolyn would say. *The bastards can't push you around if you have the goods on them.* The bastards she was referring to were men, but the takeaway for Lucy was that bastards of any gender could push you around only for as long as they had power over you. Power to hire you, fire you, make your life miserable.

Lucy realized that Carolyn, unbalanced by her desperation, or perhaps just underestimating Lucy because she had held sway over her for so long, had unwittingly handed significant power to her administrative assistant by initiating talk of a bribe.

Lucy had no embarrassing photographs … yet … but Carolyn's desperation to hide an embarrassing corpse on this day had given Lucy power she had never known before. Lucy was passionate in her dislike of her boss's disregard for others, about Carolyn's relentless drive to look out only for herself. She was angry at Carolyn for assuming Lucy would automatically go along with her illegal scheme, to put herself in legal jeopardy, simply because she was ordered to do so. She was thrilled by this opportunity to turn the tables. The car and pay raise would be nice, and Lucy had no doubt that Carolyn would give in. What most excited her was that Carolyn would pay a steep price for what she was asking

Lucy to do. An Eveready Battery of a price that Lucy would make sure Carolyn kept on paying and paying and paying.

"Fine." Carolyn didn't have time to argue. She'd deal with her problematic assistant later.

"Okay," Lucy told Carolyn, "How can I help you?"

CHAPTER 5

Officer Foreman sat in the security gym waiting for the morning briefing. Slightly out of breath, he'd thrown the handbag that he found into his locker, punched in hurriedly and sat down at exactly eight o'clock.

Security used the room for roll call, departmental meetings, birthdays and other celebrations. Fold up and stow the aluminum chairs, unroll the gray exercise mats and you had a place for calisthenics and self-defense drills.

There wasn't a lot of violence in the mall. Drunken brawls, kids carrying a grudge from school, car break-ins. Tenants bitched to management when security officers failed to give chase after shoplifters, but apprehending petty criminals wasn't their mission. Mall security would track the perpetrators and notify the Saint Commercia Police, who maintained a small substation in the mall. Security used to detain suspects themselves. Arresting officers then had to testify, requiring additional staffing while they were in court. The mall decided it was cheaper to give the Saint Commercia Police a rent-free office on the seventh floor.

A semi-autonomous unit within the security department called the X-Team existed solely to look for terrorists. Its primary jobs were to prevent physical harm to shoppers and tenants and protect the structural integrity of MightyMall. Thefts and fistfights didn't concern them. AK 47s, Ricen and C4 did. Publicly, they acted and dressed like mall guests; privately, they were a combination inside reconnaissance unit and SWAT team. The owners approved higher base pay for the unit's members, who were usually recruited out of the military or college by an ex-KGB security expert the mall had hired after 9/11. The head of security briefed senior management directly on the X-Team's activities. They liked to call themselves the X-Team, after the old *X-Files* TV show, though the security department's budget referred to them only as "IIA," which was not spelled out anywhere in the budget, but which stood for Internal Intelligence Activities. Uniformed security officers signed secrecy documents forbidding them to discuss or acknowledge the existence of the X-Team or its members. No one else inside or outside the mall knew about them.

The X-Team employed extensive racial and behavioral profiling. Because the X-Team did not belong to a public organization and kept their data private, there was no one to complain about trampled rights. Shoppers and diners with beards and guests of apparent Middle Eastern descent got a closer look than Caucasians. The X-Team looked at style of dress. They looked for behavior inconsistent with that of a person coming to shop, eat or play at the mall. The X-Team dressed in plain clothes and walked the mall looking for anyone taking pictures that the average tourist wouldn't photograph—building support columns, unmarked exits, entrances to the internal network of mall hallways, anyone spending an inordinate amount of time looking at security cameras.

The X-Team chatted up anyone they deemed suspicious. *Hello there. Are you enjoying your visit to MightyMall? Say, may I ask why you were taking photos of those exit areas?* Some of these guests might be escorted to the security office in the basement for a more detailed discussion and asked to provide copies of their ID, passport, driver's license, whatever. Hidden high tech cameras photographed the guests during interviews. Most guests were released within thirty minutes and given a coupon book or ride passes for their inconvenience. MightyMall entered the guest's photograph, copies of their ID, and the video files of the interview into a database the mall had purchased from a company in Israel. Copies were forwarded daily to the FBI. Security did their best not to ruffle feathers but chose safety over "Political Correctness."

Foreman's boss, MightyMall Security Chief Matthew "Major" Power, strode into the gym. The X-Team members leapt to attention.

"Morning, Sir!" they shouted in unison.

Power was wearing black pants, combat boots and a crisp, white shirt. His hair was blond and short. His blue eyes were deep-set. He was six-three and built like a linebacker. Fellow officers joked that he looked like Ivan Drago from *Rocky IV.*

Power had grown up in central Iowa and joined the army right out of high school. He was sent to Kuwait just after basic training and served in Operation Desert Storm. He retired five years ago, just shy of his thirty-eighth birthday. Several police departments in the area had extended invitations to Power to join their ranks, but he was happy running MightyMall security. His wife liked the regular hours and relative safety of her husband's current job. He liked the pay and the freedom to pursue his hobby of writing action novels. To date, none had been published but Power was getting positive feedback from his agent.

Conducting morning briefings for uniformed officers fell to one of the sergeants, lieutenants or captains in security.

Power supervised the X-Team directly.

"Morning, gentlemen," Power said. "And lady." He nodded to the sole female member of the day shift. "Here are today's floor assignments. Henderson," Power said, handing several sheets of paper to one of the officers in the front row, "hand these out, will you?"

"Yes, sir," Henderson said.

"All right, then," Power said. "Computers in the Security Action Center estimate we had just under two hundred thousand visitors yesterday. A tad slow for this time of year." Power flipped through several pages of reports. "Saint Commercia Police reported twenty-seven arrests, mostly shoplifting. Thirty-two car break-ins. A few dustups at *Sell-U-Right* when the store ran out of the 'gently used engagement rings' they'd advertised via text messages to the mall's subscription database and a 30-second ad beamed on the mall video boards."

Power looked up from his clipboard. "Anybody get that text message *Sell-U-Right* sent out between one and four o'clock yesterday?"

Four officers raised their hands. "Anybody not already signed up to get these things, make sure you subscribe by the end of the day. We gotta keep on top of unexpected traffic surges."

"Sir, yes, sir!"

"What a clusterfuck that was. Five hundred engagement rings at 70 percent off regular prices, and they send out ten thousand text messages. It was a stampede. What the hell did they expect?" Power shook his head in disgust. "Says here one lady pulled off some poor schmuck's prosthetic arm fighting for a place in line. Another lady kicked a guy in the nuts."

Power tossed his clipboard on the table behind him. "Other than that, a pretty standard day. The Voyageurs Room's got some press conference today about the expansion."

"Is it true they are going to announce the plans today?" Officer Kiyomi Nagata said. "For the Phase II expansion, I mean?" Kiyomi's long hair poked out in a ponytail from the back of the baseball cap she was wearing.

Kiyomi had come to Minnesota from Kobe, Japan, after high school. Her mother, Harumi, had hoped that Kiyomi, her only child, would grow up and marry a nice Japanese *salaryman*—white color worker— and give her two grandchildren. Harumi had known that was unlikely to happen from the time Kiyomi was in elementary school, when her daughter had announced that she would live in America someday. Kiyomi had always been a willful child, too independent for most potential suitors in Japan.

Kiyomi's parents sent her to The Bristol International Academy in Kobe after elementary school to give her a broader view of the world than she had gotten in the productive but regimented Japanese school system. Neither of her parents spoke English, but half of Kiyomi's classes at Bristol were taught in English and the majority of the students there were from the United States, Canada and Europe. Kiyomi graduated from high school fluent in both Japanese and English.

When Kiyomi skipped the Japanese college entrance exams, still intent on pursuing her dream of living in the United States, her father told her he would pay for one year of college in the United States; after that she would be on her own. Kiyomi used her savings and worked part-time jobs to finance her way through four years at the University of Minnesota Twin Cities.

Kiyomi had majored in pre-law but was fascinated by American spy agencies like the CIA, NSA and FBI. She was recruited straight out of the U of M because of her language skills. Eighteen MightyMall officers, including Kiyomi, spoke English as a second language. She considered MightyMall a good first step in her career plans.

"South Park North, I think," Officer Foreman said. "That's what they're calling MightyMall's expansion."

"Are you serious?" Kiyomi said.

Foreman nodded. "Pretty sure."

One of the other officers chuckled. "No, you are joking, aren't you?" Kiyomi laughed at her own gullibility. "I don't believe you."

Kiyomi was wearing a black cashmere turtleneck sweater and blue jeans. She ran thirty miles a week and was a fourth degree black belt in karate.

"It's true." Foreman thought Kiyomi looked like the Japanese actress Koyuki, whom he had seen in *The Last Samurai* opposite Tom Cruise. "There's going to be a giant statue of Eric Cartman from *South Park* greeting people as they arrive."

The other officers laughed. Security team members took their jobs and their commitment to the safety of the mall's guests and employees seriously. They felt less loyal to senior management, which had cut nine positions in security last year. Foreman had heard officers grumble that they felt like hired help, not part of the same club that other departments—marketing, public relations, events, tourism and sponsorship—were in. But to each other, and Major Power, their loyalty and support were absolute.

"Funny," Power said. When the laughter died down, he said. "Just don't let anyone from Management hear you talking like that. Especially today."

Officer Henderson asked, "You want us to patrol extra up near the Voyageurs Room during that press conference?" Henderson was covering floors six and seven today.

"Negative," Power said. "Listen, I don't give a fuck if today they announce a cure for painful rectal itch. Your job—your *only* job—is to make sure nobody blows up the mall or gathers information they can send to someone else so that *they* can blow up the mall. You just keep doing what I pay you the big bucks for."

Several of the officers groaned good-naturedly. They liked and respected Major Power and knew how lucky they were to work for him. But security department salaries at MightyMall were not high. Most officers worked there for the training they received under Major Power and the hope that they could eventually parlay their experience into a "real" job one day at an area police department or even the FBI, CIA, or Homeland Security.

"Even if one of the vice presidents or directors asks us to unlock their cars because they locked their keys inside them?" Frivolous requests from senior management were infamous.

"Especially if they ask that," Power said. "They give you a hard time, you just say, 'Yes, sir, I'll get right on it' and walk away. Then you radio me, tell me what they asked you to do, and get back to your fucking job. Everybody got that?"

"Sir, yes, sir," the officers yelled in unison.

"Okay, you knuckleheads. Now get the hell out of here."

CHAPTER 6

Officer Foreman left the security gym, retrieved the red handbag from his locker and headed to the Lost and Found department. His watch said 8:30 A.M. If it was a mall walker who had left the bag, she probably hadn't finished a complete circuit of the mall yet and might not even know she had lost her bag.

Lost and Found was located down a blind alley on the south side of the second floor of Gonzoland. Easy to find if you knew where it was, or had a map, almost invisible if you didn't. Thousands of people walked by it each day thinking it was a dead end.

The entrance to Lost and Found was through a locked door. A duty officer could view visitors via a short circuit camera before letting them in. In practice, the officer buzzed everyone in unless they were carrying semi-automatic weapons.

Foreman waved his proximity badge over a scanner next to the door, which automatically released the lock, and walked into the vestibule. He pushed the handbag through the three-by-twelve-inch slot in the Plexiglas window behind which the Lost and Found duty officer sat. Today's duty officer was Judy Engebretsen. Engebretsen was in her mid-thirties and had been with MightyMall for ten years. She was medium height and weighed one hundred thirty pounds, though she looked heavier because she always wore a Kevlar vest underneath her uniform. She'd never been shot at, actually had never been in any kind of physical confrontation at work. Her husband had made her promise to wear one anyway shortly after they got married because, he said, it was better to be safe than sorry. The vest was heavy and sticky in the summer, but she loved her husband and decided it was a small price to pay to keep him happy.

Engebretsen wrote on her clipboard that at 8:37 A.M. Officer Mike Foreman had turned in a red handbag that he had found by the bank of lockers at the first floor West Entrance. She handed him a form to sign.

Forman scribbled his name in the designated space and slid the completed form back to his colleague. "We good?"

"Good as gold," Engebretsen said. "Thanks for stopping by."

"Have a good one." Foreman waved and headed out the door.

Lost and Found duty officers logged into the computer a description of all articles brought to them. Welcome Desk computers, as well as those of the mall telephone operators, displayed general descriptions of the items in the database and the date and time they arrived at Lost and Found. *Men's gloves, November 22nd, 9:12 A.M.* If the item included a name or some form of identification, that got entered. Guests claiming to have lost something had to go to the Lost and Found office, show a valid driver's license or passport, then describe in detail—color, material, size, distinguishing markings—the items they had lost and when. Those without ID were told politely that MightyMall would keep the items in question safe and sound until the person returned with proper ID. Out of town visitors could mail in certified copies of their ID, and a credit card for mailing costs. No exceptions.

Engebretsen placed the red handbag from Officer Foreman on the counter to the left of her desk. She would catalog it after finishing up with the five remaining items turned in at closing time last night: two pairs of glasses, an umbrella—*You don't see many of them in Minnesota,* Judy thought to herself. *Must be an out-of-towner.*—a Macy's bag full of clothes, and a cell phone.

Foreman left Lost and Found and walked down the stairs to the first floor of a still-empty Gonzoland and walked briskly under idle thrill rides, past shuddered shops, around artificial lagoons and parks and headed for the West Entrance.

X-Team members patrolled two floors each per day. Kiyomi's route today was floors one and two. Another member would patrol floors two and three, someone else would cover floors three and four, and so on. Their goal was to complete three circuits around each of their assigned floors per shift. Easy to do in eight hours if you never took a break. Stopping occasionally to pretend you were looking in a store window while in truth checking out the reflection of a possible perpetrator across the hall, and chatting with the occasional shopper while carrying shopping bags around for seven miles made the task more complicated. Kiyomi's job was to look like countless other young women who used the mall for shopping and dining. She had changed into a maroon University of Minnesota sweatshirt with gold letters and matching sweat pants. She carried a Neiman Marcus shopping bag filled with empty boxes.

With her long ponytail poking out the back of her U of M baseball cap. Kiyomi easily passed for a college student. She didn't like wearing the cap—it restricted her vision—but she got tired of guys hitting on her; the cap partially hid her face.

Kiyomi started her rounds for the day.

CHAPTER 7

Carolyn and Lucy pulled and lifted and shimmied and folded and shoved the body of Greta Turnblad, now known to Carolyn and Lucy as Dead Dora, first toward the center of the Welcome Desk so they could create maneuvering room, then to the Welcome Desk's wooden gateway. The exertion left both women out of breath. The Cushman sat motionless five feet away, like an electric horse–drawn wagon.

Lucy's neck and shoulders were stiff. She sat up straight and craned her neck to the left, then to the right, generating faint grinding sounds but no satisfying "crack." Closing her eyes, she leaned her head back and hunched her shoulders. Opening her eyes as she looked up she noticed a surveillance camera on the ceiling on the other side of the shopping avenue. Startled, she dropped quickly down next to Carolyn.

"Carolyn," she whispered. "What about the security surveillance cameras?"

"What about them?" Carolyn was busy bending the knee of Dora's left leg, trying to move the woman's leg out of the way of the Welcome Desk door so they could open the gate.

Lucy turned toward Carolyn. "Well, aren't they watching what we're doing? The security guys?"

"No, they aren't," Carolyn said. "There are over 800 cameras in the mall. Until this desk opens up, that one up there," Carolyn pointed toward the camera Lucy had been looking at, "is almost always pointed and zoomed into the entrance. The officers monitoring them—if anyone *is* monitoring them at this hour with so few people coming in yet—would have no reason to train them on the Welcome Desk here. Barring that, we aren't even in that camera's line-of-sight."

"So, no one can see us?"

"I didn't say that. They *might* be able to see us when we are standing up. I doubt they can see anything inside the enclosed area here. There's that camera right above us," Carolyn pointed at a glass bubble directly above their heads. "That's always pointed down at the cash register … when it's on; I know for a fact it's never on unless someone is manning the till, and because those are emptied each night before closing, there's no sense leaving the cameras on all night. The one that maybe could look down inside here is—" Carolyn pointed to a camera located in the corner above the entrance. "That one. But no one is going to monitor that until the Welcome Desk opens in …" Carolyn looked at her watch, "ooh, it's almost eight-thirty. Later than I thought. We're lucky no one's walked by yet."

"Maybe the snow storm …?" Lucy said.

"Oh, that's right." Carolyn peeked over the counter. "We're okay for a few more minutes but we need to get a move on."

Lucy tilted her head back and almost fell backwards before grabbing the counter. *Still,* she thought, *someone might see them.* She wondered how many cameras were pointed at this desk, and if all the cameras were filming what they saw, and if so, how long security kept the video files.

Lucy stood up to stretch her legs and noticed movement. Someone was walking toward them.

"Carolyn?" Lucy hissed out of the side of her mouth. "Carolyn!"

"What?" Carolyn didn't like being addressed in that tone of voice.

"What do we do about that girl turning toward us from the main avenue?"

"Fuck!" Carolyn said, crouching down further. "What girl? Go get rid of her!"

"Me? I—"

Carolyn put a hand on either side of Lucy's hips, faced her toward the gate, and shoved hard. Lucy glanced back at Carolyn, who crouched further under the counter.

"Why can't you—" Lucy hissed.

"Because I'm *busy* here! Because I—" Carolyn pinched the bridge of her nose between the thumb and index finger of her right hand. She had read somewhere that it was good for treating migraines, which she was sure she would get any moment.

"Listen, you pathetic piece of trailer trash! You want that car and the raise you so innocently asked for? Then get your fat ass out there and make whoever is there go *away*!" She blew a strand of hair that had fallen across her eyes. "Or a new car will be the *least* of your worries!"

Carolyn closed her eyes, put her hands over her ears and pushed herself further into the corner underneath the counter overhang. Lucy glanced back at the Welcome Desk for a moment, turned to look at the young woman she had spotted in the shopping avenue, and started walking toward her.

Lucy stumbled briefly, then half ran toward the young Asian woman wearing a University of Minnesota sweat suit and matching cap. *Oh God, I hope she speaks American,* Lucy thought. The girl had bent down to tie her sneakers. She was about thirty feet away from the Welcome Desk.

Lucy tried willing the girl away from the Welcome Desk and back on to the main thoroughfare. *No good stores down here. Nothing open at this hour. Go away! Follow the light! Follow the Saks light in the other direction!*

No such luck. The girl stood up and was turning toward Lucy. Toward the Welcome Desk.

"Excuse me," said Lucy, waving needlessly. "Yoo hoo! Miss?" She placed herself in the line of sight between the Asian girl and the Welcome Desk.

Kiyomi saw one of the management secretaries jogging toward her.

"Excuse me," Lucy said. "Hello."

"Hello."

Good, Lucy thought. *She speaks English.* "You're out awfully early. Getting a head start on holiday shopping?"

Kiyomi smiled pleasantly but remained silent.

Maybe her English is not so good after all, Lucy thought.

"Shopping?" She pointed at the nearest store, a Kid's Gap. "Guess you're too young to be a mall walker." Lucy was striving for humor but her laugh sounded forced, even to herself.

Kiyomi recognized the woman as Carolyn Batch's Administrative Assistant. Shirley? Lucy, that was it. The X-Team kept extensive dossiers on the five hundred MightyMall management office employees.

MightyMall LLC, a wholly-owned subsidiary of Titanic Properties of Dallas, Texas, was landlord for the 15 million square feet of leasable space in the world's largest mall, but had relatively few of its own employees. Clerks and restaurant staff were hired and managed by the individual tenants. MightyMall LLC employed only enough people to keep the building clean, safe and structurally sound and to market it to the world.

X-Team members spent several hours a week familiarizing themselves with management staff personnel records. The database went far beyond photos, work history and employee evaluations. A powerful mainframe computer in the Security Action Center collected information from a number of data points in the mall, including all personal computers and telephones. The security database used a sophisticated algorithm to identify and monitor unusual employee behavioral trends or suspicious activities. Contents of emails, when they were sent, and to whom, were cross-referenced with known departmental functions. Emails sent within departments, or between certain departments, normally passed unnoticed. Multiple communications between people in departments that had no established business functioned might not. A string of emails between the marketing and housekeeping departments, for example, would trigger a software sub routine scanning emails for specific words. Officers monitored hundreds of surveillance cameras 24 hours a day, seven days a week, looking for people in places they shouldn't be. Phone conversations were not recorded—yet—but the system did track time, date and destinations of calls. Disparate and seemingly innocent activities, when parsed and examined by dispassionate and sophisticated computers, could turn out to be worthy of closer scrutiny. The security department didn't concern itself with spotting or preventing harmless prank emails and calls or amorous meetings in one of the mall's miles of internal hallways (though if Human Resources knew about the database's capabilities, they would likely demand access to it). It was more concerned with finding someone looking for ways to smuggle in a bomb, flooding the ventilation system with a dangerous pathogen or infecting the Security Action Center computers with a crippling virus.

Kiyomi found nothing suspicious in Lucy's walking the halls this early in the day. She had seen Lucy doing morning rounds with Carolyn Batch before. The Cushman parked by the Welcome Desk caught her attention. No sign of Lucy's boss. Probably in the nearby restroom.

Kiyomi was confident that Lucy wouldn't recognize her.

"Well," Lucy said. "It certainly is a nice day to be inside, isn't it? What with all the snow outside, and all." Her giggle was uncomfortably out of place.

"Yes." Kiyomi put on her wide-eyed, friendly, foreign student face. "It is very cold." She modulated her English accent, almost undetectable after eight years attending the international school in Japan and college in the United States, to sound more foreign. "Very cold" sounded like "BEDDEE KOHRUDOH."

"Do you come here often?" Lucy said. Just to say something.

"Oh, yes. I like at mall. It very big."

"It certainly is, isn't it'?" Lucy nodded, not knowing what to say next.

"Oh, yes." Kiyomi said, with the breathless enthusiasm of a tourist. "In my home village? In Japan? We do not have building like this." Kiyomi swept her right arm in a wide sweeping arc, like a model on The Price is Right showing what the next contestant might win.

Kiyomi wondered where Carolyn Batch was. She said, "AH YUU AHROHN HEEAA TSUU?" Are you alone here, too?

"No, I—" Lucy quickly corrected herself. "I mean, oh you mean *here*? In the *mall*? *Now*?" She nodded vigorously. "Oh, yes, I'm alone." She let out another small, nervous laugh. "Just like you. Just getting in out of the cold … taking a walk … getting a head start on shopping. You know how it is."

"Oh, yes!" Kiyomi said with the same enthusiastic voice. She wondered why Lucy had lied to her. Why would she be driving the

Cushman around early in the morning by herself? Ms. Batch always made inspection rounds in the morning and brought someone with her. She must be nearby.

And why was Lucy pretending to be a shopper? There was no reason for a mall employee, other than X-Team members like her, to keep their employment status a secret from visitors.

She decided to call Lucy's bluff.

"Aren't you cold?" Kiyomi wrapped her arms around her body and shivered.

"Me?" Lucy said. "No, of course not. It's plenty warm in here. Why? Are you cold?"

"No, I am very warm. But you not wearing coat. It very cold outside. Don't you wear coat today?"

"Oh." Lucy patted her arms on her shoulders and chest and realized her error. "I, um, no, I put my coat in the locker over there." Lucy pointed at the bank of lockers next to the Welcome Desk. She mentally kicked herself. *Don't draw attention to the Welcome Desk, you idiot!*

"Ah so," Kiyomi said. "I see." She maintained her expression of friendly innocence, but wondered about the expanding elaborateness of Lucy's lie. Could it be something as simple as Lucy not liking to interact with mall visitors?

Then why had Lucy bothered approaching Kiyomi in the first place? Why not just walk past her altogether? And what reason would Lucy have for being in the entrance hallway by herself at this hour? Kiyomi was sure that Lucy hadn't put her overcoat in one of the lockers—why would she?—she had a hanger by her desk. Her mind wandered back to Carolyn Batch. Awfully long time for her to be in the restroom.

But that still wouldn't explain Lucy's odd behavior.

Kiyomi looked down the short hallway at the Welcome Desk and the bank of lockers. Her eyes kept coming back to the Cushman.

Perhaps Carolyn had sent Lucy here alone on some errand. But why would Lucy leave the Cushman there and then walk to Kiyomi and engage her in this mindless conversation? She wanted to ask Lucy about that but needed to maintain her cover.

Lucy saw the Asian girl looking in the direction of the Welcome Desk.

"I, ah, actually, I wondered if you could help me," Lucy said.

"Yes?"

The woman seemed friendly enough but something in the directness of her gaze made Lucy uneasy. "I'm, ah, looking for a place that sells coffee this early in the morning. Do you know if there are any Starbucks or Caribou Coffees nearby?" Lucy made a show of searching intently.

What was this elaborate acting job about? Kiyomi wondered, her interest intensified.

Lucy walked to the main hallway. "Do you think there's one down this way?" She pointed to the north. "Or down there the other way?" She turned and gestured in the other direction.

Kiyomi walked and stood next to Lucy. "AYEE SINKU KOHEE SHOPPU DAHUUN ZEYAH." I think coffee shop down there. "Yes, maybe down there." She pointed north.

"Oh great." Lucy put her hand to her chest in a gesture of relief. "Say, shall we get some coffee together? Can I buy you a coffee? You've been *so* kind to me."

"Oh." The offer caught Kiyomi off guard. "Oh. Thank you very much." Kiyomi had no intention of having a cup of coffee with Lucy. "No, uh, thank you. I like to just walking around mall now. For exercise."

"Oh," Lucy said. "Sure. Well, have a nice walk." She stood in place, continuing to look at the Asian girl, waiting for her to leave.

"Yes." Though intrigued by Lucy's behavior, Kiyomi needed to resume her rounds. She headed south and made a mental note to return after completing her rounds.

Lucy watched the Asian girl walk away. Lucy turned and headed north, toward the Caribou Coffee shop she knew was about one hundred yards ahead. She stopped and pretended to gaze at shoes in the window of Johnston & Murphy. After a minute or so she snuck a look. The girl was gone, but Lucy noticed a couple of mall walkers in the distance heading her way.

Despite the weather, shoppers were beginning to arrive.

She and Carolyn were running out of time.

CHAPTER 8

Carolyn sat on the flatbed located on the back of her Cushman. Seated next to her was the petite but deceased Dead Dora. Dora had proven more of a challenge to relocate from the Welcome Desk than either Carolyn or Lucy had anticipated. A sneaker had slipped off. Her warm-up suit pants kept sliding off her bony ass. Carolyn climbed on the flatbed, grabbed Dora under the arms and heaved while Lucy half lifted and half guided the rest of the body.

Carolyn blew a strand of hair that had fallen over her eyes. She removed a silk Gucci scarf she had been wearing around her neck and tied it around Dora's head. It covered the gash on her forehead above her left eye.

"What do you think?" Carolyn said.

Lucy squinted as she scanned the corpse in front of her. "I think she looks like a cancer patient who's losing her hair from chemo," she said, "and I think if we don't get her out of here quick someone is going to walk in and see her. And us. I've already spotted a couple of shoppers in the main shopping avenue."

"Fine. You mentioned that already. Let's go."

Carolyn put her arm around Dora's shoulders. She leaned against the stiff back of the seat.

"Does she look alive?" Carolyn said. "Go over there–that's far enough. Now tell me if you can tell I'm sitting next to a corpse."

Lucy wasn't sure how to answer the question. "Well, her eyes *are* closed," she said. "And she's pretty pale. But considering how old she is ...was...." She shrugged. "Can we just go now, please?"

Carolyn jostled Dora slightly, then held her arm an inch above Dora's shoulders ready to grab her in case she started to slide. Dora didn't move.

"Okay. You've got the plan, right?"

Lucy droned the plan as if reciting the Pledge of Allegiance. "Down the service hallway behind the desk toward the fourth or fifth service elevator. Up to the seventh floor. You'll tell me when we get to some special door or room or whatever that's a big secret."

"It's not a secret," Carolyn said. "It's just so rarely used that almost no one knows about it."

"Right. Whatever."

"Just do what I tell you." Carolyn looked at the dead passenger seated next to her, warming to her plan. This wasn't going to be so hard. "Unless someone else gets in the elevator with us. In which case you stand between whoever it is and Dora and pretend you are talking to her and me. We'll continue on to the next floor, get off there, let the elevator go and wait for the next one."

Lucy's eyebrows shot up. "Talk to her? What do I say?

Carolyn sighed loudly. "Pretend you're explaining the agenda. Tell her we're going to drive to some nice stores and stop for lunch in one of the restaurants overlooking Gonzoland." Did the conniving bitch have no brains of her own? "Just deal with it."

Lucy's heart was beating like a jackhammer. This felt like one of those dreams where you are sitting in front of a piano in Carnegie Hall, yet you don't play the piano. "Who is she? I mean, who is she supposed to be and why is she here? In case, you know, someone asks."

"No one is going to ask," Carolyn said. "If they do, I'll just say it's somebody's great aunt from headquarters. That'll scare everyone away from asking follow-up questions. Nobody wants to piss off one of the owners' great aunts."

"Christ," Lucy muttered.

"Let's go."

Two rings of service corridors circled each floor of MightyMall, one just inside the outer walls of MightyMall, one just outside Gonzoland. Shoppers entered mall stores from the front of the stores. Everything shoppers saw in the stores—clothes, ceiling lights, furniture, computers, toys, kitchen appliances, food—entered from the back door, which led to a service corridor. Waste was taken out the back and dumped in designated garbage chutes. This kept unwanted (non-paying) traffic in the mall to a minimum. It also reduced the chance of someone tripping over a delivery cart and suing the mall for a billion dollars.

The service corridors were narrower than the shopping avenues. Two people walking in opposite directions could pass each other easily. If one of them was driving a Cushman, the pedestrian needed to walk carefully as they passed. If the Cushman was pulling a loaded flatbed, anyone unlucky enough to face it would duck into the nearest recessed doorway.

"Hurry up, dammit!" Carolyn said. "These things go ten miles per hour if you floor them."

"Yes, Carolyn." *And we'll be fucked if we run into someone coming around a corner.*

They arrived intact and unnoticed at the S14 service elevator. The door was open. Lucy carefully backed the Cushman in.

Elevator gates emerged simultaneously from the floor and ceiling, meeting in the middle. A second set of heavy cast iron doors closed in similar fashion.

The second set of doors had almost completely closed when a hand shot between them, tripping the safety beam that caused the cast iron doors and the gate doors to open.

Carolyn, who was facing the back wall of the elevator, hissed, "Lucy! What the fuck are you *doing*?"

"Sorry, folks." Security Chief Matthew "Major" Power jumped into the elevator.

"No problem," Lucy said. "Uh, what floor?"

"Third, thanks." Power reached over and punched the button for the third floor himself.

Lucy exhaled slowly while studying the elevator control panel.

"Can't decide?" Power said.

Lucy jumped as if she'd been caught cheating on a test. "What? Excuse me?"

"You haven't selected a floor yet. I thought maybe you'd forgotten which floor you were going to." Power's expression showed nothing.

Carolyn shifted her arm slightly, taking a firm hold of Dora's neck. She stared straight at the back wall.

"Oh, uh, no. Of course not." Lucy lurched toward the control panel and punched a button randomly. Fifth floor.

"Ah," Power said. "The fifth floor. Doing your rounds up there today, are you?"

"Yes." His tone was friendly but made Lucy nervous. Why was he asking about rounds? His face wasn't giving anything away. "We're, ah, escorting a VIP around the mall."

Power turned his head and looked briefly at the two women sitting on the back of the Cushman. He noticed the Senior Vice President for Business Development.

"Should have told me ahead of time," he said. "I could have gotten you a cart with a more comfortable back."

"We're fine, Major," Carolyn said, holding very still. "Very comfortable, thanks."

Power nodded and turned his head back toward the front of the elevator. "Yes, ma'am." That Carolyn Batch sure was an odd bitch.

The elevator arrived at the third floor. Power stepped out into the service corridor and turned around. "Have a nice day, ladies." He gave a mock salute and walked away.

"Thank you," Lucy said. "You, too."

When the elevator doors had closed, Carolyn whipped her head around and looked at Lucy with an expression of disbelief. "VIP? Escorting her around the mall? What? Are you fucking nuts?"

"But you said—"

"I said to keep your fucking mouth shut unless you had to speak, you idiot. Not chat the Major up like you're looking for a date."

"I never—"

"We're at the fifth floor." Carolyn closed her eyes tight and put her hands out, palms down, as if tamping down a fire. "Just close the door, push the button for the *seventh* floor," Carolyn opened her eyes and looked pointedly at Lucy, "and close that fucking door before some other idiot decides to jump in."

They arrived at the seventh floor without encountering another soul. Lucy eased the cart out of the elevator and stopped.

Carolyn said, "Turn left and keep driving until I tell you to stop."

"And you're sure there's a service door down this way that no one ever uses?"

"Oh, yes. It's there. I used to go up there all the time with Andy." Carolyn said. Her face glowed momentarily with the pleasure of distant memory as the realization of whom she was talking to hit her—her *secretary*, for Christ's sake, who was trying to blackmail her. Hello? The smile disappeared as quickly as if she had received an injection of botox. "I, uh, used to go there sometimes. With a friend … when I was an intern … years ago. Anyway, no one knows it's there. We'll be fine."

"No one at all?" Lucy said.

"Well, maintenance knows, I suppose. And anyone walking by can see it, of course. But I've never seen anyone use it for anything. Stop worrying."

"And we're going to hide the body there?" Lucy said.

"Just until tomorrow. We just need to get past my press conference today and give the local and national media time to digest and circulate the expansion news. Make sure that I, the *mall,* I mean, gets the publicity and recognition I deserve." Carolyn caught herself. "That *MightyMall* deserves. After that."

"Then what?"

"Well, we'll just put lovely Dora here back at the Welcome Desk first thing tomorrow morning so someone else can find her. It'll be someone else's problem then."

Two small vertical creases appeared between Lucy's eyebrows. "And you don't think anyone will catch on that, you know, that she's been moved around? Or been dead for an entire day? Won't their CSI folks be able to tell?"

"Maybe you're right," Carolyn said. "Let me think about that."

The Cushman continued along the corridor, door after tenant door. The signs above the doors, identifying all the stores and restaurants and banquet rooms and chapels and health clubs, sped past like endless stations on a high–speed rail line. Carolyn, Lucy and Greta, aka: Dora, drove along the seemingly endless service corridor on the seventh floor.

Lucy spotted a doorway up ahead that looked different than those belonging to stores, emergency exits, and storage closets. Instead of a recessed entranceway, this door was built flush with the rest of the wall.

"Is that it? Up ahead there?" Lucy removed her right hand from the steering wheel briefly to point.

Carolyn started to turn around in an effort to see where Lucy was pointing but nearly lost control of Dora and gave up. She said, "I can't tell" and turned back. Her right arm began to shake from fatigue. It was getting tired from holding onto the body for so long.

"Stop the cart and let me off. I'll know the door when I see it."

Carolyn let go of Dora as soon as Lucy had stopped the Cushman, pausing briefly before getting off to see if the body would slide off. When it didn't, she leapt off and strode to the set of double doors Lucy was already standing next to. She flexed her right arm unconsciously to get blood flowing again.

Carolyn nodded. "That's it, ML7N1." She rubbed her hands together. "Excellent. Pull the cart up ahead here, just past the door. It'll make it easier to unload old Dora."

Dora was still sitting upright in the back of the Cushman. Her legs hung over the edge of the flatbed. Her torso rested against the back of the driver's seat. Her left arm lay in her lap, palm facing up. Her right arm hung loosely outside the cart. Her head was tilted back and her mouth partially open. A passerby might have thought that, except for the gash on her head, Dora looked like a grandmother who had nodded off in front of the TV in the recreation room of an assisted living facility while watching a rerun of *The Lawrence Welk Show*.

"Hurry up," Carolyn said. "Let's get going."

Lucy got back in the driver's seat and stomped on the accelerator pedal, causing the Cushman to lurch forward. Dora's head jerked forward, lolling slightly to the right.

"Whoops," Lucy said, easing off the pedal. She looked back at Dora to make sure that she hadn't fallen off.

If the body had shifted more significantly at that moment Lucy might have been able to prevent what happened next. As it was, Lucy noticed nothing unusual in Dora's posture and didn't much like looking at her anyway. She turned back around and once again pressed down on the accelerator pedal, this time more gently. Dora, sitting behind her, with Carolyn's arm no longer holding her in place, began to tilt to the right. Carolyn, meanwhile, was focused on finding her keys. Dora's head rolled a bit more to the right, pulling first her upper, then her lower, torso along with her. And faster than you could say, "Mommy, what's a human head sound like if you drop it on the floor?" the head of Greta "Dora" Turnblad struck the concrete floor of the service corridor, sounding like a 16-pound bowling ball dropped into an empty swimming pool.

"Oh, my God, oh, my God, oh, my God," Lucy said. She squeezed her eyes tightly shut.

"Shit, shit, shit, shit, shit," Carolyn said. She rushed over to the dead woman's body. "We've got no time to waste now. Help me drag this thing through the door before someone comes along."

Carolyn grabbed Dora by the hands and shuffled back toward the doors, eventually easing Dora to the floor while she fumbled to unlock the door.

"Anyone coming?" Carolyn said.

Lucy looked first to the left, then right. "I don't see anyone."

"Okay. Grab her legs and pull back a little. She's too close to the door."

"Ugh." Dora's ankles felt clammy to Lucy.

"What?"

"Nothing." Lucy pulled Dora about two feet back toward the center of the corridor.

Carolyn swung the door open, used her left foot to hold it open and gripped Dora's hands again.

"Okay," Carolyn said. "Let's go."

"I feel like Alice," Lucy thought, as she peered into the dimly lit area beyond the doors. "Down the rabbit hole."

"Watch your step, Lucy dear. Don't want to slip in here, do we?"

CHAPTER 9

Gonzoland had over ninety rides, from tiny trains for pre-schoolers, to stomach-churning roller coasters, to "virtual" Jurassic-era rides in enclosed theaters featuring 3-D dinosaurs that grazed and fought in every corner of the room while "authentic" smells from the period wafted in through the ventilation system.

Titanic Properties had elected to self-brand the amusement park and create their own stand-alone park. Instead of paying millions of dollars in licensing fees to a Disney, Warner Brothers or Nickelodeon, they invested instead in a New York consulting firm with instructions to come up with a one-of-a-kind concept. The firm came back with Gonzoland, a park of larger-than-life characters from history and popular culture that would appeal to all the prized demographics. A seventy-foot tall superhero named Gonzoid, who looked like suspiciously like Gort from the original *The Day the Earth Stood Still*, stood at the park's North Entrance, craning his head in several directions, occasionally looking down menacingly upon unsuspecting park goers as they entered the park through his legs. A focused red spotlight shot out of Gonzoid's forehead at random intervals. Guests who were "beamed" by the spotlight while wearing a registered Gonzoland baseball cap—a chip in the hat detected when a direct hit was made—received a free family pack of passes for one of the monorails. A giant statue of Paul Bunyan, famed Minnesotan (despite what folks from Wisconsin and Michigan claimed) occupied the middle of the park, a roller coaster orbiting his head. An axe in his left hand doubled as a thrill ride, tame enough for Baby Boomers, that he lifted above his head and swung down several times every eleven minutes. A crab the size of a softball field appeared to be scaling the west wall, its claws extending toward the fourth-floor monorail, then retracting at the last moment. There was no common theme to the people, monsters, ghosts and aliens of Gonzoland except for their enormity: the largest mall in the world had the largest amusement park statues in the world, which was as it should be.

Most amusement parks added new rides every year or two, partly in an effort to draw more visitors, partly to keep existing customers happy. Park–goers, particularly teenagers, got tired of riding the same roller coasters over and over. Even one new ride, if it was big and exciting enough, had the effect of creating an entirely new reason to return. Never mind that all other rides in the park were exactly the same as last year; add just one new *Twirl and Hurl* or *Dive 2 Death* and tweens and teens were like salmon swimming upstream to their spawning grounds: they must return to the park, or die trying.

Because Gonzoland was an indoor amusement park contained within finite space, it couldn't create new buzz every year by expanding ever outward as Disney World or Six Flags had done. Gonzoland maintained its freshness by continually replacing existing rides or statues with new and improved ones. Like a basketball coach looking for the perfect chemistry between his starting players, MightyMall removed underperforming rides and replaced them with those likely to do better. Management knew which rides were making them money by monitoring ridership daily the way Wal-Mart monitored inventory.

Haunted Hollow was Gonzoland's most popular ride. Part log chute, part haunted house, the cars floated on water past ghosts, vampires, dead pirates, and alien monsters that shrieked and cackled, rose up and down, spun in circles, and flew over the heads of screaming guests. Haunted Hollow was one of several "permanent rides" partially built into the park wall on the outer edges of Gonzoland when MightyMall opened.

Haunted Hollow was designed originally to flow in a straight line from the first to sixth floors, meander in lazy eight, then finish with a steep dive back to the first floor. During construction a visiting Titanic executive had complained that Haunted Hollow wasn't exciting enough. *Why*, he had asked one of the design engineers he corralled on the construction site, *can't you just cut a few holes in the walls, have the ride disappear at one floor and then reappear from a different floor?* as if doing so were as easy as snipping holes in construction paper with two large scissors. *Instead of the ride's straight vertical drop from the seventh to the first floor, wouldn't it be more interesting*, the owner posited, *to bring the ride cars up to the seventh floor, start down, but then make a quick detour through the sixth floor wall, race down to the fourth floor in semi darkness, then make a sharp left turn back into the park, and down to a big splash at the bottom. You could even fill that area behind the walls of the fourth and sixth floors with flashing, screaming animatronics to make it even scarier. Piece of cake*, the owner had said with the blithe confidence of someone born to wealth, unconcerned with the trivialities of mechanical engineering and schedules. *Just get it done!*

The engineers and architects didn't like it but accommodated the owner's wishes. The changes increased construction costs by a million dollars, partly because some of the infrastructure needed for the original design had already been finished and had to be modified. One casualty, a five foot wide skyway from a seventh floor service corridor to what *would have been* an emergency access point for Haunted Hollow, was completed but no longer needed; the redesigned aqueduct now passed fifteen feet *underneath*. Like a Diving Board to Nowhere, the redundant skyway jutted out in mid-air and stopped. Too expensive to remove, it was easier to post a "No Admittance" sign on the double door, marked ML7N1, and keep it locked at all times.

Maintenance personnel were told to avoid the doors for unspecified safety reasons, which was enough for them; when your supervisor told you not to do something, you didn't, not if you wanted to keep your job. Security officers were told never to open that door, even in emergencies, and as most of them came from a military background, they were accustomed to following orders unconditionally, whether they made sense or not. Management staff, comfortable in their offices, had no reason to go anywhere near the doors. Eventually, it was as if the doors did not exist.

That is, to everyone except Carolyn eleven years before.

She and fellow intern, Andy Zimmer, had been looking for a place to smoke pot during lunch breaks. The mall was rife with hundreds of empty storage rooms and closets, but most of them were locked. When Nathan Parsons, then Senior Vice President or MightyMall, had flown to Texas for one of his monthly meetings at headquarters, Andy suggested they steal the master key in Parsons office.

"Dude!" Andy had said. "That key will get us wherever we want. It's like a God Key of the MightyMall Universe."

"I don't want to get in trouble," Carolyn had said, secretly turned on by Andy's brashness.

"No problem," said Andy, who liked to pretend he was Sean Penn in *Fast Times at Ridgemont High*. "We'll just borrow it while his secretary lady is out, make a copy at the Quick Key on the sixth floor, and have it back in his desk before she's back from lunch."

Most of the rooms they inspected were filled things, too close to frequently used exits, or too dirty, even for Andy's and Carolyn's raging hormones. They found one room on the fourth floor with piles of mattresses wrapped in plastic covered in dust. The two young interns made the room into their own private love nest … until one afternoon when they saw some guy from maintenance pulling a giant flatbed out of the room with several of their mattresses. Fearing the loss of their precious mattress—Andy was so stoned one time that he drew a heart on the mattress with part of that day's ejaculation—more than the room itself, they ducked into an open elevator and waited until the maintenance guy had disappeared down the hall.

Happy to see their mattress still there—"It's contains a part of us."—Andy began dragging it toward the door while Carolyn went into the corridor to look for a suitable replacement room. She spotted a maintenance door across the hall they hadn't tried, opened it and helped Andy pull the mattress through the ML7N1 door. Playing it safe, they left the mattress there for several days to see if it would be found and removed. When it was still there the following week, Carolyn and Andy decided they had found their new love nest.

Andy was eventually fired for possession of a controlled substance—Carolyn had tired of him by then—but during the year prior to his termination Carolyn and Andy enjoyed hours of uninterrupted and undiscovered lust.

CHAPTER 10

Carolyn and Lucy stood on the iron walkway inside the ML7N1 door, which had closed behind them.

"You've never been here before, have you, Lucy?"

Lucy shook her head.

"Of course you haven't," Carolyn said. "Now, this is what we're going to do. There's a metal walkway behind me here." Carolyn motioned needlessly with her head. "It goes about thirty feet straight back. It ends in kind of a 'T' shape. There are guardrails on each side and at the end so you'll be okay."

Lucy looked beyond Carolyn her eyes weren't yet accustomed to the low light.

"I don't know," Lucy said. "Are you sure?"

"Yes, I'm sure, dammit. Now listen. Stay to the center of the walkway and you'll be fine. Make sure you hang onto old Dora here at all times because she could probably slip through the railing if we aren't careful. If she goes over the edge she's falling all the way to the first floor."

"How far is it? Till the end of this thing?"

"I told you, it's about thirty feet. Now keep quiet until I finish talking."

"Okay." Lucy took a deep breath.

"You and I are going to pull Dora to the very end. Got that much?"

Lucy wasn't at all sure she got it but was too nervous to ask. She wasn't afraid of heights, exactly, but she sure as hell didn't like standing seven floors up on a plank-like walkway out of *Pirates of the Caribbean*, in near darkness, dragging a dead body.

"Can't we just leave her here? I mean, you said no one comes here, right?"

"No one has come here *that I know of.* Doesn't mean no one ever pokes their head in by mistake. No point in taking any chances. And, besides, it's just thirty feet," Carolyn said. "Now, come on. Let's get started and it will all be over."

Carolyn shuffled forward along the catwalk, pushing her feet along rather than lifting them. It was difficult to simultaneously lift and drag so much dead weight while walking. The body made a rustling sound as it scraped the floor.

"Lift her up a little higher, can you?" Carolyn said. "I think she's scraping on something." It had been too dark for Carolyn to see the candy wrapper that slid underneath their passenger—it was too dark to see much of anything—and that was what caused the faint rustling they both heard.

"I'm trying," Lucy said. Her foot caught on something and she lost her balance momentarily. She let go of the dead woman's left leg and reached for the safety rail.

"What the fuck are you doing?" Carolyn hissed.

"I lost my balance," Lucy said. "I caught on a piece of gum or something."

"Be more careful, you idiot."

It took them less than a minute to reach the other end of the platform. Carolyn dropped Dora's arms. Lucy set Dora's arms down more gently. She put her hands on the railing and leaned over to see what she could see below them.

"Oh, my God," Lucy said. "Is that what I think it is?"

"What do you think it is?"

"That's, oh my God, that's the Haunted Hollow chute ride down there," Lucy said. "Isn't it?"

"It sure is."

Lucy jerked back. "Can they see us up here?"

"You're fine," Carolyn said. "The aqueduct is going down hill, from the sixth floor to the fourth. No one is looking at us up here."

"But couldn't they see us if they looked up?"

Carolyn shrugged. "I suppose so. I never noticed."

Probably because you and your intern boyfriend were too busy doing the nasty, Lucy thought as she looked over at her boss. *Eew. What a totally disgusting thought.*

"Help me pull her up and lean her against the railing," Carolyn said. "On the right side of the 'T.'"

"Can't we just lie her flat on the ledge?"

"This is better shielded from the door. If someone does happen to open it by mistake, they won't see anything unless they walk all the way in or shine a bright light."

After much pushing and pulling and twisting, the body sat upright, legs extended straight out in front of her. Her head lolled forward on her chest. Carolyn pushed it back, trying to make it lean back over the railing. After several unsuccessful tries, she finally got the head to stay in place. Carolyn placed Dora's arms in her lap and stood back to admire her work.

"Does she look stable to you?" Carolyn said.

Lucy shrugged. *More stable than you, you bitch.* As her eyes grew accustomed to the dim light, she noticed Carolyn's head tilted to one side, as if appraising a painting she'd just finished.

"She looks okay to me." Carolyn nodded as to confirm the accuracy of her statement, then squinted at her watch. "Come on, let's go. I can't see what time it is but I've got to freshen up before my press conference."

Lucy wiped a bead of sweat that had formed on her temple. "How come it's so muggy in here in the middle of winter?"

"I don't know. Because we're on the top floor, maybe? Water heater is somewhere down there on the first floor. Engines for several of the rides, maybe." Carolyn said. "What the fuck difference does it make?"

"I just asked," Lucy said in a small voice.

"Come on."

CHAPTER 11

"*Yes*, Mr. Pankow. *No*, Mr. Pankow. Please fuck me in the *ass*, Mr. Pankow. Of course, I'm a team *player*, Mr. Pankow." Eric Lemke muttered to himself as he climbed out of the S14 Elevator on the seventh floor and headed toward the service door about one hundred feet away.

Lemke was a supervisor in the maintenance department. He was tall, lanky, with a full head of snow-white hair. He was one year away from retirement, at which time he planned to move to a nice retirement park in Plant City, Florida, where he and his wife had bought a double-wide last year.

Lemke's team did light construction in the management offices. They put up and knocked down walls between offices, erected and modified cubes, built shelves and did easy electrical work such as installing or replacing ceiling lamps. Anything more complicated went to outside contractors.

Wednesday night and Thursday morning were officially Moving Day for two-dozen members of the merchandising, leasing and advertising departments. Advertising added two new interns and one full-time staff over the summer and was unhappy that the new staff's office space was located three doors down from the rest of the advertising department. Walking fifteen feet from one clump of advertising offices, past three merchandising offices, to the three other advertising offices was, according to Tammy Dickson, the Advertising Manager, an unreasonable hardship. She complained to her boss, Jeff Patter, Director of Marketing. Patter didn't care one way or the other but was sure he didn't want to listen to Tammy bitch, so he went to Vern Pankow, Director of Maintenance, with a solution: relocate the three Leasing people to a set of cubes at the other end of the management offices, and would free up office space for the three advertising people could then be moved closer to the rest of their department. Patter had brought the idea to Pankow in the form of a suggestion, but he already had the go-ahead from Carolyn Batch so there was no room for debate. That was fine with Pankow; it was all the same to him: shuffling people and furniture around the management offices kept his people busy and helped him justify his budget. The Leasing people didn't much like the idea—"Why should *we* have to sit right next to the smelly, noisy restrooms?"—so the Leasing director went to Karl LeVander, Managing Director of Operations, with his own idea: give the three Leasing folks the merchandising department's desks, move the merchandising people to leasing's offices, then move the advertising folks into the old leasing offices. LeVander had more pull than anyone in merchandising, so the deal was done, whether it made any sense or not.

Moving these nine people simultaneously required more synchronization than D-Day. Between eight o'clock last night seven on the morning, the Information Technology guys needed to shut down, relocate and reconnect nine computers while maintenance rolled individual carts with files, photos and personal items, and favorite chairs that they hoped were all properly labeled. Painters and paperhangers removed old wallpaper or painted walls with new colors chosen by the new occupants. Old work cubes were replaced with different shaped cubes. Odd-shaped rooms with odd shapes and inconveniently located support pillars needed customized shelving built from scratch. Everything had to be packed, moved, unpacked, rebooted, painted, dried and delivered before staff arrived the next day. Staff then spent much of the day unpacking personal items, hanging up posters, putting files in new cabinets, making sure the computers on their desk was really theirs and complaining to maintenance that their walls hadn't been painted the right colors.

It seemed to Lemke that at least one manager or department head was shuffling staff locations every few months for no reason other than to assert his or her authority. This required him to pull his guys from regular maintenance work, costing the mall extra money and materials, and, from the grumbling he heard from the office staff, accomplishing nothing beyond making various mid and upper management feel better about themselves.

But that, too, was fine with Lemke.

What ticked off Lemke, and what had gotten him in trouble with his boss, Vern Pankow, was that everyone involved—Pankow, Jeff Patter, Tammy Dickson, the Information Technology guys—had weeks ago signed off on *next* week—Wednesday and Thanksgiving Day—as Moving Day, not *this* week. Lemke planned his vacation time around this. He was scheduled to take a long weekend off, starting Wednesday, and drive down with his wife to Beatrice, Missouri to visit his son, daughter-in-law and grandchildren. His two kids and their children—Lemke also had a daughter in Hayward, Wisconsin—always spent Thanksgiving with him and his wife in Minnesota. His son's family couldn't do that this year because Suzy, his daughter-in-law, had just had an ovarian cyst removed and couldn't travel. Lemke figured he and his wife could travel to Beatrice for an early Thanksgiving with his son's family, then a second Thanksgiving at home with his daughter and her boyfriend next week.

That was the plan until Tammy Dickson on Monday that the move just *had* to happen a week earlier. Too many of her staff would be off next week for Thanksgiving, she said. She needed to get everything done before everyone left.

That, also, was fine with Lemke. His guys knew the routine. IT said they could adjust their schedule. Management wanted to move a week early? Fine. Lemke wrote up a new schedule and emailed it to Vern Pankow on November 13th.

Pankow called him into his office and their meeting went like this:

"Hey, Eric," Pankow said, getting right to the point. "What's with this construction report?" He flicked the page he was holding with his finger.

"Slight change of plans," Lemke said. "Tammy Dickson rescheduled the advertising area move ahead a week. But we're good to go. Skip and Tony can do this kind of stuff in their sleep."

"I don't see your name anywhere on the duty roster." Pankow flicked the report twice, then turned it around so that Lemke could see it.

Alarm bells began sounding in Lemke's head but he fought to keep his voice even. "I'm visiting my son, Brett, and his family Wednesday through Sunday this week. They won't be coming up for Thanksgiving this year so we thought we'd go down there instead and visit them. Down to Missouri."

"But without you there's no supervisor on duty during the move." Pankow spoke as if he were addressing a dull child.

"Oh, c'mon, Vern," Lemke said. "It's three offices and six sets of cubes. My guys can do that blindfolded. They don't need no supervisor to tell 'em what to do. IT does the computer stuff on their own. If I *was* here—and I was going to be here if it was next week as it was supposed to be—I'd just be working along side 'em. There's no real supervising to do on a job like this. You know that."

"I understand that," Pankow said. "But mall rules state that a supervisor has to be present on all construction projects."

Lemke scratched his nose. "I know the rules, Vern, I teach them to every new guy that comes in. But you know as well as I do that those rules are meant for big projects, like complex rewiring, new tenants coming in, plumbing … stuff like that. Moving offices is a piece of cake."

"I get that," Pankow said again. "And I feel for ya. Really, Eric, I truly do. But you're a supervisor. You're paid more than them other guys. You're paid to supervise."

An extra seventy-five cents an hour, Lemke thought to himself. *Thanks so much for nothing, prick.*

"Supervisors gotta be dependable," Pankow said. "They gotta be around when needed. Otherwise, why pay anyone extra for that?"

"Dependable?" Lemke spoke more loudly than he had intended to. He took a deep breath, struggling to keep his temper, and let it out slowly. "Vern, I put in sixty hours last week, and I can't remember putting in fewer than forty-five for Christ knows how long. I cover for every one of my guys when one of 'em calls in sick. Hell, I've had more six-day weeks than five-day weeks this past year. You know damn well that if anyone's a team player, it's me. The fact is, if I needed to be here, I'd be here."

Pankow tilted his head back slightly and looked down his nose at Lemke, pursing his lips and sticking out his chin with what he believed was an air of superiority. "You saying you maybe need to drop down a step? Move back to regular staff?" Pankow let the words hang in the air. "You thinking that maybe this supervising stuff has gotten to be a bit too much responsibility for you, you think?"

"What?" Lemke's eyes were wide open. "Of course not, Vern. You know I didn't mean that. It's just that—"

"Not much I can do then, is there? Regulations is regulations." Pankow shrugged his shoulders and put up both hands, palms facing out, to fend off further argument. "Way I see it, you have a choice to make. You can either spend Wednesday night and Thursday morning supervising your team—remember, it's *your* team—and make sure the job gets done the way it's supposed to. Or, if you won't be here, let me know now and I'll be glad to reassign you and find someone else who can do your job."

Lemke looked down at his hands, clenched tight in his lap, and sighed. "Fine." He nodded in resignation. "I'll be here." He continued looking down for a few seconds, then slapped his hands on his thighs, stood up and headed for the door.

"And you might want to work on that attitude of yours while you're at it, Eric. Maybe just a little bit," Pankow said. "I'm just letting you know, friend to friend. You don't wanna forget we got the annual Personnel Improvement Statements coming up at the end of the year, and as you well know, they play a big part in deciding next year's pay raise." Personnel Improvement Statements, known among the rank and file as "PISS Reports," were the mall's latest attempt to put a positive spin on employee evaluations.

"Yes, Mr. Pankow," Lemke had said. "I'll remember that."

That was how Eric Lemke had ended up in MightyMall on Thursday morning, November 15th, instead of on the road to Beatrice, Missouri, with his wife, visiting his son's family.

Lemke and his team had worked through Wednesday night moving, unloading, building and rebuilding. They were finished before six this morning and Lemke had sent the rest of his team home. Lemke decided that, since he was already here, he might as well stay a few hours longer and find things to do until noon. He could always use the extra money and he felt like screwing the mall out of a few extra dollars for ruining his travel plans. And since his weekend was blown already, he figured to get ahead on a few projects he needed to finish before the end of the year.

One was the annual check of the service ladders located behind Gonzoland. The ladders stretched from the first basement up to the top of the building above the seventh floor. The inspection climbs were slow, tedious and dangerous. Maintenance workers and ride engineers used several of the ladders regularly. Some had no practical use, other than to serve as alternate or emergency access points. State law, however, required that each ladder be inspected annually to ensure proper working condition.

Lemke was finished inspecting four of the twelve ladders. He opened the service door on the seventh floor marked, "ML7N2" and stepped on to the ledge. He gave the ladder a shake, not expecting it to detach from the wall, but it never hurt to be safe. He made sure his tool belt was fastened, placed his hands on the ladder, stepped on with his right foot, then his left, and started climbing down.

It took Lemke about two minutes to descend to the sixth floor. He climbed slowly, pausing to look for significant corrosion on the ladder itself, loose or missing bolts and cracked concrete in the walls. Lighting was dim, just two lamps pointing toward the ladder from above each service door.

Lemke continued down, looking intently at the ladder's joints and the bolts connecting it to the concrete. Step, look, step, look. Monotonous. Tiring on the eyes. Hard on the knees.

Lemke heard a sound from above. He stopped to listen more intently.

"Anyone there?" He always expected an echo but the vastness seemed to swallow up most sounds.

Lemke looked to his right and saw that he was just below the sixth floor service door. He removed the flashlight from his tool belt and pointed it at the door. The door was closed and he couldn't see anyone.

"Fucking rats." He placed the flashlight back on his tool belt and resumed his climb down the ladder.

CHAPTER 12

Officer Judy Engebretsen of Lost and Found emptied the contents of the red handbag Officer Foreman had brought her earlier in the morning. One pair of lined women's gloves, crumpled credit card receipts, a key ring with a big Buick insignia on it, a bottle of prescription medicine, a mall-issue car locator medallion, and a wallet. Engebretsen unsnapped the wallet clasp and found what she was looking for: a driver's license. Greta Turnblad. But no cell phone and nothing with her home phone number printed on it. No way to contact her immediately. Judging by the date of birth listed on Ms. Turnblad's Minnesota driver's license, Engebretsen concluded the woman was a mall walker. Security or housekeeping would have found the bag if it had been left overnight. The lady probably set it down while putting her bag in a locker before starting her walk and then forgot it. Lots of the older folks did that.

Photo IDs made Officer Engebretsen's life easier. No need to interrogate people before letting them see what she had behind the counter. *What color did you say that bag was? What were your gloves made of?* Photo IDs allowed Mall security to be proactive, instead of having to wait for someone to come in asking for something. Even without a phone number for Ms. Turnblad, she felt good about reuniting the lost handbag with its owner.

Engebretsen accessed MightyMall TV, the internal broadcasting system for the mall. Air time on the one-hundred-forty high-definition screens around the mall was in high demand; the marketing people wanted to promote store sales; Sponsorship sold ads to credit card companies, soft drink makers and cell phone providers; Events pushed upcoming celebrity appearances and book signings.

The security department's computers had immediate override capability. The designers had 9/11 and hurricane season in mind when they included that upgrade a few years ago. The system could be used to broadcast Amber Alerts or evacuate the mall; security had once posted a photo of an escaped convict from North Dakota after one of the officers spotted him on an internal camera. They never did catch the escapee, and tenants weren't happy about the mall shutting down for four hours while security checked every exiting mall guest, but the local press gave the mall high marks for trying.

The system was most often used as a lost child locator. "*Five-year-old boy named Marty is waiting for Mom at the Welcome Desk near the Costco bubble on North 7. Please come immediately or call extension 8936*" could be displayed on all 140 screens instantly via any security department computer.

Engebretsen typed "*Greta Turnblad: your bag located. Please come to Lost and Found in Gonzoland or ask a security officer for assistance*" into her terminal and punched the Enter button.

"There," Officer Engebretsen said. "I'll bet Greta Turnblad comes power walking in here any moment now."

CHAPTER 13

From close up, MightyMall looked like any other gigantic shopping mall with a huge amusement park in the center, it just happened to have more things to do than Orlando and had a daytime population, during holidays, larger than Milwaukee's. Where else could you find an Emporium Armani, a full-service bank, a Banana Republic, a pet store, a real estate agency, a skating rink, a Ruth's Chris Steakhouse, an Arby's, a Hertz Rent-a-Car, a Delta ticket counter, a plastic surgery clinic, a dinner theater and a McDonald's all within two hundred yards of each other, all indoors?

People didn't behave much differently at MightyMall than at other malls in towns large and small around the United States. Kids came to hang out with other kids, except for Friday and Saturday nights when they had to leave by four o'clock unless accompanied by a parent or guardian. Local shoppers bought clothes and shoes, had their hair done and saw a movie. Tourists, who accounted for fifty-five percent of MightyMall's visitors and seventy percent of the money spent in the mall, bought the same things they bought back home. On vacation, though, it was more exciting to buy them here.

Hoping to capitalize on the public's growing interest in healthy menus, the mall once hired a consulting company to create restaurants in each of the food courts featuring organic low-calorie menu items designed by celebrity chefs to be both good tasting and good for you. Handmade gourmet tofu and turkey burgers on whole-wheat buns with sides of salads, fruit cups, fruit juices and non-fat milk. They called the restaurants *MightyHealthy*. People knew and trusted the MightyMall name. They traveled great distances to spend time and money here. Why not demonstrate the mall's ability to tune into current sentiments, and its commitment to people's health, by creating restaurants that were available only at MightyMall?

The venture was a flop. People didn't want to eat at a restaurant they had never tried before, with menu items they didn't recognize. Families wanted Whoppers and Big Macs; business travelers wanted expensive steaks at places with names they knew from trips to Seattle and New York. People wanted the familiar; they just wanted it in a cool place like MightyMall. And while most visitors accepted the notion that they should make healthier food choices, the last place they wanted to do so was at a shopping mall or on a vacation trip. MightyMall's real draw was: All Familiar, All The Time. The last *MightyHealthy* restaurant closed earlier in the year.

It was necessary to look at MightyMall from the outside to see why people would drive thirty minutes to get here instead of five minutes to the mall closer to home. Why did people come by the busloads from Saint Louis, by the planeload from Rio, or by car from Boise? You could find well-known clothing stores, banks, restaurants, spas and jewelry stores anywhere. Viewed separately, MightyMall's individual components weren't that special; collectively, the mall was unique in its audacious size and breadth. People wanted to be able to say to friends and family, "I *went* there! *You* should go, too." People felt incomplete if they hadn't been to MightyMall, like not owning the latest cell phone or video game console. People wanted to belong. Visiting MightyMall made them believe they did.

The difference between MightyMall and a regular mall was like the difference between seeing a movie in a packed theater and watching a DVD at home: shared excitement. Even the best home theater system couldn't reproduce the sensation or experience of watching an action movie with people next to you "oohing" and "aahing" at the same time, magnifying your emotions in a giant feedback loop. Wherever you were in MightyMall, you heard sounds of people screaming in Gonzoland and felt vibrations from the rides. You saw thousands of people carrying shopping bags, eating cotton candy, kids carrying souvenir stuffed animals. All that sound, that energy, trapped inside a building the size of the Pentagon and as tall the Statue of Liberty. Studies showed that people were more likely to wait in a moderately long line than go immediately to a restaurant next door with no line because the line itself was proof of the quality of the experience. If so many people like this restaurant, it must be good. Another study showed that people drinking a wine with a high price printed on the label expressed higher satisfaction than people drinking wine from a bottle with a low price printed on it, even if the two bottles contain the same wine. People want to believe that what they are spending money on is satisfying.

MightyMall successfully capitalized on these human characteristics. It didn't matter that the individual stores and parks were the same as any in their hometown. If it was big, and if so many other people came here, it had to be good.

MightyMall was a self-fulfilling prophecy.

CHAPTER 14

Kiyomi had finished a circuit of the first floor and was halfway around the second floor when shoppers started showing up in numbers. November 15th wasn't officially holiday shopping season yet but most of the stores already had taken to offering specials from the beginning of November. Hundreds of green wreaths sporting red bows hung suspended at identical heights along every MightyMall shopping avenue, like giant lime lifesavers. Miles of colored lights traced storefronts and exits. One hundred thousand red, green and white lights on MightyMall's roof created a wreath large enough to see from jets passing overhead. Rumors that the MightyMall wreath could be seen from the International Space Station could not be verified.

November 15th was especially busy this year because it coincided with the annual Minnesota Education Association teachers' conference. Moms came seeking sales, dragging their elementary-school-age children with them. Tweens and teens took off on their own or with friends after receiving discount brochures and stern warnings from Mom to stay together at all times, not to talk to strange men and to not even think about getting a tattoo. For most Dads it was still too early to worry about Christmas shopping; those visiting from out of town with families headed immediately for Best Buy, Bass Pro or Hooters to bide time until lunch or until it was their turn to watch the kids while Mom went off shopping on her own in the afternoon. Few visitors were "just hanging at the mall" on this day.

MightyMall encouraged people to take souvenir photos during their visits. Train and bus passengers snapped shots of the four-story "Welcome to MightyMall" signs at the north and south entrances. Gonzoland was always popular with shutterbugs thanks to the excellent lighting and multitude of beautiful sights within its 30-acres, especially during the holidays. Hardcore shoppers were usually too busy shopping to worry about taking pictures, but foreign tourists regularly asked fellow shoppers, security officers or complete strangers to take pictures they could send to friends and family back home.

Kiyomi Nagata was on the lookout for a specific kind of photographer, one who walked alone, carried few bags and who stopped in locations that had little to do with shopping, eating or playing. The pictures such people took were not for sharing with friends, unless such friends were intent on murdering people.

Service doors from the shopping avenues into the back corridors remained unlocked at all times. The *Employee Only* signs on the doors were intended to discourage use by unauthorized personnel. The backlit *Exit* signs above the doors provided legally required access points on all floors to emergency stairs leading to the first basement, through tunnels running under the road surrounding MightyMall, and out street-level doors on the other side.

Security dedicated significant numbers of hidden cameras and frequent monitoring by officers to preventing unauthorized access by lost shoppers, amorous sweethearts, absconding shoplifters, or terrorists. Most people saw the signs on the doors and continued on their way. Kids sometimes snuck in on a dare or to find a place to make out. Shoplifters fleeing stores most often tried to blend into the crowds around them or head to their cars, which they could only find by going out the way they came in. Occasionally, higher profile, and embarrassing, crimes took place; a mentally handicapped woman was raped in one of the service stairwells several years back, prompting weeks of negative press and a thorough review of security policies. Hidden sensors scanned proximity badges, worn by all management staff and authorized store employees, every time one of them passed through a service door. Cameras inside the doors took photos at regular intervals. Security computers used facial recognition software to cross-reference the images with stored photos. If the photo matched the badge, nothing happened. If the photographed face was not in the security database, or if the face did not match the ID on the badge that passed through the door, a security officer was dispatched immediately. The security photo was sent to cell phones of all on-duty officers. Sensors in the corridors followed the movement of the unidentified subject and relayed his or her location to the dispatched officer, who could intercept the potential intruder in three minutes or less. One of the duties of uniformed security officers on patrol was to identify anyone displaying unusually high interest in the service doors or the security cameras near them.

Kiyomi kept a casual eye on the many back hallway doors when she passed but didn't spend significant time inside. Security officers covered them. Dressed undercover as she was, there was a risk that someone might see her going in and report her, wasting time and potentially blowing her cover. If she did see someone ducking into a service door, she had a small microphone inside the collar of her sweatshirt that she could activate by pushing against her neck, connecting her instantly to the Security Action Center.

Kiyomi was more interested in people standing around for no apparent reason. The cameras were well hidden, but you could spot them if you looked hard enough. People staring intently at one of the cameras earned Kiyomi's attention. People taking notes also caught her eye; organized shoppers brought shopping lists and checked things off quickly as they moved from one store to the next. People writing lengthy notes warranted a closer look, especially when glancing furtively around them.

Kiyomi's mind kept returning to the episode this morning with Lucy Evans as if caught in a feedback loop. She could find no reason for Lucy to pretend she was not an employee or to approach Kiyomi in any case. And why had she seemed so fidgety?

She was anxious to get back to the Welcome Desk near Northern Lights West 1.

Officer Foreman's territory today was Gonzoland. Three of the rollercoasters raced along as safety technicians ran them through their paces. A housekeeper was sweeping the glass-bottomed skyway that spanned the seventh floor from east to west, high above the dozens of rides, bungee jump stations, rock climbing walls, blimps and gondolas. Mega Monorail Alpha connected the northern and southern most points of the fourth floor. Mega Monorail Beta ran on a suspended sixth floor track crossing from northeast to southwest.

The job of watching the park differed from that of X-Team members who patrolled the shopping avenues. Foreman today would spend more time looking at what people were carrying and doing while walking around the park or waiting to board one of the rides. Any suspicious bulges from an overcoat that might be a gun or a bomb to be dropped from a rollercoaster? Someone clutching a handbag a little too closely?

Anyone with a distant look in their eyes, as if preparing to meet their maker?

Foreman didn't like the contrast: people planning death and destruction in a place dedicated to joy and laughter. There was probably no good place for mayhem, Foreman supposed, but he was sure it didn't belong here.

That was why he liked the park early in the morning, empty of potential terrorists. It was clean and quiet and full of promise.

CHAPTER 15

Carolyn looked out with satisfaction at the two-dozen-or-so newspaper, radio and TV reporters in the VIP Premium Voyageurs Room. Most were seated at the six round tables near the front of the room, each table with an unhindered view of the projector screen pulled down from the ceiling. A few were scribbling notes. Some looked bored. Three cameramen were making last minute adjustments to their equipment. Reporters from the *Star Tribune* and *Pioneer Press* chatted amiably in the back. A dais sat atop a miniature stage to the left of the screen; Carolyn had told her staff that she needed to be able to make eye contact with reporters wherever they stood or sat.

Mayor Calvin Gleason of Saint Commercia sat at the table nearest the dais. Carolyn had met the Mayor at the Voyageurs Room entrance herself, personally escorting him to his table. She then sat with him for a few minutes to demonstrate her respect. Carolyn found the Mayor, with his vain but fruitless attempts to hide his male pattern baldness by growing his few remaining hairs on one side of his head several inches long—she and her staff referred to him as CombOver Cal—to be comical. But he was mayor and one of the reasons MightyMall ended up in Saint Commercia. He was mayor when Titanic Properties formally decided to locate their new mall in Saint Commercia—though negotiations had begun during the tenure of his predecessor; MightyMall *did* bring in over $20 million annually to the city's coffers, allowing Gleason to reduce property taxes to the lowest level of any municipality in the state, and the mall was a major employer of Saint Commercia residents. When voters considered mayoral candidates during election years, Gleason reminded everyone that he alone was responsible for the city's robust economy.

Follicular challenges and a predisposition for self-aggrandizement aside, Carolyn knew that Mayor Gleason was a dependable friend of MightyMall; one whose help she would need more if her plans for the expansion of MightyMall were to be realized.

An attractive blond wearing a navy skirt and jacket with a white silk blouse sat next to the mayor. Billie Brandt was President of the Saint Commercia Chamber of Commerce. Brandt had cocked her head towards the mayor, as if straining to hear something important he had said. Carolyn noticed the mayor's surreptitious glances towards Brandt's ample breasts. She knew that the second button on Brandt's shirt hadn't been left open by accident. The cow.

Brandt constantly lectured Carolyn on the need for a closer partnership between the Chamber and MightyMall, of the need for the mall to help the Chamber in their efforts to attract a more diverse, less service-oriented, business base. She wanted more high tech and financial corporations, businesses that would provide higher paying jobs and make the economy less cyclical than one dependant solely on the retail industry.

Early meetings between MightyMall and the Chamber had gone well. The mall owners understood and supported the need to be good community citizens. The mall had set up a foundation to provide tuition support for at-risk youth in Saint Commercia and committed a six-figure donation to it annually. Phil Kahn at Titanic Properties had instructed Nathan Parsons to make good-faith efforts to support non-profit groups in need of public space for fundraising events.

Relations between the Chamber and MightyMall had chilled when Brandt began questioning why an enterprise as large and successful as MightyMall paid such low business and property taxes. Why their corporate tax rate was lower than what other Saint Commercia businesses had to pay. *Are you forgetting*, Carolyn had tried to explain, *the thousands of jobs that wouldn't exist here—that might have ended up out of state, maybe even in Wisconsin, for Christ's sake—without MightyMall? Or the millions of dollars in taxes the mall already paid? Or the economic impact of all the money tourists spent in local hotels, restaurants, museums and theaters?*

That may be true, Brandt had said quietly while sitting across the desk in Carolyn's office. *But that was then. People take your mall for granted now. The jobs, the corporate taxes, have been here for as long as their short attention spans can remember. The economy is not as strong as it was. Everyone is being asked to make sacrifices. Why shouldn't the big, strong MightyMall do the same?* It was at that moment Carolyn had realized the truth about Billie Brandt. This slutty bitch was going to run for mayor someday and her campaign would be something like, "Why Shouldn't The Mighty Help The Rest of Us?"

Carolyn looked at the mayor and Brandt, who seemed to be chatting happily. *Are you blind, you horny old fool? Or are you two somehow in cahoots? You planning to move on to bigger and better things and leave Saint Commercia to Billie as a going away gift?*

Fantastic Catering had come through in spades. Gone were the oatmeal cookies Carolyn had complained about earlier in the morning. Three long tables on the left side of the room were covered with enough fruit Danish, croissants, fresh-baked chocolate chip cookies and cut fruit for fifty. Few reporters had touched the food, but interns and younger office staff were already grazing.

The chairs around the tables covered in crisp white linens were almost full. Each table had a vase of fresh flowers in the center. The semi-circle of tripods in the back with their cameras all pointed at Carolyn looked like a firing squad. *Bring it on,* she thought to herself. *I'll show you. I'll show you all.* A few of the reporters had chosen to lean against the side walls. They were speaking softly into their cell phones or jotting notes on small notepads.

Everyone had come to find out if the rumors were true, if MightyMall was finally moving ahead with the expansion plans they had promised since before MightyMall had opened. Was it really going to happen? Now, after years of grand announcements followed weeks or months later with quiet press releases clarifying and spinning the earlier "misstatements" and "circumstances beyond our control?" Where was the money coming from? Why did Minnesota even *need* a larger MightyMall? Wasn't this one, plus that one in Bloomington, enough already? Some people thought MightyMall shouldn't have been built in the first place. Carolyn had walked through this press conference in her mind hundreds of times, anticipated every possible question. Or so she hoped.

Carolyn gave a short nod to Rakhshanda, the Pakistani IT techie seated in the back who was running her presentation, then looked to the right at the screen to confirm that the projector was on. She usually used a clicker so she could advance presentation images herself; today she wanted no distractions, no chance of foul-ups like frozen screens or missing files. If anything went wrong today, she wanted someone to blame, and a diminutive, dark-skinned foreigner would serve well in that role.

Carolyn looked with reverence at the on screen image, one she used in all her presentations, shining like a religious icon: the MightyMall logo—a muscular super hero on one knee named MightyMan, who looked suspiciously like Superman minus the cape. He was holding a family of four in his left hand and a stack of nameless department stores, kiosks, restaurants, amusement parks and hotels in his right. MightyMan looked off into the distance with an expression of strength, confidence and kindness. The miniature Dad in his left hand looked successful, trustworthy and unadulterous; Mom, slightly shorter than Dad, appeared simultaneously loving, career-minded, and shapely—but not so shapely that women would resent her; the kids looked happy, intelligent and not overly mischievous. Skin tones were beige and everyone's features were so non-specific that the same images worked equally well in ads targeted at white, Latino, Asian and African American markets.

Carolyn checked her watch. Ten past eleven. Only ten minutes behind schedule, not bad. She looked at Patter, standing in the back with arms crossed, wearing a look of smug satisfaction. He nodded. Everyone who was planning to attend the press conference had arrived.

Show time.

CHAPTER 16

"Ladies and gentlemen." Carolyn stopped to clear her throat and take a sip of water. "Ladies and gentlemen. I'd like to first of all thank all of you for coming here today. What I have to tell you is extremely exciting news."

The chatting stopped. Worthy of skepticism or not, this announcement was what everyone had come to hear. People put down coffee cups, took final bites of food, returned pastries to plates, brushed crumbs off hands, turned on voice recorders and cameras, and picked up pens. All eyes were focused expectantly on Carolyn Noxon Batch.

"But before I go any further I have a few people I must acknowledge," she said. "First and foremost, our beloved mayor, the Honorable Calvin Gleason," Carolyn motioned for Gleason to stand, "who as we all know, and who will remind anyone who forgets," she paused to allow chuckling at her gentle ribbing of the mayor, "is one of the main reasons that MightyMall is here today." The mayor stood briefly to acknowledge the warm applause.

"Billie Brandt." Carolyn smiled radiantly at the woman sitting ten feet away. *The evil bitch*, Carolyn thought. "The Saint Commercia business community would be nowhere near as strong as it is today without your tireless efforts." Carolyn was gratified to hear only tepid applause for her arch nemesis.

Carolyn took a deep breath and smiled at the audience, caught the eye of a young cameraman in back, turned to one of the tables on the left and finished with a wink at a young woman near the front who used to be her intern. *You must project confidence and calm*, her three-hundred-dollar-per-hour consultant had coached her, *but also convey warmth.* Connect *with the audience. Make them like* you, *and they will like what you say.*

"I was a little worried that some people might not make it today. And not just because of the snow outside. Some of you may be thinking, and with good reason, that you have heard all of this before." Carolyn smiled somewhat sheepishly, pausing again to allow for appreciative laughter. Dick Cross, her PR director, had suggested the line as an icebreaker, chuckled loudly, hoping to get the ball rolling. No one in the audience took him up on it.

"Today, however, is the day when it all becomes real. When myth becomes reality. Years from now, people will remember today as the day MightyMall's long-promised expansion plans passed from speculation to reality. No more abstract ideas based on insurmountable obstacles. Today the long rumored future begins. Right here, right now."

Carolyn raised her eyebrows and nodded imperceptibly to Rakhshanda. "Ladies and gentlemen…."

The screen filled with an animated rendering of MightyMall from a point directly above the top floor of the building. The roof and floors were opaque but clearly delineated, making it easy to see inside. Thousands of miniature shoppers scurried along shopping avenues. Monorails zipped back and forth along their tracks. Park rides in Gonzoland spun, swung, twirled, rose and fell in perfect detail. Motorcoaches and cars and trains streamed into the transit centers, disgorging arriving visitors and gobbling up replacements for the rides home.

The image shrank down to a small circle about one-tenth its former size and slid to the lower left portion of the screen. An icon representing MightyMall's parking lots and ramps appeared as a simple square just to the right. The remaining four fifths of the screen above was blank. The perspective changed, from a two-dimensional overhead view, to a three dimensional view one might see from an airplane at a thousand feet, making its final approach from the south to Minneapolis / Saint Paul International in the distance, MightyMall visible in the left foreground. The MightyMall image began to vibrate, as if in a strong earthquake, and a small, grey triangular-shaped object poked through the upper right hand portion of the screen. The object grew larger and was joined by other triangles nearby, rising up in concert like a chorus of indefatigable monoliths from the earth's depths. The rapidly expanding images revealed more details—snow, fissures, conifer trees, valleys, plains, rivers, villages, houses, railroads, a massive body of water—until the elements filled the entire area north of MightyMall and it became obvious that the elements were not separate components, but one, single, interconnected ecosystem. The perspective rotated again, the viewer now thousands of feet up, directly over the area encompassing MightyMall and the newly emerging entity.

"I give you … *Rodinia*."

The outlines of *Rodinia* onscreen resembled a pizza crust in need of further rolling, pushing and pulling. The body of water, looking like an inverted image of South America, occupied much of the southwestern region, narrowing as it moved north. Tributaries emptied into the lake at several points from the east. A mountain range traced the eastern border, culminating in a single, sharp, snow-covered peak to the northeast. To the west of the mountain range were gentle green hills, merging into lush forests. Along the base of the mountain range were several communities containing individual homes, low-rise apartment buildings, markets and public gathering places. Vast plains in the center showed grazing livestock, assorted crops grew in farmland closer to the lake.

Carolyn stuck out her chin and looked out triumphantly at the audience.

No one spoke for a full minute. Someone Carolyn didn't know finally said, tentatively, "You are making a ... what? ... a new ... ecosystem? A new ... planet, maybe?"

A few people in the audience chuckled. Carolyn maintained her look of conquest.

"*Rodinia* will be the 21st Century's first lifestyle bionetwork," she said. "Rakhshanda, zoom in to MightyMountain One. " The onscreen mouse hovered briefly over the tallest mountain and clicked on it. The image sped toward the viewer, became opaque, then disappeared, replaced with an approximation of what the mountain would look like if you had sliced off the south face. A hotel occupied a dozen floors at the bottom of the mountain. Tiny stick figure guests were checking in at the front desk, riding elevators, entering rooms, swimming in pools, shopping at boutiques, eating at restaurants, sitting in theaters. One of the hotel's elevators ran all the way from the first floor to the peak of the mountain—on the inside.

"Okay, Rakhshanda," Carolyn said. "Full view." The previous view from 5,000 feet returned.

"Good. Now let's go next to the lake, shall we? Any point on the surface."

Carolyn felt her confidence swelling. This project was her baby, her future. She had spent months convincing Titanic Properties to abandon the design their own team had come up with the previous year, *Patriot*

Park. Times had changed; the mood of the country had shifted. Overt religiosity and aggressive patriotism were out. People wanted a bolder vision now, they wanted newer, bigger, audacious. The time was right for Minnesota to leapfrog competition around the world with a show-stopping plan of its own. When the owners saw the projected revenue, and her brilliant plans for financing the project, they bit.

The onscreen mouse had moved to the northern part of Lake Interior and zoomed to a point a few dozen yards above the surface, showing gentle waters reflecting blue skies and twinkling sunshine. Motorboats pulled water skiers. Kids leaped off houseboats. Fishermen sat contentedly in small boats, lines in water, bobbers bobbing.

The *Star Tribune* reporter turned to his counterpart at the *Pioneer Press* and said, "How the hell big is this thing going to be?" His friend shrugged and shook his head. Carolyn overheard the question.

"MightyMall has purchased nine square miles of farmland directly north of here.

Carolyn turned her attention back to the screen. "Submerge One, Rakhshanda." The IT technician continued staring slack-jawed at the screen, as was everyone else in the room. She had glanced briefly at the presentation's first two slides in the morning while setting up, paying little attention to the contents. Her job was simply to make sure the software and hardware functioned properly, and to advance slides when Carolyn told her to. She had been expecting a bunch of stale architectural drawings.

"*Rakhshanda!*" Carolyn said. *"The lake!"*

Rakhshanda snapped her attention to Carolyn. "Oh! Sorry." She looked back down at her laptop screen, confirmed that the mouse was still on the lake and clicked.

The vantage point now glided underwater. Scuba divers inspected an ancient shipwreck, with a small passenger submarine hovering nearby.

Lake trout and large-mouth bass, muskies and walleyes swam lazily back and forth. Underwater fencing indicated a fish farm.

"Rakhshanda?" Carolyn made sure she had the techie's attention. "Go ahead with Submerge Two now."

The perspective sank deeper into the lake, entering a transparent tunnel, glass-walled on four sides.

"Carolyn, can I ask a question?" A reporter raised his hand. "Bob Tatreault from the *Star Tribune.*"

"Yes, Bob."

"Is that tunnel in the middle of the lake? Or ocean … or whatever that is?"

"We call it Lake Interior. And, yes, that tunnel is in the middle. Actually, about two thirds of the way to the bottom, to be precise."

"How deep is that lake going to be?"

"One hundred feet. Our plans call for six different underwater tunnels, four along the bottom—you can just see one of them off in the distance …" Carolyn aimed her laser pointer at a point near the top of the screen. "… up there. You can't see it in this image but two tunnels will run north to south the entire length of *Rodinia.* Two will go east to west, intersecting with the north/south tunnels near the center of the lake. Two express tunnels will be suspended fifty feet from the bottom and will run from MightyMountain to MightyMall. All will contain both walking paths and high speed conveyor belts."

Several other hands shot up, shouted questions merging in a cacophony of excitement. Ignoring all of them, Carolyn said, "Rakhshanda. Slippidy-Do-Dah."

"Slippidy-Do-Dah?"

Carolyn smiled sweetly at Rakhshanda, walked back to her lone table in the back and spoke softly into her ear. "First time using this software?"

"No, but nobody told me it had—" On the left side of her laptop screen, invisible to the audience, was a vertical strip of thumbnail images labeled with single word identifiers. "Oh … here it is." She clicked on the one labeled, "Slippidy." Carolyn was already walking back to the dais.

The vantage point shot up several hundred feet above the surface. Visitors were once again ants down below scurrying in all directions. The mountain, the lake and MightyMall looked like thumbnail images on an atlas.

Carolyn gazed at the screen for several moments, then turned to the audience. "See anything unusual?"

Everyone leaned forward in their seats; eyes squinted, hoping to be the first to find whatever it was Carolyn was talking about. No one said anything.

"Nothing?" Carolyn said in the tone of a slightly disappointed homeroom teacher speaking to a group of dim kindergarten students unable to find the Easter Eggs. "Anybody?"

"Give us a hint," someone said. Several people laughed; it felt like a game.

Poor children. "Don't you see something suspended a few hundred feet off the ground? Beginning at MightyMountain, at the top, extending toward MightyMall near the bottom?"

More silence. Then: "What's that fuzzy thing?" Tatreault said, pointing. "Looks kind of like the camera was out of focus. Makes the ground underneath it look blurrier than the rest of the picture. You see that?" He turned to his colleague at the *Pioneer Press*.

"Yeah, I see it. Running diagonally from right to left."

"Yeah. That thing."

"Very good." Carolyn clapped once. "Rakhshanda. Click on the Slippidy-Do-Dah image."

The blurry area came immediately into focus. A long band, rippled like a playground slide, stretched the entire length of *Rodinia*, from high atop MightyMountain in the northeast, to the border with MightyMall in the south. The rendering began to animate; children and adults in swimsuits emerged from the elevator at the top of MightyMountain, stepped out onto a fenced-in ledge and jumped into a shallow swimming pool which magically funneled everyone to a multi-lane slide where each person *whooshed* down a near vertical drop that quickly lessened to a gentler gradient, the slide continuing to undulate as it moved its sliders along. Adults and children waved arms excitedly and gazed at the breathtaking vistas encompassing the entire nine square-mile park. Slippidy-Do-Dah continued inexorably southward, approaching the basin near the entrance to MightyMall where it plunged into a shallow pool where everyone easily stood and walked to the shore.

"No way!" someone shouted.

"Get *out* of here!"

"Holy crap!"

"Sweeeeet!"

Bob Tatreault said, "What is going to hold that thing up? The slide thing."

"Cutting-edge nanotechnology," Carolyn said. "Now, I can't explain the science behind it, but the slide material is translucent, strong as titanium, yet lighter than fiberglass."

"Who makes it?"

"Manufacturer's name, please?"

"I can't tell you that now," Carolyn said.

She pointed her laser at the top of MightyMountain and continued. "One end of the slide is anchored to the top of MightyMountain and the other, as you can see, empties into the southern end of Lake Interior. The mountain and three support columns—one at the south end and the two other each about a mile apart—will bear the weight of the Slippidy-Do-Dah and up to five thousand people at one time. Ten-foot high translucent retaining walls make sure no one falls off."

"Carolyn? Jim Gunther, Pioneer Press."

"Yes, Jim."

"Can you give us the dimensions of this thing?"

"Of course," Carolyn said as she consulted her notes. "Just under three miles long and fifty yards wide." She looked out at the audience. "And here's a number for your readers, viewers and listeners: the north end of Slippidy-Do-Dah will be over nine hundred feet high—right here in the Midwest! MightyMountain itself, at nine hundred twenty-six feet, will be the tallest structure in Minnesota." She smiled. "Or the highest mountain, if you prefer."

Reporters scribbled furiously on notepads and checked to make sure tape recorders were still running.

Onscreen, summer changed to winter. Watersliders disappeared, replaced by skiers and snowboarders. The final descent of Slippidy-Do-Dah now terminated in a frozen lake. The lake was peppered with ice fishing huts, skating rinks and several hockey games.

Carolyn basked in the appreciative *oohs* and *ahs*.

"Still," someone said. "That's just two seasons. What do you do the rest of the year?"

The season changed again. Forests became a riot of reds, yellows, greens and browns.

Gunther said, "Are those luges that people are riding on?"

"Something like that," Carolyn said. "Flexible plastic sleds covered with gel pads on top for comfortable rides. Both the sleds and Slippidy-Do-Dah will be encased in a non-stick alloy. This animation is representing autumn, obviously, but we can use these sleds during warm winters and springtime as well. Whenever we want, really."

Bicyclers onscreen dressed in light jackets raced along winding, paved paths up and down rolling hills, in and out of colorful woods. Couples held hands as they walked along beaches. Families camped and barbequed.

Carolyn said, "Let's take a break from visuals, shall we? Rakhshanda, back to main screen." The bird's eye view of both MightyMall and the expansion once again filled the screen.

"Questions?"

Everyone's hands rose.

"Whew. Where to start?" Carolyn said, feigning bewilderment. She pointed at a familiar looking man in his 40s sitting near the back. "You, sir. I'm afraid I don't know your name." Carolyn had noticed him speaking with one of the cameramen several times during the presentation. He rose to his feet.

"Yes, thank you, Ms. Batch," he said. "Paul Ruvio. I'm with MSNBC."

"Yes, Mr. Ruvio."

"We've seen a lot of nature—mountains, camping, farming, the lake. Can you tell us more about the revenue-generating aspect of the park? How you expect to make enough money to pay for what will certainly be a huge construction bill?"

"Certainly. And I'm glad you asked that, Mr. Ruvio." Carolyn shuffled her notes, scanned them briefly and looked back up. "*Rodinia* will become, quite simply, the one destination that every person in the world will want to *be* in, whether to visit, work, or live in. People today visit Las Vegas for facsimiles of pyramids, miniature Eiffel Towers, large swimming pools made to look like beachfronts. They travel to mixed-use facilities like MightyMall and our friendly competitor to the south, Mall of America, to enjoy indoor amusement parks and shopping avenues protected from the elements. They live in suburbs and brave daily traffic jams to work downtown, or vice versa. Think about what a waste that is. A waste of time and energy.

"*Rodinia* will be the ultimate reality experience because it will be non-stop. Visitors will swim in an ecologically perfect lake; ski and slide on the world's longest slide. Climbers will scale real boulders—the façade of the mountain *will* contain actual boulders, rocks and trees—to the highest point in the Midwest."

Carolyn paused to give her audience time to think.

"Imagine being able to walk directly from your hotel room to the top of MightyMountain, ride on a high-speed elevator, and walk along a three mile long underwater tunnel—twenty-four hours a day. Imagine visiting a real farm to harvest organic vegetables, watching our world-class chefs prepare them—and the fish your husband caught earlier in the day—for you that evening. Wake up one morning and tell your family, 'Hey, let's go camping down by the lake or on the mountain tonight' and being able to actually do it."

Someone raised a hand but Carolyn waved her off.

"Imagine finishing the greatest vacation ever and wishing you could preserve your experiences, replay them for your family and friends, for all time. Next generation GPS badges all guests will wear upon entry to *Rodinia* will make that dream a reality. Your every move outside of your hotel rooms will be recorded on any of five thousand video cameras strategically placed throughout the park filming your every move. Want a disc of your two days here? Our onsite production staff will have access to all relevant footage—or specific hours and days of your visit, your choice—and will put together a Hollywood-level movie of your vacation, complete with soundtrack and a trailer to send to your friends.

"Now imagine *living* in a place like that. Micro communities will offer comfortable homes, shops you can walk to, public gathering spaces.

Monorails will connect your community with several other communities and office parks in *Rodinia*. Our office parks will contain businesses spanning the economic spectrum—from clinics and research facilities and libraries, to the arts, to convention centers, to light manufacturing, and everything in between. Our residents will be working on those farms, in those hospitals, in the hotels and convention centers, helping our guests create memories."

"She may be the world's biggest bitch," Patter whispered to Dick Cross, Public Relations Director in the back of the room, "but she sure has vision. I'll give her that."

"We estimate fifteen thousand permanent residents and 150 million visitors a year, twenty percent local and eighty percent of them tourists, half of those from abroad. These visitors will stay in our hotels; shop in our stores; purchase our manufactured products, our organically grown produce, fish and meat products; visit our research facilities, our convention centers, rent climbing and ski and camping equipment, bicycles, boats. The project will more than pay for itself. More importantly, it will do so in a way that has a positive impact on the community, the state and the environment."

Carolyn pointed at a tall, lanky man leaning against the right wall. "Sorry, you've had your hand up the longest."

"Yes," he said. "Pete Brannigan, Minnesota Public Radio."

"Yes, Pete."

"Earlier development plans MightyMall presented included stipulations that the state, local counties, or Saint Commercia, or all three, finance part of the construction costs through direct grants, tax rebates, or a combination of both. Can you comment on whether this plan includes such stipulations? And if not, can you give us details of how you plan to pay for the construction of *Rodinia?* And, finally, can you give us a total price tag?"

"I'd be glad to, Pete," Carolyn said. "Though you might want to sit down for this part: neither MightyMall nor Titanic Properties will be asking for *any* government support for *Rodinia*. The entire project will be financed privately."

"What?" Brannigan said. "Are you saying that Titanic Properties has enough money to pay for this on their own?"

Carolyn held up her hands. "I am not prepared to name names at this time," she said. "But I can tell you that we have signed contracts with several partners who will provide one hundred percent of the funding required to make *Rodinia* a reality and open to the public within seven years. Total cost: $43.6 billion dollars."

CHAPTER 17

Mike Foreman sat at a table in one of the food courts eating lunch. He packed his own lunch most days, partly to save money and partly because he didn't like eating fast food. The mall had over two hundred restaurants, one hundred thirty of which served fast food. Even where "healthy choices" were available, Foreman often found himself making unhealthy choices. Who goes to McDonald's for a salad?

Today he had brought a cucumber sandwich on whole wheat bread, a Tupperware filled with *edamame* beans and a wedge of apple pie his mom had sent home with him last weekend. Foreman didn't know if his lunches contained fewer calories than restaurant food, but they felt healthier and tasted a hell of a lot better.

Foreman looked up after taking a bite of his sandwich. Kiyomi Nagata was stepping off an escalator. He noticed that she was carrying a brown paper bag.

Foreman said, "Hey, Kiyomi! Over here!" Most of the security officers called each other by their last names. Kiyomi was the only officer Foreman had met whom everyone called by her first name. At least he thought that Kiyomi was her first name.

Kiyomi headed toward Foreman's table. Several male diners stole furtive looks as she passed. Foreman speculated, as he often did, about what it was that made Kiyomi so attractive. Not her fashion-model good looks, though they didn't hurt. Or her dancer's posture that somehow reminded him of the actress Summer Glau. It was something in her facial expressions: she projected confidence without arrogance, was always friendly but not needy. She was comfortable in her own skin. Kiyomi, Foreman decided, was the type of woman that guys would gladly spend Saturday night with and then bring to Mom's for Sunday brunch.

"Foreman." She walked up to his table, placed a paper bag next to her chair and sat down. "How are you doing today?"

"Oh, business as usual. You know. I was expecting *Gonzo* to be busier. Maybe everyone's Christmas shopping." Foreman looked at Kiyomi while taking a swig of water from his bottle. "How about you?"

"Busy!" Kiyomi said. "Or I should say crowded, at least on one and two." Foreman knew she was referring to the first and second floors. "The uniformed officers have their hands full. I saw them escorting this one man—how do you say when a guy has long, very dirty hair and looks very mean?"

"'Skanky,' maybe? 'Skuzzy'?"

"Skuzzy, that is it. I have heard that word before. He was definitely skuzzy. I don't think he took a bath in many weeks. His jeans were torn and he had this leather jacket, like motorcycle gangs wear?"

"Skuzzy. That's your word. Was he in a fight, or something?"

"I didn't see. He rushed by me surrounded by four officers just after opening time. Later I was on the second floor and saw two girls punching each other, pulling out their hair. Uniforms were just arriving."

Foreman nodded. He liked listening to Kiyomi speak. Her voice had a singsong quality that was both soothing and alluring.

She sighed. "Not much for me to do, however." Her mouth curled down in an exaggerated frown that Foreman guessed was supposed to indicate she was pouting. "A lot of watching, harder with so many people walking all over the place. I saw a guy playing with one of those new Sony digital cameras but I don't think he was doing anything wrong; the camera was just new and he didn't know how to use it. I was going to chat him up, just to make sure, when his wife and two kids got there ahead of me." She looked at Foreman's sandwich and giggled. "That looks healthy."

Kiyomi had a bubbly laugh that Foreman liked. "Everybody says that. I swear, I just like cucumber sandwiches. Don't they have them in Japan?"

"I don't think so." Kiyomi brushed a strand of hair from her eyes. "Maybe at a hotel coffee shop. I have never seen one."

"But Japanese people eat healthy food, right? Fish and stuff? Don't you guys eat lots of stir-fry vegetables? Egg rolls?"

"That's Chinese. Japanese fry almost nothing. Traditional dishes are mostly fish, meat or vegetables; served raw, broiled or boiled. I don't mean to be rude, but I do think Japanese eat more balanced meals than Americans."

"Oh, I hear you," Foreman said. "Americans eat crap, no question about that." He watched Kiyomi take a long, slender case out of her paper bag and place it on the table in front of her. She then removed a large package wrapped in white cloth covered with blue dots. The four corners of the cloth were tied at the top.

"What have you got in that bandana there?"

"It is not bandana," Kiyomi laughed. "It is called *furoshiki*. It is holding my lunch. Can you say *furoshiki?*"

"*Frowsh* ... say it again?"

"FU-ROH-SHEE-KEE. Four syllables."

"FOODOH—"

"No," Kiyomi said, firmly but without a trace of impatience. "Japanese Rs sound like a mixing of American Rs, Ds and Ls. Try again. FU ... ROH ... SHEE ... KEE." She over enunciated each syllable. "Make each syllable longer."

"FU-ROH-SKEE-KEE."

"Very good, Foreman! You speak very good Japanese."

Foreman didn't believe a word of it but was pumped that Kiyomi had said so.

"*Furoshiki* is made of a piece of cloth and can be used to carry anything. It comes from ancient history in Japan." Kiyomi untied the two knots at the top and splayed the corners open on the table like a blooming flower petal. Two square boxes were stacked one on top of each other. "See? I put my box lunch, called *obento,* in the center, then tie the *furoshiki* like this." She retied the four corners. "It makes the boxes easy to carry. I just hold onto it like this—" Kiyomi hooked her index finger through one of the knots. "And I can reuse again and again."

"Very cool. Do you make the lunches yourself?"

"Of course!" Kiyomi laughed again. "My parents live in Japan. Nobody else will make this for me." She removed the top box and placed it next to the bottom one, unclipped fasteners on each box, removed the tops and stacked them to one side.

"What have you got in there?" Foreman said, pointing.

"This box is rice, as you can see."

"What's that red thing in the aluminum foil thingy in the corner?"

"*Umeboshi.* It's kind of a pickled plum. Try."

"Are you sure? You've just got the one."

"Please. I have many other foods. Try it." Kiyomi expertly plucked the *umeboshi* with her chopsticks and placed it in Foreman's outstretched hand. "Careful. It still has the, what do you call it? Seed?"

Foreman put it in his mouth and took a tentative chew, not knowing what to expect. "Pit," he said, mouth full. "Too big for a seed. We call it a pit." It was bitter, sour and salty. Not something Foreman would choose to have again.

"How do you like it? Most Americans can't eat it."

"This is great," Foreman said.

"Really? Are you teasing?"

"No, I'm serious. It's different, that's for sure. I like trying new kinds of food." Foreman quickly chewed the remainder of the *umeboshi* and swallowed. "Kind of salty, though. Makes me thirsty." He took a swig of water to wash out the bitter aftertaste, which tasted to him vaguely like a plum soaked in salt water.

"What else have you got there?" he said, pointing at the second *obento* box.

"Well." Kiyomi was pleased that Officer Foreman was interested in learning about her native food. Most of her acquaintances thought that *sushi*, *tempura*, and *teppanyaki* of the type served in Benihana restaurants were everything that Japanese ate, and lost interest if she talked about other dishes. Foreman seemed different, Kiyomi thought, more open to new things. He was also cute and in very good shape.

"This is spinach mixed with ground, roasted sesame seeds." The second box had built-in partitions that reminded Foreman of TV dinner trays. Kiyomi aimed her chopsticks in a section that took up about a fifth of the box's space. "Here try a little," she said.

"No, I—" Foreman hated spinach but Kiyomi had already dropped some on the piece of discarded plastic he had wrapped his sandwich in. "I don't have anything to eat it with—"

"I'm sorry I don't have a fork." Kiyomi pulled out a second set of chopsticks. "Can you use these?" Before Foreman could respond that he didn't think he could, she gently grabbed his right hand and opened it. She had long, slender fingers and Foreman felt a jolt of electricity where she touched him. Kiyomi placed the fat end of both chopsticks in the base of the joint between thumb and index finger. The barrel of one stick rested on his middle finger, with the index finger providing control; the other stick rested on his third finger. Kiyomi took her set of chopsticks and demonstrated their proper use, snapping the ends together several times like lobster claws. "They are much better, much more … how do you say in English … precise … for picking things up than a fork or spoon." She then proceeded to pick up a single grain of rice with her chopsticks and put it in her mouth. Kiyomi smiled at Foreman with a mixture of satisfaction and, maybe something else, *challenge*? "Now you try," she said, looking at him in mock innocence.

Foreman liked a good challenge. And he didn't want to fail Kiyomi's test, if that's what it was.

"I'm game," he said. "The spinach, right?"

"Yes," she said.

Foreman thrust his chopsticks deep into the mound of spinach. He retracted the two chopsticks as Kiyomi had instructed him, but with markedly different results. His chopsticks did not meet at the tips, but instead crossed like scissors, the gastronomic equivalent of crossing one's skis on the slope and falling flat on one's face.

"Well." Foreman smiled good-naturedly at Kiyomi. "Somehow it worked better when you did it."

Kiyomi laughed more loudly this time, then covered her mouth with the fingers of her right hand, as if embarrassed that she had made too much noise. She removed the chopsticks from Foreman's hand and carefully replaced them in their proper positions. She paused briefly, her expression becoming serious. Foreman watched in fascination as Kiyomi drew something in the air with the fingers of her right hand. Her look of intense concentration was just as attractive to Foreman as was her smile. She said something to herself in what Foreman assumed was Japanese.

"I'm trying to remember a *kotowaza*, an old saying. I think you say in English, 'Practice makes perfection?'"

"Close!" Foreman said. "We say, 'Practice makes perfect.'"

"Yes! That's it!" Kiyomi said.

"Meaning, you want me to keep trying."

"Yes, yes," Kiyomi said, nodding, as a satisfied teacher might nod to a good student.

Foreman plunged his chopsticks once again into the spinach. He paused, squeezed the tips gently together, and pulled the chopsticks up slowly, like a fisherman reeling in his line, hoping to discover he had caught something. He was gratified to see that his chopsticks held a small portion of spinach. Foreman prepared himself to fake an expression of satisfaction—if the spinach tasted anything like that salty plum it would take some effort—and popped it into his mouth. To his great relief and surprise, he loved it. "This is delicious!"

Kiyomi's face beamed. "I am glad you like it."

"No, I'm serious. I've never tasted anything like this." Foreman continued to chew meditatively for a moment. "What else did you say was mixed in?"

"Ground, roasted sesame seeds. Sesame is fairly common in Japanese food."

"Amazing."

"Here is a piece of grilled fish marinated in *miso*, a kind of fermented bean paste." Kiyomi broke off a small piece of fish and pushed it to one side. "Try it."

Foreman picked the fish up—looked proudly at Kiyomi when he didn't drop it—and put it in his mouth. "This is unbelievable. I'm running out of words to describe it. I just love this stuff. I've never had anything like it in my life."

"And this too," Kiyomi said, pointing to another area of her *obento.* "It is called *tamagoyaki.* Please try."

"It looks like a sliced piece of omelet," Foreman said. "With tree rings."

"Sort of. We scramble eggs, then add soy sauce and a few other things. You pour it into a square pan, little by little, rolling it up as it browns. That is what makes the rings that you see."

"Sounds complicated," Foreman shoved it into his mouth. "But delicious. Yum." He sat back suddenly. "But now I've eaten half of your lunch. I'm sorry."

Kiyomi shook her head quickly, "No, it is okay. I'm so happy that you like my cooking."

Foreman pushed his Tupperware closer to Kiyomi. "Then share these beans I brought."

Kiyomi looked at Foreman's Tupperware. "*Hora!* See? Those are *edamame* beans. You already know Japanese food very well."

"No, no, I don't. Really. Some guy in dreadlocks in my co-op was pushing this so I brought some home. I like the taste."

Kiyomi took one of the *edamame* shells and put it in her mouth, sucked the beans out, and placed the empty shell next to one of her *obento* boxes. *Way, way overcooked,* she thought. She smiled at Foreman. He had probably tried boiling them until soft enough to chew both bean and shell, like he would for snap peas or green beans, instead of stopping when just the beans were cooked. She said, "Pretty good. It is maybe better if you soak them in salty water overnight, then boil for just a few minutes."

"Sounds good," he said. "You'll have to show me how sometime." Foreman hoped he didn't sound too pushy.

"Maybe I will," Kiyomi said. If she was embarrassed she didn't show it. "Now, try this. We call it *tsukemono."* Kiyomi placed a pinkish-green slice of something on the plastic wrap in front of Foreman.

"SU-kay-MOno," he said.

"Close. TSU-KAY-MOH-NOH. Don't put accent on any syllables. All even."

"TSU-KAY-MOH-NOH."

"Very good. Some people call it a Japanese pickle."

Foreman popped into his mouth. "This is very crunchy," he said, between bites. "What is this vegetable? It *is* a vegetable, isn't it?"

"It's made from *daikon*, a kind of Japanese radish. Sometimes we make it from other vegetables. It's very good for your health. I see *daikon* in American supermarkets sometimes."

Foreman continued chewing.

"How do you like it?" Kiyomi tilted her head to the right and raised her eyebrows. "Many Americans think it is sour."

Something inside Foreman, or maybe it was Kiyomi's relaxed nature, made him feel he could be honest and that it wouldn't hurt her feelings. "Well …" He shrugged and held up his hands.

"I knew it!" Kiyomi laughed, covering her mouth.

"Wait!" Foreman said. "I *loved* the fish. Honestly. And the spinach stuff and the egg omelet thing."

Kiyomi pointed at Foreman, continuing to laugh. "You also hated the *umeboshi*, didn't you?"

"No, no. Well, I …" He tried to keep a straight face but couldn't hold it. "All right. I hated it!" Both now laughed uncontrollably.

"You're so brave," she said. Kiyomi was bent over laughing. "And a little strange."

"Strange? Hey!" Foreman was embarrassed and happy at the same time. Kiyomi's laugh was almost childlike, innocent. The opposite of the serious professional he saw each morning at roll call.

A large clock on the wall caught Foreman's attention. He wanted to keep talking with Kiyomi but had to get back to work. "Thanks for sharing your lunch. This was delicious *and* entertaining."

"No, *you* are entertaining," she said, giggling as she reassembled her *furoshiki*. "I have to go, too."

"What floors did you say you've got today?" Foreman tossed his paper bag in a nearby garbage can.

"One and two," Kiyomi said. "You're in *Gonzo,* aren't you?"

"Yup. Come on, I'll ride down the elevator with you." They walked together to a bank of five elevators just outside the food court. Foreman punched the Down button.

"Thanks again," Foreman said, able to think of nothing else to say, but wanting to say something.

Kiyomi said, "So, when would you like to learn how to properly prepare *edamame?"* She felt a warm thrill at speaking so boldly as they stepped into the arriving elevator.

"Anytime," Foreman said. "You're an amazing cook." He wanted to look at Kiyomi but felt suddenly shy. He watched the floor numbers flash by at the top of the elevator car.

"How about tonight?" Kiyomi said. "If you are not already busy, I could make a Japanese dinner for you. And you can help me."

"Sure! I'd like that. Don't know how much help I'll be, though."

"You are not busy tonight?"

"No," Foreman said. Even if had been, he would have cancelled his plans. "What time should I come?"

"Please come at seven." Kiyomi wrote her address and phone number on a notepad she kept in her pocket, tore off the sheet and handed it to Foreman.

"Can I bring anything? Wine?"

"Just bring beer," she said. "Japanese food goes best with beer."

CHAPTER 18

Foreman got off the elevator on the second floor and headed to Gonzoland. He passed Officer Engebretsen of Lost and Found walking the other way.

"Engebretsen," he said.

"Foreman."

He had just passed her when he stopped and turned back. "Hey, Engebretsen," he yelled. "Hold up."

"Yo," she said.

"That bag I dropped off this morning. The red one. The owner already come and claim it?"

"Not yet," Engebretsen said.

"Really?" Foreman was puzzled. Anyone missing a handbag should have noticed it by now. Can't do much in MightyMall without your wallet. "That's weird."

Engebretsen shrugged.

"Any ID inside?" Foreman said.

"A driver's license. But no cell phone or home phone number. No way to contact her, except maybe asking the Department of Motor

Vehicles. Figured it was kind of early for that. People usually turn up eventually."

"You put her name on the plasmas?" He meant the one hundred forty-seven high definition plasma screens scattered around the mall.

"Around 10 A.M."

"Doesn't that seem strange to you?" Foreman said. "It's not like she lost her gloves and wouldn't notice them missing until she was ready to leave. Once the stores open and she went to buy something she'd have to notice pretty quickly she didn't have her bag, don't you think?"

"Yeah, maybe," Engebretsen said. "Her license says she's kind of old, which means she's probably a mall walker. She might have met up with friends and got to talking and lost track of time. Maybe they're having lunch and her friend paid." She shrugged.

"Could she maybe have gotten sick? Fainted, maybe?"

"Nothing like that on InCom." InCom was the internal communication system interconnecting all management office departments. Calls for medical assistance, ambulances or police help were announced there.

"Hmm," Foreman said. "Do me a favor, will you? Let me know right away if she picks it up. Or if you hear of any ambulance calls for old ladies."

"Sure," Engebretsen said. "But you wait and see. She'll turn up okay."

Five floors up, Haunted Hollow cars were floating out of the boarding platform every two minutes, twisting and turning, *clackety-clack-clacking* from the first floor to the fifth, bouncing off the tube walls as they descended to the third floor, *clackety-clack-clacking* again on the way to the seventh floor, then tumbling down to the sixth floor, where the tube poked through the wall. Then down to the fourth floor, where it emerged back into the park. All that *clacking*, bouncing and tumbling caused vibrations in the tubes, which created sympathetic vibrations in adjacent areas.

The unused maintenance skyway on the seventh floor trembled each time one of the cars passed by.

The body of Greta Turnblad, sitting against a safety rail at the end of the maintenance skyway, began to shift. Her head tilted to the left. Her shoulders sagged, just a little, but enough to cause her body to continue moving. As her head and left shoulder struck the middle of the ledge, Greta's right shoulder rolled slightly, causing her right arm to hang over the ledge. Her torso turned. Her right shoe came to rest an inch from the edge as her body ceased moving.

CHAPTER 19

Carolyn was standing in front of the dais, chatting with a clutch of reporters. The press conference had ended several minutes before. Mayor Gleason and Billie Brandt and other VIPs wished Carolyn well and left. A few of the cameramen were still stowing their equipment.

Carolyn was answering a question from Jim Gunther of the *Pioneer Press* on how *Rodinia* would affect the environment.

"The environmental impact study we commissioned was quite positive," Carolyn said. "We used that every step of the way in creating our blueprint and will abide by it religiously going forward."

"Has the Department of Natural Resources given their approval?" Gunther said.

"We've had several discussions with the DNR and are very pleased with the tone. The State knows how committed we are to building *Rodinia* in a way that creates positive environmental and economic impact."

Dick Cross caught Carolyn's attention and pointed to her watch, then drew an imaginary circle around it, indicating that she needed to finish up.

"I've got time for one more question," she said, " and I'm afraid I've got another commitment waiting."

The other commitment was a taped interview with Paul Ruvio of MSNBC. He'd spoken to Cross during the presentation. Cross had run up to Carolyn immediately after her presentation and told her. "Ruvio wants a taped interview," he'd said breathlessly into her ear. "Right now. For airing tonight right after Keith Olberman. What do I tell him?"

"Tell him yes and that I'll be ready in fifteen minutes." Cross had run back to Ruvio, spoken to him briefly, then given Carolyn a thumbs up. That was ten minutes ago.

"What about Lake Interior?" Bob Tatreault of the *Star Tribune* said. "Where do you plan to find enough water to fill it? Are you planning to divert water from a nearby stream? Build a dam?"

"There is an area community—I am not at liberty at this time to tell you which one–that consists of large acreage but has a small tax base; the tax base being restricted because too much of the town consists of lakes, with little room to build tax producing businesses and homes. Their Board of Supervisors has for some time been quietly considering a plan—since well before MightyMall became involved—to drain out a few of the lakes and use that land to develop a downtown area, a new business park and additional housing units."

Tatreault said, "So, you're going to buy their lakes and, what, pipe the water over to Lake Interior?"

Pete Brannigan from Minnesota Public Radio jumped in before Carolyn could speak. "What town are you talking about?"

"I'm afraid I really can't tell you any more at this time. But you will be hearing from our PR department in the near future with more details as soon as we can share them." Carolyn started wading through the crowd. "Now, I really do have to get going. Thanks again for coming today."

Dick Cross was waiting for her at the door. "They're out on Lost Deck."

The *Gonzoland Observation Deck*, nicknamed the Lost Deck by mall employees, was an area of unused space behind the Saint Commercia Police Substation. The triangular deck jutted out twenty feet over the park from the seventh floor like a giant arrowhead. Its two sides provided a spectacular view of Gonzoland beneath. The low metal fencing had been erected for temporary use during mall construction. Plans had called for the fencing to be replaced with a ten-foot-high Plexiglas wall and the area made into a public observation deck. Management had shelved those plans when they gave the area adjacent to it to the Saint Commercia Police. SCP didn't like the idea of allowing so many people outside of their door; they had demanded that the observation deck be closed as a condition of their moving in. Management agreed, reluctantly, because they wanted the visible presence of the local police on premises.

An intern during that period had nicknamed the area The Lost Deck, after The Lost Forty, a section of prime forestland in northern Minnesota that had "disappeared" in the nineteenth century due to a surveying error. As the forestland had been divided into parcels for logging, boundaries on all sides mysteriously never met, carving out forty acres that could not be used because they didn't officially exist. By the time the surveying error was discovered in the 20th century, the height, age and beauty of the trees inside the Lost Forty were such that the Minnesota legislature enacted legislation making the area a permanently protected area.

The Lost Deck was similarly "invisible." The space had to remain off limits to the public due to its inconvenient proximity to the SCP Substation. The temporary fencing was never replaced—why spend the money on something the public would never use? The temporary fencing was, technically, a safety hazard, so extra precautions were put in place: the only access to Lost Deck was through a single door located next to the SCP Substation. The dead-bolt lock in the door required an old fashioned key to open. Only three master keys in the mall would open the door: one belonged to Carolyn, one to Karl LeVander, and one to the Saint Commercia Police. These safeguards did not fit strictly within the official guidelines of the City of Saint Commercia, but the town Safety Inspector received as many Gonzoland passes and no-questions-asked MightyMall Hotel certificates as he wanted. Besides, Lost Deck was almost never used. The Titanic Properties owners liked to bring their kids when they were in town. Management brought the occasional VIP tours. Public relations conducted filmed interviews there because the views were so exciting. A few people a year. No harm, no foul.

Paul Ruvio's producer had clipped a microphone onto his lapel and was now busy with Carolyn.

"Will this location work for the interview, Mr. Ruvio?" Carolyn said.

"'Paul', please," he said. "And yes, this will be fine." He looked to his producer, who nodded and went over to the cameraman to stand. "Ronny," he said to his cameraman, "everything working?"

"I can hear you and Ms. Batch fine," Ruvio's cameraman said. He was leaning against the overlook's metal fence, pointing his camera at Carolyn and Ruvio.

"Lucy, go over and tell him he can't lean on that fence." Carolyn whispered to her assistant, pointing at Ruvio's cameraman. "Can't have him falling into Gonzoland." A little click in the back of her mind. She continued staring at the cameraman for a moment.

"All right, then," Ruvio said.

"Sorry?" Carolyn said. "I was thinking of something else."

"Not a problem," Ruvio said. "I think we're about ready to start if you are."

"Of course."

Ruvio's producer and cameraman indicated they were ready. "Carolyn, today's a big day for MightyMall."

"Thank you, Paul. But it's just the beginning of a long journey. *Rodinia* will be, we are confident, a huge win for Saint Commercia and for the State of Minnesota, just as MightyMall has been. And with all the additional foreign tourism dollars that will flow in, for the entire United States."

"Earlier plans you showed to the press were more traditional, a bigger amusement park plus stores. Where did you get the ideas that went into *Rodinia*?"

"Simply put, the status quo doesn't work anymore. The public won't accept more of the same: bigger buildings, bigger amusement parks, bigger shopping malls. The user experience doesn't change just because it takes longer to walk around–you need to give them new reasons to walk around, new things to do. Computers and cell phones were on the verge of maxing out a few years ago until someone invented YouTube and free internet porn and Facebook. Suddenly people needed bigger and better computers and cell phones to access those services."

"So you're saying that *Rodinia* is going to provide new services."

"*Rodinia* will provide *all* services! *Rodinia* will be the largest construction project in American history providing unparalleled variety and seamlessness of products and services. Our mission will be to respond to every person who says, '*This* is fun, but I wish I could also do *that*–right now' by saying, 'No problem. You *can* do that right now.'"

"The ultimate in immediate gratification," Ruvio said.

"With absolutely no need to feel guilty later!" Carolyn said. "Active vacations. Tours of organic farms, fish hatcheries, research facilities.

Recycled water, waste used as fertilizer. Solar, wind and thermal power. A virtually self-sustaining ecosystem that you can study, experience and show as a home movie."

"And you think MightyMall and Titanic Properties can build a facility to provide that gratification profitably?"

"People will pay a lot of money not to be disappointed."

"Well, I think that went well, don't you?" Carolyn said. She and Lucy were riding the elevator back to the management offices in the first basement. "Good turnout by the press. Good questions. Good reaction to the news." Carolyn nodded to herself, satisfied.

"Great," Lucy said, without enthusiasm.

"And did you see that poor Billie Brandt's face? Always talking about putting *the rest of* Saint Commercia on the map, developing an independent business identity *apart from* MightyMall...and I just announced that we have, for all intents and purposes, *bought up* the rest of Saint Commercia. The mayor will be happy; tax revenues will skyrocket and his budget will balance for the rest of the century."

"Won't that also be good for the Saint Commercia Chamber?" Lucy said.

"Be great for existing businesses," Carolyn said. "They'll feed off this like Remoras on a shark," Carolyn said. "But there won't be much further need for a Chamber of Commerce if there isn't any more opportunity to develop business. Might as well change the name of the town to MightyMall-ville."

The elevator arrived at the first basement level. MightyMall had two basements; the first housed the management offices, security, maintenance, housekeeping and IT. The second basement consisted of storage space, for MightyMall itself—seasonal decorations, stage equipment for large events, unused furniture—and rental space for tenants who needed to warehouse extra merchandise onsite.

The two women emerged from the elevator at an intersection of four service hallways. They started down the hallway toward Carolyn's office about one hundred feet away.

"Oh, hold on a second," Carolyn said. She turned left and headed down a different way. "Let's go this way. I have to stop by the Reception Desk. I'm expecting a package."

Carolyn and Lucy walked along a stretch of grey hallway wide and high enough to drive two large trucks through. Not for the first time, Lucy thought this would be the ultimate place to have a game of hide-and-seek. The miles of service ways, hallways and spokes on this floor alone could allow someone who knew their way around to elude capture for days. Weeks, maybe.

Carolyn was in a good place.

Lucy looked behind her to confirm that the two of them were alone. "Carolyn," she said. "About that body…."

Carolyn looked like she had been disturbed from a pleasant dream. She turned her head slightly away from her assistant, putting up a hand between them like a barrier. *Yes, of course, that damned dead woman.* Carolyn leaned her head back a little and closed her eyes to think. She had worked out part of the problem–how to get rid of the body. That bit of inspiration had come to her up on the seventh floor while waiting to shoot the MSNBC interview on Lost Deck. She nodded happily to herself. Lucy noticed the movement and looked over at her questioningly, but Carolyn ignored her. Getting rid of Dead Dora would no longer be a problem.

Now, what to do about Lucy? She couldn't allow that conniving little bitch to continue holding Dora over her head.

They arrived at the entrance to the reception area, a holding area where guests signed in and waited until an authorized mall employee came to escort them into the bowels of the management offices. Carolyn ran her ID badge over the proximity sensor and walked in.

The lone attendant, Caitlin, was talking on the phone. Her job was to welcome and sign in guests, then page the appropriate mall employee.

Carolyn walked up to the counter and leaned on one elbow. She waited until the Caitlin had finished on the phone.

"Good afternoon, Mrs. Batch," Caitlin said.

"Hi," Carolyn said. *What was the girl's name again?* "Any packages come for me this morning? I was expecting a FedEx."

"Yes, Mrs. Batch," Caitlin said. "I signed for it at about ten and had someone bring it down to your office."

"Great," Carolyn said. She started to turn away and stopped suddenly. "Oh, damn!"

"What's the matter?" Caitlin said.

"Oh, it's not you. It's my bag. I left it up on Lost Deck after the interview."

Caitlin said, "Well, I can have someone go get it—"

"No, that won't be necessary," Carolyn said. "Lucy, be a dear. Can you run up and get it? You know what it looks like. I think it put it down in one corner just before we stepped out on the deck."

"I—" Lucy didn't understand why Carolyn didn't send someone from security to get her bag, but what could she do? "Um, sure. I'd be glad to," she said and headed for the door.

"Oh, hold on," Carolyn said. "You'll need the master key." She removed a single key from her key ring and handed it her Lucy. "Here you go." Most doors in MightyMall could be opened with a wave of a mall ID badge. Certain doors that were seldom used, either because they required high levels of clearance, or were deemed dangerous areas, required a master key, of which only senior management had copies. The door to Lost Deck required such a key.

"Just leave the bag and key in my office when you get back. I'll be in meetings the rest of the afternoon." Carolyn turned to head into the management office, then stopped. "Oh, and keep your schedule open at the end of the day. We have things to discuss."

"Certainly, Carolyn," Lucy said.

CHAPTER 20

Kiyomi looked at her watch. Four-thirty. Thirty minutes left until her shift was over. The day had been uneventful, as were most days. Terrorists had never attacked MightyMall. According to the FBI, with whom security held daily teleconferences and monthly sit downs, it had never been mentioned as a target by al Qaida or any other organizations bent on raining death and destruction upon the United States. But, as Major Power frequently lectured everyone in security, you don't plan for what the enemy might do; you plan for what they could do. Terrorists could target MightyMall, and if they did they could use explosives, guns, poison chemicals, or a combination of all three. They could also use planes again, as they had with the attacks on the World Trade Center; MightyMall security couldn't control what someone might do with planes, so they didn't worry about them.

Uniformed security checked for weapons and explosives via multiple means: sniffer dogs, "sniffer" sensing equipment and, on occasion, "aggressive hospitality," greeting guests as they came in with a warm welcome and a request to search their bags. Most of the knives, small arms and illegal substances—mostly pot—turned up this way.

Kiyomi had never found anyone who it later turned out was a known terrorist, or had been convicted of abetting terrorist groups. She was ever vigilant, but not surprised when, as her shift neared its end, she had nothing significant to report.

She had used a portion of her concentration during her rounds this afternoon thinking of what to make for Mike Foreman for dinner tonight. What was I thinking, she thought to herself, inviting him to my apartment for dinner on our first date? It was exciting, though. He was such a nice man. And cute! She had considered several dishes and rejected them. Broiled fish, rice and *miso* soup? Too boring. *Sukiyaki* or *shabu-shabu?* Eating out of the same pot was too intimate for a first date. She was still running through the possibilities when she noticed that she was near the Northern Lights West 1 entrance, the place she had had that strange encounter with Carolyn Batch's administrative assistant.

Kiyomi turned down the spoke hallway connecting the main shopping avenue with the West entrance. The elderly man working at the Welcome Desk didn't know her and there was no reason to blow her cover by introducing herself to him. She walked past the desk and entered the recently remodeled Ladies Restroom; she wasn't looking for anything in particular, didn't know what she was looking for. She looked at herself in the mirror, noticed a pimple on the right side of her chin that she would have to deal with before Mike Foreman arrived, and went back outside.

Kiyomi walked up to the Welcome Desk and glanced casually at the brochure rack, removing one of the mall maps and opening it up. When she saw that the attendant was helping a customer, she peeked over the edge of the counter and scanned for anything out of place.

"Something I can help you with, miss?" The attendant had noticed her.

"No, thank you." Kiyomi smiled winningly at the man and moved away. What could Lucy have been doing here that she felt she had to hide her identity? She had also felt that Lucy was trying to get rid of her with that lame invitation to have coffee together, then standing there, watching Kiyomi as she had walked away.

Kiyomi looked at the wall behind the Welcome Desk displaying products and services and their prices. The suspicious activity, if it was a suspicious activity, had taken place in this area, either inside the Welcome Desk, or in the Ladies Restroom. Kiyomi felt sure of this. Something that Lucy had needed the Cushman for? If she was alone, why hadn't Lucy just walked, as most staff did? *Had* Carolyn Batch been with Lucy, after all, in the bathroom, when Kiyomi had happened by? If so, what were they doing?

Kiyomi stepped further away from the Welcome Desk, almost to the yogurt stand on the other side. She looked to her left, at the main shopping avenue, at the relentless tide of shoppers flowing past. She tilted her head to one side, as she often did when confused, or when thinking especially hard about something. Nothing came to her. She turned back to the right and looked at the people entering the mall, happy to get out of the cold. She looked again at the Welcome Desk and noticed the maintenance door; something she hadn't noticed in the morning while talking to Lucy. Nothing suspicious there, senior management drove their Cushmans on the shopping avenues before and after opening. Service corridors could be used anytime, before, during or after business hours.

So why had Lucy gone to such lengths to hide her identity from Kiyomi?

Less than a half mile away, and one floor down, Mike Foreman was walking into the X-Team office. He had finished his round early and wanted to catch Judy Engebretsen before she punched out.

Foreman dialed Lost and Found's extension on the office phone.

"MightyMall Lost and Found," she said. "Officer Engebretsen speaking."

"Hey, it's Mike Foreman again."

"Yo."

"I assume because you never contacted me that that old lady never turned up."

"Nope."

"Damn," Foreman said. He twirled his pen in his hand.

"You want me to check the Security Action Center computer? See if anything's in their database?"

Foreman could have done that himself but he could hear Officer Engebretsen already typing away on her keyboard. "Thanks."

"No problem," she said. "All right, here we are. Reported events for the day … nothing related to a Greta Turnblad in the mall … nothing on any unidentified blue hairs in the mall … ooh, wait a second." Renewed typing sounds. "No, never mind. I thought I had something, a multiple car accident right in front of the mall this morning early. One of the victims was an old lady whose Lincoln Town Car got rear squashed by a monster truck driving in for the auto show this weekend. Not pretty."

"Leaving the mall or coming in?" Foreman said. He thought the owner of the red bag might have forgotten completely about it and been heading home.

"Coming in," Engebretsen said. "But it's not our gal. The victim was a Charlene Goblirsch. Jaws had to cut her out of her car, paramedics sent her to Hennepin County Medical Center."

CHAPTER 21

Lucy sat at her corner cube outside Carolyn's empty office playing solitaire on her computer. She dragged a red eight onto a black nine. Lucy's duties consisted primarily of screening calls to Carolyn, scheduling her meetings and taking dictation. She sat with her back facing the wall of Carolyn's office. The wall closest to Carolyn's door was a counter low enough to allow eye contact when her boss decided to talk to her from her own desk without leaving her office. The wall behind her computer was about six feet tall and gave her a certain amount of privacy. Lucy used to have her computer placed against the wall of Carolyn's office, but that made it too easy for people walking by to see what was on her computer screen. Things like computer solitaire. She had maintenance rearrange things last spring. Easier to keep track of people visiting Carolyn's office, she had told the maintenance guy.

She drew a card from the pile. Ooh, a black seven! She put it on the red eight.

Lucy's cube was situated across from a group of eight cubes, manned by lower level assistants or interns for one of the other departments. She was proud to have her own space. It underscored her higher rank in the admin hierarchy. If anyone spoke too loudly on the phone, or laughed, or made Lucy feel left out, she had the authority to tell them to quiet down.

Lucy had spent most of the afternoon thinking about the new car Carolyn was going to buy her. She had never had enough money to buy a new car. Carolyn could certainly afford it. And it wasn't like Lucy had wanted to get involved in this thing; she had wanted to call security immediately, and she would tell everyone that in case they were caught. She was afraid. It was her boss, for God's sake; what could she do? Say no, and Carolyn would have found an excuse to fire her for sure. Hard enough to get a job in this economy as it is, without getting fired from your current one, even if it does suck. No, it was Carolyn's idea, Carolyn's plan: Carolyn's bullying caused all this. Blame her, not me.

Besides, Carolyn was pretty smart, after all. A bitch, for sure, but she had risen up this high in the company, hadn't she? She knew what she was doing. And if anyone did find out anything, like security, she could just order them to be quiet. Maybe buy them a car, too. Pretty exciting, a new car.

Lucy heard Carolyn approaching from down the hall before she saw her. She quit the solitaire, after saving the current game, and made sure the calendar was open. She looked at it intently.

"Lucy," Carolyn said. "In my office. Now." Carolyn walked into her office, then stepped back out immediately, holding her handbag. "Oh, thanks for getting this for me, Lucy," she said, then went back inside and sat down. "Hurry up," she waved at Lucy, "get on in here."

Lucy grabbed her note pad and walked into Carolyn's office.

"And close that door behind you," Carolyn said.

Lucy closed the door and sat down in the chair in front of Carolyn's desk. Carolyn had no sooner called Lucy in than she began doing something at her computer. Looked like she was checking emails, Lucy thought to herself. She looked at shelves behind Carolyn's desk. A photo of Carolyn with the governor. A large one of her standing with John Travolta when he had visited MightyMall to promote his new line of aftershave. A poster on the wall showed Carolyn standing somewhere in Rome with the Coliseum in the distant background. No pictures of her children.

Carolyn finished what she was typing and swiveled her chair around. She looked at Lucy for several seconds without speaking.

"We've got some work to do." Carolyn smiled at Lucy the way a shark smiles at a sea otter. "Don't we?"

The smile made Lucy nervous. She nodded, hesitantly.

"We are going to make this work," Carolyn said. "This morning's presentation was fantastic. Everyone wanted follow up interviews. Dick Cross told me that the local stations are already airing teasers for tonight's news, and the tone is completely positive. This is going to be huge." Lucy assumed that Carolyn meant that news of *Rodinia* was going to be huge, not the dead woman on the seventh floor.

Carolyn picked up a pen and started doodling on the notepad on her desk. "I got an idea while riding back on the elevator with you after the press conference," she said. "How we can turn a potential negative into a positive."

"You mean…?" Lucy said.

"Yes, of course I *mean*." Carolyn said. "Now picture this." She went to her office door and quietly turned the lock. "An elderly woman, out on her own when perhaps she's too old, is wandering around the seventh floor on a Friday morning, tomorrow, when she becomes disoriented, loses her focus. Maybe she's got Alzheimer's, or has a stroke. Doesn't matter. Following me so far?"

"I guess so," Lucy said. "But we don't really know what happened to her, do we? What if she was attacked or had a heart attack, or something? Won't the CSI people be able to tell that?"

The smile on Carolyn's face expanded mechanically, as if a contraption inside her was drawing back the skin, trying unsuccessfully to create a reasonable facsimile of a human smile.

"That *might* be a problem," Carolyn said, "except that there won't be an autopsy."

"But why not?" Lucy said. "Don't the police always do those kinds of things?"

Carolyn said, "Not if the cause of death is obvious. Not when a body is so badly mangled that an autopsy would be pointless."

Lucy recoiled. "You're not suggesting we chop up the body or anything."

"No need." Lucy listened in rapt horror as Carolyn detailed her plan for dealing with the body they knew as Dead Dora.

"Now," Carolyn said after she had finished. "I want you here in my office at five sharp tomorrow morning. We're going to be quite busy."

Lucy emerged from the basement stairs onto the first floor with a roaring sense of disquiet. It wasn't that she and her boss had discovered a dead woman, failed to report it to the police and then relocated the body to a different part of the mall. Or the fact that she didn't understand how they could pull off Carolyn's plan without something going wrong. It wasn't even that, if caught, Lucy could lose her job and go to jail. What made Lucy's blood run cold was Carolyn's increasingly hollow and menacing gaze.

CHAPTER 22

Mike Foreman punched out right at five o'clock and ran to his car. The MightyMall Weather Channel, displayed periodically on mall plasma monitors, said that the main arteries in and out of Saint Commercia had been plowed and salted and that the traffic foul-ups from this morning's storm had mostly abated.

Foreman got home in less than twenty minutes. After a quick shower he put on a brown turtleneck and faded jeans. He stopped at the liquor store near his apartment to buy Japanese beer. He was spared the need to choose one beer over the other when the store manager told him they carried only one Japanese brand: Asahi Super Dry.

Kiyomi lived thirty minutes south of MightyMall in the part of Minneapolis known as Uptown, which, counter-intuitively, was located just south of Downtown. Downtown Minneapolis had museums and Broadway theaters and expensive restaurants, sports stadiums and tall glass buildings, rowdy bars and plenty of police driving around at night to make sure revelers didn't become too revelrous. Living in a Downtown Minneapolis condo was convenient for work, and it was green—the Light Rail was within walking distance of most buildings—but quite expensive.

Uptown was mostly older three and four-story buildings filled with trendy restaurants, art shops, bookstores, and movie theaters specializing in foreign films. Uptown had more affordable apartments and was less prone to violent crime than Downtown. Uptown had no Light Rail but plenty of bus stops. The gorgeous Midtown Greenway, a 10-mile long paved bicycle path replete with exit ramps, rest areas, gardens and emergency call boxes, ran through the middle. From the Greenway you could bike north to downtown Minneapolis, south to Bloomington, east to Saint Paul across the Mississippi, or west to several suburbs.

Kiyomi's apartment was on Dupont Avenue, just off Hennepin Avenue, the primary conduit between Downtown and Uptown. The refurbished three-story brick building consisted of one and two-bedroom apartments occupied exclusively by women in their twenties and thirties. The floors in Kiyomi's apartment squeaked, the walls were thin and she wished her next-door neighbor would have less exuberant sex, at least at three o'clock in the morning, but she loved the place. The landlord had replaced the major appliances before she moved in and put in a hardwood counter facing the living room. Plenty of space for the smaller Japanese appliances Kiyomi had brought with her. The co-op she frequented was nearby, carried excellent produce and was staffed by people who looked and acted like 1960s-era hippies. She was within an easy walk of several coffee shops not named Starbucks, and felt that every day was a shiny adventure.

Kiyomi was chopping cabbage when the building's video intercom chimed. She rinsed her hands in the sink, dried them off and went to her door. She activated the black and white monitor and saw Mike Foreman's face smiling back at her.

"You order a pizza, ma'am?" Foreman said.

"What?" Kiyomi's eyes went wide with surprise.

Foreman pretended to open up a pizza box. "Pepperoni? Double mushrooms?"

Kiyomi laughed loudly. "Oh, you are teasing me again! You are a terrible American man, Mike Foreman!"

"How about beer?"

"All right, Mike," Kiyomi said in mock seriousness. She always used his last name at work but it seemed somehow more appropriate to use his first name off duty. She hoped he didn't mind. "Yes, you can come in. I'm on the third floor, Apartment 312." She pushed the buzzer and watched Foreman open the door.

Kiyomi ran to the bathroom to check herself in the mirror. She decided that she looked fine and gave the kitchen and living room final once over. Everything was neat and clean. She heard a knock on her door and went to answer it. Foreman was standing at the door holding a brown shopping bag and a bouquet of flowers.

"Oh my, these are beautiful," Kiyomi said. "Thank you! And please come in."

Foreman was stunned at the change in Kiyomi's appearance from what he saw at work to what he saw now. As undercover officers they both wore civilian clothes. Foreman never thought much about the clothes he wore at work; if it was clean and comfortable, he wore it.

He had never seen Kiyomi look like she did this evening. She always looked good at MightyMall—really good—pretty, healthy, confident, always with an expression that said what she was doing at that moment was the only thing of importance in the world. That was one reason Foreman enjoyed talking with her so much. He tried to pinpoint what was different tonight: her hair was different; she always kept it in either a ponytail or up in some kind of bun. Her face tonight was … brighter? More glowing? He couldn't see any makeup on her eyes but they were bigger, darker, somehow. Her lips were, well, plumper. The sweater and jeans gave her body more definition than he had ever noticed. I'm out of my league, he thought to himself.

Foreman caught himself staring. He extended his left hand, gave Kiyomi the bouquet and entered the apartment. "I wasn't sure what kind of flowers to get so I just asked the lady at the shop to use her judgment."

Kiyomi said. "They're wonderful."

"And here is the Japanese beer," Foreman said. He pulled three 32-ounce cans out of his bag and placed them on the counter. "I didn't figure we'd drink all of them but…" he shrugged.

Foreman noticed that Kiyomi was wearing only socks. "Should I take off my shoes?"

"Yes, please." Kiyomi pulled a pair of slippers from a small cabinet by the door and placed them in front of Foreman. She took Foreman's black leather bomber jacket and hung it in the closet.

"Oh, I almost forgot," Foreman said. "Here." He pulled a piece of paper out of his pants pocket.

"What's this?" Kiyomi said. She looked closely at the piece of paper, turned it over, and then back. "A Minnesota Hot Lotto ticket?" she laughed. "You bought me a Minnesota Hot Lotto ticket?"

"See, it's like this," Foreman said in mock consternation. "I gave a lottery ticket to a friend in college as a housewarming present. I didn't have much money back then and thought: you never know. If it pays off, it's the best present ever."

"Did they win?" Kiyomi said.

"They did not," Foreman said. "But it was fun, and cheap, and so I continue to do it whenever I visit people's homes."

"But you already gave me the beautiful flowers and the beer."

"True," Foreman said. "But it's only a buck. And kind of fun. You can split it with me if you win."

"You are very silly," Kiyomi said, "but very kind. Thank you."

Foreman put out his hands, face up, hunched his shoulders and put on his best Tony Soprano face and voice. "Fuh-get-a-bout-it."

"Please sit down at the counter," Kiyomi said. "You can watch me make dinner." She opened one of the beer cans and poured two small glasses of beer.

The counter had an array of dishes and bowls, each with an individual ingredient, some of which Foreman recognized.

"We're going to have *okonomiyaki*." Kiyomi said it slowly and allowed Foreman several opportunities to master its pronunciation. "Some people call it a Japanese pancake because it's flat and cooked on a hot pan," Kiyomi pointed at the large round hotplate sitting directly in front of Foreman, "but it's not sweet. To me, it is more like a pizza. It's round and tasty; Japanese people like to eat this with friends because it's cheap and you can find *okonomiyaki* restaurants everywhere."

"Is that cabbage?" Foreman said, pointing at a large bowl. "And did you chop that up yourself?"

"Yes. And yes," Kiyomi said. She reached into the bowl and removed two large handfuls and put them in a smaller bowl. She poured in a thick batter, added a raw egg and several pieces of something bright red.

"Carrots?" Foreman said.

"Ginger," Kiyomi said. She handed Foreman a wooden spoon. "Your job is to mix everything together and then we will pour it on this hotplate and cook it and then eat it."

They each made one six-inch wide *okonomiyaki*. After turning each one over once, Kiyomi placed two strips of thinly sliced pork near the center and pushed them gently into the still-soft batter. She turned the two *okonomiyaki* over a few times until both sides were brown.

Kiyomi squirted a thick brown liquid onto her *okonomiyaki* in round circular motions. "Now you do the same." She handed Foreman the bottle.

"What is this?" Foreman said. "It smells good."

"I'm not sure." Kiyomi shrugged. "Maybe Worcestershire sauce and ketchup? We just call it *okonomiyaki* sauce." Next, she sprinkled on a layer of what looked to Foreman like very thin wood chips. They seemed to be writhing.

"Are those things alive?" Foreman said.

Kiyomi giggled. "No, it's just dried fish flakes."

"Dried … fish … flakes," Foreman said. "Hmmm. Like, they just dry out an entire fish and then … what? … scrape that stuff off with a knife?"

"Kind of," Kiyomi said. "The heat makes them wave like that."

Foreman didn't know if "kind of" explained it, but he wasn't sure he wanted to know any more so decided to let the matter drop. "Okay." He grabbed a handful of the flakes and sprinkled them on top as Kiyomi had done.

Kiyomi finished up with mayonnaise and homemade mustard. "Be careful," she said while spooning a large, yellow dollop on top, "this is hot."

"Oh, I like hot," Foreman said. "No problem there."

"Um hum." Kiyomi smiled to herself as she swirled everything together. "I see."

When Foreman had finished adding his own ingredients, Kiyomi handed him her swirling knife.

"Done," Kiyomi said. "Look what you helped me make!" She used a spatula to place the two *okonomiyaki* on plates. "If we were in Japan we would eat them while still on the hotplate, but this one is not really built for that style so we will use plates."

She handed him an implement that looked like a knife with a two-by-two inch square head. "You cut it with this. And eat with chopsticks."

Foreman cut off a bite-sized piece and put it into his mouth. "Mmm. What a great mix of all these different flavors," he said with his mouth full. He suddenly inhaled sharply, swallowed, and took several drinks of beer. "And hot!"

"I told you," she said, looking mildly reproachful, but smiling. "Japanese mustard is spicy."

"Like horseradish," Foreman said. "Boy, it really clears out your nostrils." He had already cut off another piece and was about to put it in his mouth. "But delicious. I must have been Japanese in my previous life."

In between mouthfuls of *okonomiyaki* and drinks of Japanese beer Foreman and Kiyomi talked in that random way that people do when they feel comfortable with each other but don't yet know much about each other. Movies, books, hobbies, favorite TV shows, where they went to school. Kiyomi brought out photo albums of her family, their house, her hometown of Kobe. Foreman was fascinated with Kiyomi's life before she moved to the United States—*Young kids* really *go to school in the afternoon and late evening, after regular school? One hundred dollars for a specially grown cantaloupe? Tell me again why kids study hard in high school and not much in college.*

One of the photos, a raised highway, reminded Foreman of something he had seen on TV. "Wasn't there a giant earthquake over there a few years ago?" he said. "I saw something on Discovery Channel, I think."

"You are right," Kiyomi said. "It was very bad."

"Did anyone … was everyone in your family okay?"

"My mother, father and brother, yes," Kiyomi said. "But my aunt died."

"Man," Foreman said, "I'm so sorry." He wasn't sure how sensitive the topic was for Kiyomi, or how Japanese felt about discussing death. He decided it safer to just continue leafing through the photo album.

After a few moments Kiyomi said, "My aunt's house, the roof and second floor, collapsed on top of her, killing her and her husband. The house across the street had almost no damage. It was, I guess you would say, fate." She picked up one of the other photo albums and flipped through a few pages. She pointed to a picture of an elementary-age girl standing next to a woman in her 30s. They were on top of a mountain, the ocean visible in the distance behind and below them. "That's my aunt," she said.

Kiyomi stared at the photo for several moments before putting that album down and picking up the one they had been looking at before.

She turned the page and smiled. "That is me wearing *kimono*, when I was five years old."

"Cute kid," Foreman said. "And you look just like you. Do Japanese wear them a lot?"

"Only on special occasions," she said. "Ooh," she pointed at a different photo, "here is me and my tennis circle … and my best friend, Kyoko … and my high school graduation ceremony. And…."

Looking at the hundreds of photos of Kiyomi at various ages, her family, home, school, vacations and everyday scenes, and listening to Kiyomi describe the significance of each, gave Foreman a better idea of how she became the person who now lived in the United States and did the same job he did. Foreman had lots of questions; sometimes he was content just to listen to Kiyomi's soothing voice.

A few times Kiyomi stopped talking and they looked at photos together in silence. Foreman loved listening to Kiyomi's voice, loved asking for the stories behind the photos, but what he was sure he would remember years later about the evening were the moments of comfortable quiet, the instances when neither of them had anything to say and both were fine with that, neither felt the need to fill gaps with meaningless words. Foreman didn't know if Japanese were good at silence or if it was chemistry or something unique to that evening, but Foreman felt certain that he and Kiyomi together represented infinite possibility.

CHAPTER 23

Foreman noticed the clock on the wall above Kiyomi's TV. Five minutes past nine. He didn't want to wait until it was so late that Kiyomi would kick him out so he started picking up plates and glasses and headed to the sink.

"No, please!" Kiyomi said. "I will do those later."

"It's the least I can do before I leave," Foreman said. "This was the best dinner I've ever had."

"But I didn't make it myself. You helped, too."

Foreman was already scraping plates into the small garbage can he found under the sink. "Then let's do the dishes together," he said. "How about I wash and you dry."

"But—" Kiyomi said.

"I don't know where the dishes go," Foreman said.

"Well," Kiyomi said. "That is very kind of you." She picked up a dishtowel hanging near the sink.

Kiyomi would not normally have allowed a guest to do the dishes like this, man or woman. Her mother would be so horrified! She had been taught since a young age that guests must be treated with the utmost respect. On the rare occasions growing up in Japan when there were guests for dinner at her home—Japanese entertain as frequently as Americans—her mother had spent most of the time in the kitchen cooking or bringing in dish after tiny dish of food.

Kiyomi had to admit that she was glad Foreman had insisted on helping. She had enjoyed the evening immensely and was not anxious for it to end. Foreman wasn't as fond of talking about himself as most American men she had dated. He listened. He asked questions. He thought about what Kiyomi said. He was open about not knowing a lot about Japan but seemed to enjoy hearing about it. So many Americans looked bored as soon as the conversation progressed beyond sushi, *anime* and Japanese baseball players in the Major Leagues.

Besides, she thought, feeling herself flush slightly, he had very strong hands and a wonderfully tight butt, as her American women friends would say.

Kiyomi saw her favorite kettle on the stove and realized that she had gotten so caught up in their conversation that she had forgotten to offer Foreman tea. "Oh my goodness," she said. "I haven't made you tea yet."

"That's fine," Foreman said. "I'm fine."

"No, please have a cup of tea before you leave," Kiyomi said. "It's cold outside and it will warm you. It will be done before we finish the dishes. Is green tea okay?" She picked up the small red can on the counter where she kept the green tea powder her mother sent from Japan every few months. "Or I have some ground coffee if you prefer." Kiyomi opened the cabinet over the refrigerator and removed a small bag of ground coffee."

"Green tea sounds great," Foreman said. "I've never had that."

"Okay," Kiyomi said. As she was replacing the ground coffee in the cabinet she noticed the Starbucks logo on the side of the bag. She froze, keeping her hand on the bag as it sat on the cabinet shelf.

"You okay?" Foreman said.

"Hmm?" Kiyomi said. She still hadn't moved.

"You look like you might have forgotten something," Foreman said.

Kiyomi closed the cabinet door. "No, I'm fine," she said. "I was just thinking about something strange that happened this morning during my rounds."

Kiyomi told Foreman about the encounter with Lucy, how Lucy had pretended to be a mall customer and had seemed so intent on getting Kiyomi out of the area as quickly as possible.

When Kiyomi had finished, Foreman said. "That *is* weird. Where did this happen?"

"Northern Lights West 1," Kiyomi said. "I wasn't planning on walking down that spoke toward the Welcome Desk or Entrance area; I'd just stopped to tie my sneakers. When I looked up, Lucy was walking straight toward me."

Foreman turned to look at Kiyomi. "The Welcome Desk?" he said. "You say she was by the Welcome Desk?"

"Yes," Kiyomi said. "Well, it could have been the restroom, they are near each other, but it looked like she was walking away from the Welcome Desk. Why?"

"And what time was this?"

"Between eight-thirty and nine," Kiyomi said. "It was during my first run around the first floor after Morning Briefing."

Foreman turned back to the sink, finished washing the last of the dirty dishes, turned off the water and handed the bowl to Kiyomi. "It's probably nothing," he said. He dried his hands on the dishtowel, hung it back on the rack, turned around and leaned against the sink.

"What is it?" Kiyomi said. "Tell me."

Foreman tilted his head up and scratched under his chin. He either had a significant five o'clock shadow or was growing a beard; either way, Kiyomi thought it looked sexy.

"I found a woman's handbag on the way in this morning," Foreman said. "I was running in because I was kind of late. Just after I got into the building I saw something out of the corner of my eye. I stopped and found this red handbag sitting on the floor by the lockers."

"Which are near the Welcome Desk," Kiyomi said.

"Yeah," Foreman said. "I didn't have time to look around much; I took a quick peek in the women's room and didn't see anyone. I just grabbed the bag and ran to the security gym."

The kettle whistled. Kiyomi put a small amount of powdered green tea into a small teapot and filled it with boiling water. She waited a few seconds and poured the contents into two small handle-less ceramic cups.

"Let's go sit down," Kiyomi said. She put the two cups on a round wooden tray and led Foreman into her small living room. She put the tray on a coffee table and sat on the couch at a discreet distance from where Foreman was sitting.

"Where is the bag now?" Kiyomi said.

"That's the other thing," Foreman said. "I turned it in to Lost and Found after Morning Briefing but no one had claimed it by the time I left."

"Any ID?" Kiyomi said.

"Yup. A driver's license. An old lady," Foreman said. "I figured she was a mall walker and would come looking for it after she was done with her walk. But Judy Engebretsen still had it at the end of the day."

Foreman picked up his teacup. "Careful," Kiyomi said. "It's really, really hot."

He took a small tentative sip. Then another. "Do you like it?" Kiyomi said.

"I'm not sure," Foreman said. "It's mild, maybe, but not bland. A little bitter, but not unpleasantly so." He took another sip.

Kiyomi was pleased but said nothing.

She said, "So where is the old woman?"

"Exactly," Foreman said. "Her bag's got her car keys, her driver's license. Who goes home and forgets about that?"

"Sen ... seen...." Kiyomi said. "I'm not sure of the word. Maybe she has seen—"

"Senility?" Foreman said. "You mean like Alzheimer's?"

Kiyomi shrugged slightly. Japanese didn't shrug much but she found herself doing it more often since moving to America. "Maybe she's very forgetful."

"Could be," Foreman said. "That would mean she probably left with a relative or friend, maybe. But she didn't call anyone because she didn't have any money."

Kiyomi said, "Maybe a fellow mall walker found her and brought her home?"

"If someone from security had found her they might have called an ambulance," Foreman said. "That's easy enough to check tomorrow morning. I'll ask someone in SAC." Kiyomi understood that SAC stood for Security Action Center.

Foreman and Kiyomi both paused for sips of their tea. Foreman noticed that holding the cup warmed his hands.

"Still pretty odd," Foreman said. "I find a handbag that no one claims in the same area that Carolyn's assistant decides to pretend she's a customer. And you said that Carolyn wasn't anywhere nearby?"

Kiyomi shook her head.

"Which is weird all by itself," Foreman said. "No reason for Lucy to go riding around by herself at the same time she's normally riding around with Carolyn doing morning rounds."

"I didn't find anything when I went back to the Welcome Desk later," Kiyomi said. "Though, I wasn't looking for anything special. I just thought I should look."

"Could the two events be connected?" Foreman said. "The bag and Lucy? Maybe the old lady was Lucy's relative."

"You mean Lucy found her grandmother? Then why didn't she check with Lost and Found and then claim the bag for her?" Kiyomi said. "And why would her grandmother's losing her bag make Lucy behave so strangely?"

Foreman looked down at his teacup and nodded. Kiyomi filled it for him without asking if he wanted any more. He was getting to like the taste more with each sip.

"Should we talk to Major Power?" Kiyomi said. "See what he thinks?"

"And tell him what?" Foreman said. "We don't really know anything except that a lady lost a handbag and never claimed it on the same day that Lucy was acting weird."

Kiyomi nodded and said something that sounded to Foreman like WAKATTA. He assumed it was Japanese.

"What was that?" Foreman said.

"Oh, sorry. The Japanese? I just said, 'I see.'" Kiyomi sipped some tea. "Unless we can learn more about when and how the bag ended up by the lockers," Kiyomi said. "Why don't we access the security video files for the cameras nearest the Welcome Desk? We select those starting at seven o'clock yesterday and move backward. See if we can see the woman who left the bag there."

"And then follow her from one camera to the next." Foreman nodded. "Good thinking."

Kiyomi was so thrilled that Foreman liked her idea that she thought she might explode.

"We could even track Lucy's movements," Foreman said. "See where she was just before she saw you and just after you left, and whether Carolyn was with her or not. Or if she was with someone else."

Kiyomi nodded excitedly. "And what she was doing around there that made her want me to leave."

"Okay, how about this?" Foreman said. "Are you up for getting to work a couple hours early tomorrow?"

"Sure." Kiyomi said.

"Let's use the SAC computers to get some answers. I'll start looking through the video files for cameras near the Welcome Desk from say, six to seven. Once I locate her, I'll follow her from the moment she sets her bag down until she walks out of view. Based on the angle she is headed, I can tell which camera picked her up next and I'll open the view file for that time period. While I'm doing that, you look at clips later in the morning for the same camera from just before and after the time you ran into Lucy. See who she came with, what she did there, what she did after she left. Can't hurt."

"I feel like a real police detective," Kiyomi said.

"Hey," Foreman said. "Worst case, we waste an hour of our time. But if we find something interesting, Major Power will be pretty happy. " Foreman stuck out his fist and Kiyomi tapped it with hers. "See you there at five?"

"Yes," Kiyomi said. "I will be there."

Kiyomi got Foreman's leather jacket from the closet and watched as he put it on. She noticed that he didn't lean against the wall while putting on his shoes, as most Americans did, but was able to maintain his balance on one leg while he pulled on and laced first one shoe and then the other.

Foreman was buttoning his coat when he stopped suddenly. "Oh my God," he said. "I almost walked out of here without thanking you for such a fantastic dinner. And for showing me your photos. And telling me about Japan. Everything. It was great."

"Me too," Kiyomi said. "And thank you for the beautiful flowers, Mike. I enjoyed this evening." *And I can't wait to see you tomorrow morning.*

FRIDAY, NOVEMBER 16TH

CHAPTER 24

MightyMall in the early morning was an intimidating place. Although mall access between closing each night and unlocking the doors to the public each morning was restricted, the place was never completely empty. Officers manned the Security Action Center 24/7. A store was being remodeled or readied for opening most nights. Movement of construction workers was limited to the stores they were working on; they were escorted from a secured service entrance to and from their work sites. Movement to any other part of the mall—the restrooms, for example—required chaperoning by a security officer, who was not always readily available. Coffee-guzzling workers had been known to recycle empty paint cans for Emergency Urination Purposes.

In a building capable of holding over 200,000 people, there were rarely more than a few dozen souls inside it between two and six in the morning. A small contingent of security officers patrolled the floors and Gonzoland to make sure no one stayed beyond bar closing either by accident or by design. The threat of arrest or banishment from MightyMall kept most people in line. The few that braved such punishment normally lost their nerve quickly and tried to sneak out;

security officers usually turned a blind eye if the interlopers were less than thirty minutes overdue—who needed the extra paperwork for a couple of innocent pranksters? Security officers were few and far between after four o'clock; they spent most of their time making sure store gates were down and locked and that store doors in back were properly closed. There were no Saint Commercia Police Officers after business hours; their responsibilities in MightyMall consisted solely of public safety and compliance with local ordinances.

The SCP Substation was empty between midnight and 7 A.M.

As Carolyn Noxon Batch well knew, and was counting on.

"Where the *fuck* have you been?" Carolyn was sitting at her desk as Lucy entered her office.

"What?" Lucy was unprepared for the attack. "It's five. You said be here at five o'clock."

"It's already five *past* five, you stupid twit. We don't have all day!" Carolyn stormed past Lucy into the main office area. She peered to the left and right, confirming that no other management office staff had yet arrived, then headed for the door nearest to the maintenance corridor.

All right already, you psycho bitch! Lucy thought to herself. *If you don't get off my case, you may end up buying me a Lexus instead of a Prius. Fuck the environment.* She followed Carolyn out of her office.

"You understand the plan?" Carolyn said, as she hopped onto the Cushman. She punched the acceleration pedal to the floor before Lucy had finished climbing in, throwing her assistant against the seat.

"Jesus!" Lucy said, grabbing the metal bar located between her seat and Carolyn's. "Yes, I know the plan already. We're going to sneak Dora—" Lucy said.

"Fine. Let's go." Carolyn sped down the corridor.

They encountered no one in the elevator going up to the seventh floor or in the service corridor in the ten minutes it took them to arrive at Service Door ML7N1. With her left hand on the door handle, Carolyn stopped suddenly and held the index finger of her right hand to her lips. "See if you can hear anyone," she whispered to Lucy. After several seconds of silence, Carolyn pushed the handle down, opened the door and went in.

Once they were both inside and had closed the door behind them, Lucy said, "Be nice if we had a flashlight." As in their previous visit, there was little ambient light, just a dim glow emanating from the small bulb over the door.

"Too dangerous," Carolyn said. "On the off chance someone from maintenance is on one of the floors below us, they might come to investigate, or call security. We're fine with the light we have. All we need to do is carry her out the same way we came in."

Carolyn started along the walkway with the confidence of someone who had done this many times before. Lucy walked more slowly and kept a firm grip on the railing. She knew the platform at the end was coming up but the farther they got from the door, the darker it became.

"All right, I've found her," Carolyn said. Then: "Oh shit."

"What?" Lucy said.

"She's moved."

"She's *what*!" Lucy pictured an image of Dead Dora rising from the dead and walking away.

"*Shhh*," Carolyn hissed. "Be quiet, you *imbecile*! She's not in the same position we left her, that's all. Looks like she's kind of tipped over."

"*Gross*!" Lucy said. "How did that happen?"

"How the hell should I know?" Carolyn said. "Vibration, maybe ... from one of the park rides...?" She nudged the body gingerly with one foot to make sure it was done shifting. "I guess we're lucky she didn't fall completely off the ledge."

"But wouldn't that have been better?" Lucy said. "I mean, body falls over the ledge, falls to a lower ledge or all the way to the first floor, somebody else finds her? Then we don't have to worry about getting rid of her."

Carolyn shook her head. "Wouldn't work. Too many awkward questions. There's no way a non-employee could have gotten through that Service Door. I'll bet there hasn't been anyone besides me in here for years." Carolyn looked over the railing, then back at the door. "It would be too hard to explain how an old lady wandered down a half mile of restricted hallway out of the blue and then opened a door that's always locked."

What does it matter as long as it's not us *who finds the body?* Lucy thought. *Just get rid it and let someone else come across her, for Christ's sake!*

Standing next to Lucy, Carolyn was thinking happier thoughts. *My plan is much more … efficient? It takes care of old Dora here,* and *eliminates your little plan to blackmail me, my lovely Lucy, in one neat stroke.*

"Here, put these on." Carolyn handed Lucy a pair of rubber gloves and put on her own. "We can't leave any evidence." *Yet.*

Carolyn bent over and sat Dead Dora back up. *Please return all seat trays and dead bodies to their upright position.* The dead woman had grown cold and stiff with rigor mortis in the past twenty-four hours. The shifting of her body had caused various body parts to twist at such odd angles that her posture no longer looked human. The legs pointed straight out. The torso was bent forward at the waist, but rotated to the left. The head faced forward. Her right arm, which had flopped over the ledge, now pointed straight up. The left arm was locked tight at her side. Dead Dora now looked like a Raggedy Ann doll sitting on the floor, turning toward something on the left but waving to something straight ahead, off in the distance.

"Looks like a fucking mannequin from the Halloween Store," Carolyn said. She pushed the right arm down once, gingerly. It snapped back up, like a diving board. She pushed again, adding her body weight. A loud *crack* came from somewhere in the body's shoulder, like a log popping in the fireplace. Carolyn jumped back.

"Shit."

"*Eeew,*" Lucy said.

"C'mon. Help me with this," Carolyn said.

Lucy backed away. "Can't we just leave the arm the way it is?"

Carolyn briefly considered pushing down hard enough to break the arm bone so that it would hang more obediently at the body's side but rejected the idea; if Lucy got too spooked at the cracking sounds and ran off now, Carolyn's beautiful plan would fall apart.

"Fine," Carolyn said, "we'll leave her the way she is. It'll be fine."

Why don't I just run out of here now? Lucy thought to herself. *Run straight for the door, down to security, tell them the whole thing. "Listen guys: Carolyn and I found this dead woman, see, and yesterday and she and I hid it up on the seventh floor … but I didn't want to—Carolyn made me do it—and it's not my fault!" All right, forget that. My word against Carolyn's and no one's going to believe me. How about I just run for the nearest exit and leave the building forever? Head for my car and go home and never come back. Move some place far way, like Eau Claire. What could Carolyn do? The worst I'd get is a bad reference for my next job. "Lucy was an unreliable assistant who ran off when I needed her to help me move a corpse. Not a team player." Fine, I can live with that.*

"Come on," Carolyn said. "Let's get her out to the Cushman. We'll each grab an arm," she said. "Or an armpit."

Lucy considered her options for a few more seconds, then returned her attention to the task at hand. *I'd never make it anyway,* Lucy thought glumly. *Carolyn would find a way to screw me.* "Fine. Let's just get this over with."

Standing on the right side, Carolyn reached down and took hold of the body's right arm, still pointing straight ahead like the Scarecrow pointing down the Yellow Brick Road. Lucy's side of the body was less cooperative. The left arm pressed firm against the body, like a frozen chicken wing. Lucy was barely able to wedge her hands between the arm and the torso. The fit was so tight she immediately felt her fingers beginning to go numb.

Lucy straightened up, laboring to lift the body with her. "How can she be this heavy? She's, what? … five feet tall and about 100 pounds?"

The two of them struggled a few feet toward the door when Lucy doubled over, letting the body drop to the metal walkway with an audible thud. "My fingers!" she said. She dislodged her hands and began massaging her fingers.

"Careful, you idiot!" Carolyn hissed.

"Ow!" Lucy said. "It was pinching my fingers. Her arm is locked against her shoulder like a vice. I can't carry her that way, I'm sorry."

Carolyn straightened up and stretched her neck. She moved to the front of the body. "Okay, let's try a different way," she said. "You get back there and take her legs. I'll take her head. Think you can handle that?"

"Whatever," Lucy muttered to herself.

When they got to the Cushman, they discovered another issue. Once on the flatbed, the rigor mortis was causing the body's legs to stick straight out, like those of a wooden doll. Dead Dora and Carolyn could no longer sit side-by-side on the back of the Cushman, dangling their legs off the flatbed like two old friends going for a hay ride, sharing the latest gossip. Her legs were locked at the knees.

"Great," Carolyn said. "Help me push her the other way."

They slid the body toward the front of the Cushman so Dora leaned flush against the back of Lucy's seat. The body's legs now rested entirely within the flatbed. Odd for an adult to sit like that, but not out of the question, Carolyn decided. She climbed in and sat to Dead Dora's left. She placed her right arm around the Dora's shoulders, the way a dutiful daughter might tend to a frail grandmother. Carolyn gave the body a once over, nodded once in silent satisfaction and looked toward Lucy.

"What do you think?" Carolyn said.

"Jesus!" Lucy thought, *"Dead Dora's arm looks like someone saluting Hitler, her head is tilted up toward the ceiling, her face looks like it spent the night on a waffle iron, she's got a gash on her head, and her eyes, wide open like she's seen a ghost, are more white than blue. She looks scarier than anything I've ever seen in a movie and if the lights suddenly snapped on I'd start screaming and never stop for the rest of my life.*

Lucy looked away, pretending to study something down the corridor. "Great," she said, without enthusiasm. "Let's go." She climbed into the driver's side of the Cushman.

"You don't think she looks strange?" Carolyn said, the same way someone might say, *Do I look fat in this?* "With her arm pointing up the way it is?"

Lucy wanted to scream. *You* don't *think so?* "No, she's great," she said. "Now can we go? Please?"

"Okay, let's go," Carolyn said. "You know the plan. Keep to the service corridor. It'll take a little longer than going straight over on a shopping avenue but we're less likely to run into anyone. Got it?"

"Got it."

"When you get to the service door by that pizza shop, stop the Cushman. That's the door nearest to the Lost Deck. Then I'll run out and make sure no one is around."

Lucy closed her eyes and took deep breaths. When she didn't respond, Carolyn said, "Got it?"

"All right! Yes, I've got it," Lucy said.

Just hang with me a little longer, you little twat. "And when I'm off checking the area near the Lost Deck," Carolyn said, "What do you do?"

"I keep an eye on the service corridor," Lucy said. "If I hear anyone coming, I should drive away and call you on my cell phone."

"Good," Carolyn said. "Hurry up. Can't this thing go any faster?"

CHAPTER 25

Friday morning at 5 A.M. found Eric Lemke in a far sunnier mood than he had been in the previous day. Thursday afternoon one of his maintenance guys, Joey, asked if he could take Saturday and Sunday off next week to make a long Thanksgiving weekend. He said he would be willing to trade his normal days off, next Monday and Tuesday to anyone willing. It immediately occurred to Lemke that he and his wife Stella might still be able to spend Early Thanksgiving with Brett; it would just be tomorrow through next Tuesday, instead of yesterday through Sunday as he had originally planned. Same difference: four days with his son, daughter-in-law and the grandkids. He didn't need the Saturday and Sunday off after Thanksgiving anyway because he and Stella were staying home this year. Lemke checked the work calendar and confirmed that there were no construction projects scheduled for next Monday and Tuesday.

He and Stella were headed for Beatrice after all.

Apart from the office move day before yesterday, the past week was quiet for the maintenance department. Smaller Christmas decorations had been popping up the past few weeks but the biggest changes would occur next week, from Wednesday night after closing through Thanksgiving Day, one of the two days a year when MightyMall was closed. A flurry of activity would create a seventy-five foot Christmas tree covered with Tiffany Christmas ornaments. Hundreds of wreaths would hang from the ceilings of each of the seven floors. One hundred miles of LEDs would snake around the complex, forming snowflakes, candles, snowmen, spruce trees, wrapped packages, mistletoe, poinsettias, reindeer and other assorted politically correct / non-religious icons on the outside of the building.

The week before Thanksgiving was, however, for the maintenance department, generally quiet.

Lemke decided to begin the day by finishing up the service ladder inspections. He had only one left to check: MN1. With any luck, he would be done in less than an hour. A couple of hours to finish up the paperwork and to make sure the thousands of pounds of Christmas tree parts and decorations, and all the LED lights, were where they should be in storage and ready to go for next week. He could then coast through the rest of the day.

Lemke had entered on the first floor from the ML1N1 Service Door and climbed up the first six floors. He stopped to hook his left arm on the ladder rung for balance and reached in his pocket for his handkerchief. The long climb, combined with the mugginess of the shaft, had left his underarms damp. He dabbed away the drops of sweat trickling down his forehead and returned his handkerchief to his pocket.

Lemke froze as he heard a sound like air escaping a balloon, like a parent blowing on a baby's stomach, or a prolonged fart. It lasted about ten seconds. He thought it was above him but wasn't sure; sounds echoed oddly in the shafts. He felt for the hammer hanging on his utility belt. The size and weight of it were comforting. What the hell was a deflating balloon doing in this shaft?

"Hello?" Lemke said. He had no reason to be afraid. He'd never encountered anyone on these ladders or any of the catwalks. It was the *type* of sound that put him on edge, more than the fact that he had heard something. He knew every sound that one would normally hear in the back corridors, shafts and storage rooms of the mall. The ticks of machines cooling, doors opening or closing, rats squeaking, ambient sounds from Gonzoland seeping through the walls. Lemke knew every creak and groan the building could make.

He'd just never heard a balloon deflating in a service shaft before.

"Anyone there?" Lemke said. He took out his hammer and rapped it once on the ladder, as if that would cause the sound to recur. Or warn an intruder of his presence.

After thirty seconds of silence, Lemke resumed his climb. He was just below the seventh floor catwalk; the source of the sound was most likely there.

He stopped again, just below the catwalk and peered up at the door. It was closed. One more step. His head was now level with the catwalk. He stretched his neck up and craned it to the right. Nothing on the catwalk by the door.

A second farting sound caused Lemke to jerk his head back so far that he banged the left side of it on the ladder.

"Godammit to hell!" Lemke yelped as he squinted his eyes shut in pain. He touched his head gingerly with his left hand, already sensing a growing welt.

"I swear to fucking *Christ* if anyone is up here who shouldn't be here there's going to be *hell* to pay!" Lemke said.

More angry than afraid now, Lemke ascended several more rungs of the ladder and stepped onto the seventh floor catwalk. He pushed his shoulder against the door and confirmed that it was closed and latched.

Lemke removed the flashlight from his belt and switched it on. He pointed it toward the end of the catwalk and saw a human shape. Even at thirty feet it was obviously human. He saw pink and a head and white hair.

"Excuse me," Lemke called, then mentally kicked himself. What was he being so polite for? *He* was *supposed* to be here. Whoever was at the end of the catwalk was not.

"Hello. Um." Lemke wasn't sure why it took him so long to act, but he finally started walking down the catwalk toward the body at the end. He hadn't even seen it close up or checked for a pulse but already he was thinking of it as a body and not as a person asleep or passed out. The posture was too unnatural to be a living, breathing person. Maybe that was why he was so hesitant to approach.

He stood over the body and traced the body with his flashlight. Out here there was no light beyond what his flashlight supplied. It was a woman, he was sure.

"Hello," he said, giving the body one more chance respond and prove him wrong.

Lemke crouched down beside the woman, his boots half a foot from her head and neck. Now that he knew that it was a indeed a dead body he was dealing with, not an intruder, and that this was the source of the strange sounds he had heard, his fear left him. The known, no matter how gruesome, was much less terrifying than the unknown.

Yet he was hesitant to touch the body. Was this a crime scene? Maybe: how did she get in here anyway? But his reticence came from a different place and that realization bothered Lemke, even as he did nothing to fight it. The truth was, he didn't want to touch the body because he simply didn't want to get involved. Not today. Not as he was getting ready to visit his kids with his wife. If he reported finding a body now, he might have to stay for hours. Maybe have to come in tomorrow. Lemke was no expert but he knew this was not a normal death, no old lady who had a heart attack while shopping with her friends or mall walking.

Thinking of mall walking caused Lemke to wonder when she had died. He reached out with his left hand, then drew it back. Would his finger leave some kind of trace evidence that the CSI folks would find? Fuck it, he didn't think so, and anyway, he didn't plan to stick around long so how would they think to check his DNA or fingerprints or whatever it was they checked? He reached out a second time and cautiously touched the woman's neck to check for a pulse. Nothing. He touched her neck again, this time with the back of his fingers. He touched his own neck, then the woman's neck again. The body was cool. Not cold, but definitely cooler than his was. And stiff. He ventured a light nudge of her shoulder. Stiff as a board. She was dead, all right.

Lemke's creaky old knees were beginning to ache. He placed a palm on each of his thighs and pushed himself up.

He was still looking down at the woman and already feeling guilty for what he was planning to do. There was no telling what the fallout of finding a dead mall guest in a supposedly secure location would be. Would maintenance get the blame because his guys were the only ones to ever venture into these areas? Lemke couldn't remember the last time he had been on this particular catwalk; it didn't go anywhere except straight out. He only used this service door, ML7N1, to get to the ladder.

Would security take the heat for letting this woman somehow get into the service corridors unnoticed? Lemke wondered, not for the first time, how many of the surveillance cameras in the mall were actually monitored and how often. He'd noticed fewer security officers doing patrols than right after 9/11. Or if all of the cameras were even real–he'd heard rumors for years that some of the units were just plastic fakes, meant to deter would-be terrorists.

In any case, Lemke could imagine several scenarios that would not only force him to cancel his travel plans, something he was in no mood to do again, but also put his job in jeopardy. Yet he could think of no upside for doing the right thing and notifying the authorities. The woman was obviously dead and he couldn't do anything about it. It would make no difference to her if she was found now or later by someone else. Lemke felt a brief pang of guilt as he thought about the woman's husband or children who might be looking for her, but pushed those to the back of his mind. Not my problem, he kept repeating like a mantra. Not my problem.

Lemke crouched down again and placed his hand gently on the woman's shoulder. "Sorry old girl," he said. "You're going to have to wait here a little longer."

Lemke stood up, walked to the entrance of the catwalk and opened the door. He stepped out and paused momentarily as he confirmed that no one was in the area. He thought he might have heard faint voices coming from the corridor to the right, so he immediately turned left and walked rapidly away.

CHAPTER 26

The Security Action Center looked like a cross between NASA's Mission Control Center and a movie theater with stadium seating. You entered at the back, which was the highest point in the room. Six semi-circular tiers, each lined with twelve workstations facing forward, led to the main floor dominated by two 100-inch screens. The rest of the wall space was lined with 50-inch monitors.

The SAC underwent major renovations after 9/11 when panic had caused a brief period of exuberant capital spending by the mall's owners, including $21 million for the security department to upgrade its technical and personnel requirements. Some of the money had gone to the formation and training of the X-Team. The rest had gone to new SAC facilities.

The SAC ended up with seventy-two workstations, partly out of then-current needs and anticipated needs for the mall expansion. Major Power's wish list was fulfilled, leaving a $6 million surplus that he had no intention of giving back. He had learned early on that ending a budget cycle with leftover money was the fastest way to having one's subsequent budget cut. Owners tended to believe that surpluses indicated waste, and that waste was best dealt with by cutting next year's budget. So Power had spent all $21 million that year, which was why SAC ended up with more workstations than it needed. There were never more than forty officers in SAC at any one time, except when owners were visiting, when, miraculously, all seventy-two workstations were manned with busy officers.

Power's plan worked well the first few years after 9/11; his budget requests sailed past the owners' desks with nary a cut of any kind. Eventually Power's cleverness was done in by a disappointing lack of terrorist activity in the US and his own team's excellent record of preventing any violent crime other than the occasional bar brawl; the Chief Financial Officer at Titanic Properties ultimately reached the point where he could no longer justify spending so much money when the threat of physical attack had been diminished. Thus began a series of annual cuts to security's budget, particularly to the labor line. Clearly, there was no longer the need for so many officers and certainly no need to increase their pay beyond the inflation rate. The irony of the situation was not lost on Major Power; it occurred to him more than once that the shortest route to a larger, better-paid staff would be a series of successful attacks on MightyMall.

Power looked for ways to reduce costs that had the least detrimental effect on actual security. Cutting the midnight-to-seven shift was the easiest of the low-hanging fruit to pick. By putting extra uniformed officers on the floor at peak shopping times and just before bar closing, shoppers and potential troublemakers were convinced they saw a large security presence. All entrances were locked, from both the inside and outside. Surveillance cameras were always recording, though without anyone to redirect or zoom in, the recordings were limited to events that occurred in the cameras' lines of sight. As there had never been a serious crime during those hours, security staffing had never been an issue.

Mike Foreman walked into SAC a few minutes before five in the morning wearing blue jeans and a Vikings jersey with the number 28 on the back. He spotted two officers sitting next to each other in the front of the room. They turned toward him when he walked in and he acknowledged them with a nod of his head. X-Team members were allowed to use SAC computers as necessary.

Kiyomi was sitting at one of the workstations in the back.

"Hey," Foreman said.

"Morning," Kiyomi said. She was wearing beige UGG boots over black Mia Ultra-Skinny Leg jeans from Express and a light gray heather ribbed open cardigan over a turquoise cotton v-neck top, both from Banana Republic. A bit overdressed compared to her normal work attire, but Kiyomi knew she would be seeing a lot of Mike today and she had had a great time last night, and ... well ... why not dress up?

Foreman walked over to the workstation on Kiyomi's left and did a double take. Was she dressed differently than usual? He didn't pay much attention to fashions so he couldn't be sure. Whatever it was, Kiyomi looked drop-dead gorgeous. And was she wearing some kind of perfume? He handed her one of the large paper cups he was carrying and tried not to stare.

"Starbucks!" Kiyomi said. "Yeaaay!" She lightly clapped her hands, finger-to-finger style, in the way she had told him last night that young Japanese children clapped. It didn't seem childish when Kiyomi did it.

The two uniformed officers sitting in front turned around to look at what was causing the commotion. The SAC was normally as quiet as a library.

"Sorry!" Kiyomi said in a loud whisper, covering her mouth and bowing her head slightly in what Foreman assumed was the Japanese way of apologizing.

Foreman placed his coffee on his desk. He took off his coat and hung it over the back of his chair.

Kiyomi reached down by her feet and picked up a pizza-sized cardboard box.

"Dunkin' Donuts!" Foreman said, happy but careful to keep his voice low. "I didn't know we even had Dunkin' Donuts in Minnesota."

"There's a new one near my apartment," Kiyomi said. "It opens at three every morning. I hope you like them."

"I *love* donuts." Foreman picked through several before deciding on a jelly donut.

"*Yappari!*" Kiyomi said, and giggled.

"What does that mean?" Foreman froze, his donut inches from his mouth.

"In Japanese it means, 'I thought so' or 'I was right after all'," Kiyomi said. "You Americans all like everything so sweet."

"Hey! You bought them." He bit into his donut. "Yum."

Kiyomi smiled, picked out a plain donut for herself, broke it in half, dunked one piece daintily in her coffee, took a small bite and chewed happily. "Mmm," she said. "Just right."

"Do Japanese dunk donuts in their coffee?" Foreman said. "Do they even have donuts in Japan?"

"We have donut shops. My favorite growing up was Mr. Donut. Some of the donuts are the same as what you have in America; some are different. You'll also find some with mashed Japanese sweet beans inside, or ground beef, or curry—"

"Yuk," Foreman said.

"They're *good*!" Kiyomi said. "But no dunking in coffee. I learned that here from my first roommate in college. It is one of your American customs I like best." She dipped another piece of donut in her coffee and popped that in her mouth, emitting a satisfied sigh.

After Foreman finished his jelly donut he logged onto his computer. Video surveillance files were cross-referenced by location, specific camera, date and time. If he knew the names of the cameras in the area of Northern Lights West 1 he could call up all its files immediately. He didn't know the names of any cameras offhand, so he first pulled up "Northern Lights," then "Level 1," then "West." Under Keyword he typed in "Welcome Desk," which displayed a diagram of the entire hallway leading from the main shopping avenue, "Northern Lights," to the exit.

The diagram showed three cameras: one directly above the Welcome Desk, one over the mall entrance and one at the intersection of the hallway with the Northern Lights shopping avenue. Foreman clicked on the Welcome Desk camera and typed in yesterday's date. He moved the slider to five minutes to seven. The screen was blank.

"That's weird," Foreman said.

"What is weird?" Kiyomi said.

"There's no file for seven yesterday morning for the camera just above the Welcome Desk."

Kiyomi leaned over to peer at Foreman's computer screen. "Try typing in another time a few hours before or after."

Foreman typed in "10:00:00."

"Oh, there it is," he said.

Kiyomi said, "I think certain cameras are programmed automatically to shut off at certain times."

"I never heard anything about that."

Kiyomi shrugged. "Major Power mentioned it at one of the morning briefings last year, I think before you joined. He didn't explain why, but he was not in a good mood that day."

"Maybe budget cuts," Foreman said.

“Video files do take up a lot of space,” Kiyomi said. “And you know how the IT department is always telling us to delete unneeded files to free up space.”

“Damn,” Foreman said. “I hope we never have to depend on video evidence to nail some criminal and then find out too late that the file doesn’t exist.”

“Try another camera,” Kiyomi said. “Try that one over the shopping avenue—the one facing the entrance.” Kiyomi pointed to one of the icons on the diagram. “That should be active all the time.”

Foreman clicked on the camera and moved the slider to five minutes to seven. The camera was pointed straight ahead. The majority of the screen was filled with the eight glass doors at the entrance. He could see one set of benches sitting back to back. He knew there were three sets of those benches and he instinctively looked for the button that would pull the zoom back. It took him a moment to realize that he couldn’t do that–he wasn’t looking through the camera at a live image but at a recording.

Sighing quietly, Foreman pressed PLAY, then the FAST FORWARD button. At 07:02:36 an elderly woman wearing a parka and carrying a handbag strode through one of the doors.

“Hey,” Foreman said. “Look at this.”

“Ooh,” Kiyomi said. She pointed at something the woman was carrying. “Is that the bag?”

“I think so,” Foreman said. “Hard to say in black and white like this, but it sure looks like it.”

Foreman and Kiyomi watched the woman stomp her feet, sit down on the bench, put down her bag and remove her boots. She put on a pair of sneakers, picked up her bag, stood up, took two steps to the left and disappeared from view.

“Damn,” Foreman said.

"Yes," Kiyomi said. "Damn."

When the old woman failed to reappear after an additional minute of viewing, Foreman used the slider to skim ahead several more minutes. There was no further sign of the old woman. By 7:31 A.M. no other person had entered the field of view.

"Odd that no one else came in by that time, don't you think?" Foreman said. "Oh, that's right—" Foreman knocked himself on the forehead with a closed fist. "The snow storm. Traffic was all tied up the first few hours yesterday. Of course there weren't many people in the mall yet."

"Maybe after she put down her bag she just started thinking about her walk, or had to meet someone somewhere else, and walked away," Kiyomi said. "You know, people do forget things sometimes."

"Maybe," Foreman said. "Let me try the camera over the entrance."

"Wait a second," Kiyomi said. "I'm going to write down the file names."

"Good idea. Easier to find them later."

Foreman opened the next file, typed 07:02:00 in the TIME field and pressed PLAY. This view showed a portion of the Welcome Desk counter in the lower left portion of the screen, several stores along the sides of the hallway and the main Northern Lights shopping avenue off in the distance. He and Kiyomi watched several minutes of the video in real time and used the slider to skim a further twenty minutes. No sign of the old woman.

Kiyomi said something in Japanese that Foreman couldn't understand, then: "I don't understand. She *has* to be there. She didn't exit the mall and she didn't walk into the mall. Where else could she be? Are you sure we are looking at the correct segment of tape?"

Foreman pointed to the screen date and time: November 15, 07:25:05.

"She could have gone into the bathroom, I suppose," Foreman said. "Maybe she had stomach trouble and stayed there for a while." Foreman slid the clip ahead to 07:59:00 until he saw footage of himself racing down the hallway. He reopened the other video clip and slid from 07:00:00 until he saw himself entering the mall at 07:58:02.

"And you checked the women's restroom when you came in, didn't you?" Kiyomi said. "So we know she could not have gone on to the Northern Lights shopping avenue, and she didn't leave the mall."

Foreman nodded.

"The only other way out of that area that wouldn't be caught on tape is the door to the service hallway next to the Welcome Desk," Foreman said. "But why would she go that way?"

Kiyomi shrugged. "Alzheimer's, maybe…?" she said. "She looked old. Maybe she became disoriented. Changed her shoes, had a stroke or something? Stood up and wandered off?"

Foreman located the diagram for the service hallway nearest the Welcome Desk. They checked video files for the period between seven and eight o'clock. No one entered or exited the service hallway door by the Welcome Desk during that time.

"Impossible," Kiyomi said. "This is impossible. That woman could not disappear like that. No one could."

Foreman scratched his head. "Now I'm really confused." He reached for a glazed donut, took a large bite and chewed meditatively for several moments. After taking a swig of lukewarm coffee, he shook his head and said. "I'm stumped. I've got nothing. This is really starting to piss me off."

Kiyomi dipped the remaining half of her plain donut into her coffee and took a bite. She smiled at Foreman and said, "Well, the coffee is very good. It was very kind of you to bring it."

Foreman chuckled. "And the donuts are good."

Foreman and Kiyomi resumed their silent meditation while they ate their donuts, drank coffee and pondered the wonders of vanishing septuagenarians.

"All right," Foreman said. "Let's go over what we *do* know. We know an old woman came in the West entrance. We know she changed out of her boots into her sneakers. We know she walked in the direction of the lockers."

"Carrying her boots," Kiyomi said.

"That's right!" Foreman said. "And I didn't see any boots when I was there at eight. Wherever she went, she isn't likely to have brought her boots with her."

"Which means she must have put them in a locker," Kiyomi said.

"Exactly!"

Kiyomi typed on the keyboard in front of her. "Here is a list of the lockers at the West entrance," she said. "And here," she entered a few more strokes and then pressed ENTER with a flourish, "are the lockers that are currently empty."

The screen displayed the numbers of all forty lockers at that entrance; flashing red squares next to the lockers, #232, #233 and #501, identified them as currently occupied. Sensors built into all lockers were activated by anything weighing more than four ounces, whether locked or unlocked.

"We can sign out the master key for the lockers when we finish with this," Kiyomi said.

"Okay," Foreman said. "Back to our original question: where did the woman go after she left our field of view? We know she didn't disappear into thin air." He opened a file showing an architectural drawing of the hallway between the entrance and the shopping avenue. He pointed at the entrance. "Here are the lockers, the Welcome Desk, the restrooms, the stores—"

"What about the Welcome Desk?" Kiyomi said. "Could she have gotten inside and taken a nap?"

Foreman frowned as he continued to stare at his computer screen. "That's a stretch, don't you think? The wooden gates are latched—"

"But not hard to open if you know where the latch is," Kiyomi said.

"True."

"Perhaps she became fatigued or ill and decided to ... no, that doesn't make any sense—why would she do that?" Kiyomi shook her head in frustration. "And she certainly wasn't there when I went back to the Welcome Desk at the end of the day. If the attendants had found her we certainly would have heard about it."

Foreman's face brightened suddenly. "But," he said, "We still haven't checked the video files from your experience with Carolyn Batch's administrative assistant."

"Lucy Evans," Kiyomi said.

"Yes."

Kiyomi said, "I forgot all about her." She turned to her computer. "You keep your files open on your computer. I'll use my computer to show what we have of Lucy."

CHAPTER 27

Carolyn opened the door from the service corridor slowly, bending forward as she peeked out like a child sneaking out of her bedroom looking for signs of grownups. Seeing none, she straightened up, stuck out her chin, and stepped fully out into the seventh floor shopping avenue, adjusting wrinkles in her skirt that weren't there and patting her hair. She scanned the area. Store gates were all down. No tenants were yet in their places of business; no security or management office personnel were anywhere in sight.

Carolyn took several more steps, tentatively at first, then with more confidence, standing erect, looking more and more like the Vice President she was. *I have every right to be up on the seventh floor at this time of day. I run the place. I can go anywhere I please.*

Carolyn noticed a Tim & Kevin's Minnesota Style Pizza on her right, confirming that she had chosen the correct exit door. Across the shopping avenue she saw the Saint Commercia Substation, lights out, as she had expected. To its left, a nondescript door that was the only way to their final destination. She turned to go back inside the service corridor, then quickly changed her mind and headed out to the middle of the shopping avenue. It was simultaneously exhilarating and terrifying: if anyone came along in the next two minutes her plan would be ruined, or worse, she would be discovered with the body. But they were so close. All she needed was to get the body through that small door and her plan would work perfectly. She scanned one direction, then another, searching for open store gates, lights on that shouldn't be, security officers on foot or Segway patrol.

Nothing. The coast was clear.

Carolyn hurried back inside the service corridor and found Lucy and Dead Dora right where she had left them. *Probably wasn't smart to have left Lucy unattended like that; if she ran off now leaving the Cushman and the body I'd be really screwed.*

"Okay," Carolyn said. "I want you to slowly edge up to the doors, nudge them open, then just drive through. They'll close automatically behind you."

Duh, Lucy thought to herself.

"Once we emerge, I want to get across the avenue as quickly as possible," Carolyn said. "Zip on over, circle in front of the Substation, point the Cushman back out toward the avenue, then back up as close to the Lost Deck door as you can. Got it?"

"Yes, I've got it," Lucy said, between clenched teeth.

Carolyn took a deep breath, rubbed her hands together and exhaled. "Okay. Let's go."

Lucy pointed the nose of the Cushman at the double doors and gently pumped the accelerator pedal, moving the vehicle forward. As slowly as they were moving, the metal of the Cushman striking the metal of the doors created a loud *crack* that reverberated in the long service corridor. Both Lucy and Carolyn froze momentarily, waiting for the SWAT team to surround them. When that didn't happen, Lucy pushed the Cushman through the doors.

Free of the doors, Lucy raced across to the other side of the shopping avenue. She curved sharply to the left in front of the SCP Police Substation, forgetting her two passengers in back.

"Fucking *hell!"* she heard Carolyn whisper/scream from the behind her.

"Oops. Sorry," Lucy said, removing her foot completely from the accelerator, causing the automatic braking system to engage, throwing Carolyn and Dora against her seat.

Carolyn reached behind her and slapped Lucy in the face. "You retarded, white-trash, shit-eating, *slut!"* She continued swearing as she leapt off the back of the Cushman. "Have you totally lost your *mind?"*

Lucy's face stung where Carolyn's hand had struck her, igniting a fury she had kept repressed until now. She jumped out of her seat and stood face to face with her boss. "Back off, you fat cow." She spat the words. "Back off right now or I swear I will call 911, give them your name and wait for the police to show up." Lucy balled her fists at her side, her face red with rage, shaking with the desire to kick her boss in the stomach, pull out her hair and gouge out her eyes.

Carolyn was so shocked at the outburst that she stood motionless, eyes and mouth wide open.

Lucy looked her boss straight in the eyes, unblinking, for the first time. "Carolyn." The gates to Lucy's emotions now swung wide open. "*Dear.* I am sick and tired your constant daily abuse. Of letting you talk me out of calling security when we found the body and into helping you drag this … this *thing* all around this *fucking* mall! All so you can make sure your stupid presentation gets front page coverage in the newspapers and you get your annual zillion dollar bonus!"

After the initial shock of being addressed in such a way had worn off, Carolyn clamped her teeth together and took several deep breaths. She stopped listening to Lucy somewhere after, "I'm sick and tired…."

and forced herself to focus on more important things, namely her Plan. Properly executing her Plan would render Lucy's impudence and rudeness moot. *Just a little bit longer,* she told herself. *You've put up with worse.*

Carolyn's Plan had begun to take shape yesterday afternoon during the post-press conference interviews out on the Lost Deck. Like all of her best ideas, including catching her philandering worm of an ex-husband rutting with those two hussies up north, what began as a series of unrelated thoughts had eventually coalesced into a whole that was greater than the sum of its parts. The initially disparate thoughts that formed Carolyn's Perfect Plan were:

1) Carolyn had a body she needed to get rid of in a fashion that would not be connected to her.
2) Lost Deck was almost always empty.
3) Lucy Evans was the only person who could connect the body to Carolyn.
4) Lucy Evans had threatened to blackmail her and was becoming increasingly impudent.
5) Because Lost Deck was not open to the public, security cameras were almost never trained on it.
6) Access to Lost Deck was limited to a single door next to the SCP Substation.
7) Only three keys existed that could open that door.

Viewed separately, the random thoughts were of no use. Mixed together creatively, they formed the ingredients of The Perfect Plan.

Carolyn began yesterday by loaning her master key, very publicly, to Lucy Evans while they were both at the reception desk following the press conference. Carolyn had made sure that, Caitlin, who was manning the reception desk, had overheard her instruct Lucy to retrieve her bag from Lost Deck. Carolyn also presented Lucy her key with such a flourish that Caitlin could not have missed it.

So far as anyone would ever know, Lucy was the last person to visit Lost Deck on Thursday. With that seed planted, the rest of the plan would fall perfectly into place:

Who is to say that, after retrieving Carolyn's bag on Lost Deck, Lucy didn't simply forget to lock the door behind her? Human error happens. Who is to say that some old lady, after suffering a stroke, for example, or allowed by uncaring children to wander the mall despite late-stage dementia, hadn't wandered off last night and somehow found her way onto Lost Deck? And maybe, after wandering into Lost Deck, this poor old woman had fallen asleep and spent the night there. Or perhaps she went through that door looking for the police—it didn't matter. At some point the woman, barely coherent with Alzheimer's, must have shuffled over to the observation deck and been overwhelmed by the amazing view of Gonzoland. But it was dark, so she wanted to get closer. The fence brought back a happy memory from her childhood. She decided to climb over the fence to get a better view of what lay beyond. The fence was only five feet high, so all it would take was a single step up. She lost her balance, sadly, fell seven stories to her death, grey matter splattering all over Gonzoland, precluding the possibility of identifying a conclusive cause of death. Besides, the woman was old, wasn't she? She fell. What need would there be for an autopsy? Let the grieving family take the body home and lay her to rest.

An internal investigation, later confirmed by police, would uncover the unfortunate chain of events that led to Dora's death: Lucy Evans, a mall employee, must have left the door to Lost Deck unlocked when she went back to retrieve Carolyn's bag. An unfortunate but minor case of negligence; after all, the door was clearly marked as off limits to the public. Warning signs were posted all over Lost Deck. The woman had no business on Lost Deck. The mall's lawyers could probably buy off the relatives for less than $100,000; if it went to court, MightyMall would surely win.

Carolyn would feel pity toward Lucy for her negligence but would have to fire her, with a full pension of course, for the sake of the company. Couldn't allow that level of negligence. If Lucy went to the police with some crazy story about her and Carolyn finding the dead lady the previous day, stashing the body overnight and then moving it, she'd be written off as a nut job and buried with countersuits.

The woman's death would draw headlines for a few days or months, maybe forcing Carolyn to close off Lost Deck permanently. By this time, interest in *Rodinia*, and the huge economic benefit it promised the local and state economies, would eventually trump public interest in some dead old bag and a cockamamie story concocted by a money-grubbing disgruntled former employee.

Almost too easy, Carolyn mused. She needed to remain calm for just a few more minutes.

Carolyn forced the muscles in her face to relax, conjuring up her best impression of someone overwhelmed with stress, shaking her head ruefully. "Lucy, you are absolutely right. I've been a complete bitch." Carolyn put her hands to her face, pushing the balls of her thumbs into her eyes. "I just don't *know* what's gotten into me. I didn't sleep a wink last night. Haven't slept in days preparing for that damn *Rodinia* presentation." A sigh. "I've been *awful* to you, I know. But how often does something like this happen?" She gave Lucy an expression she hoped was both humble and conspiratorial. "We're in this together! Let's work our way out of it as a team! Help me get through this and I promise I'll make it up to you. Can you do that for me? I'm begging you."

Lucy was embarrassed at her own loss of temper but also because she had never heard Carolyn apologize to anyone before. It felt as real as Dick Cheney apologizing to Scooter Libby. The shock left her speechless. "Sure," she said. "I, uh, it's okay."

"All right then!" Carolyn was immediately back to business. "Let's not waste any more time, shall we?" Carolyn took Dead Dora's legs and began to pull. As the body slid to the back of the flatbed, Lucy was unable to get a good grip around the shoulders. The body slammed to the floor. Lucy jumped behind the body to reestablish her grip as Carolyn made her way to the door. The linoleum made push/pulling the body easier than it had been on the iron catwalk. In fifteen seconds they had moved the body to the door.

Carolyn unlocked the door with her key, hoisted Dora's legs and dragged her inside, barely waiting for Lucy to pick up the head and torso.

CHAPTER 28

"Oh boy," Foreman said. "Here we go."

The timestamp on the video clip read 08:29:46.

"There!" Kiyomi said. "It is them!"

Playing in real time on Kiyomi's computer monitor the clip showed a Cushman carrying two women entering the viewing area from the bottom right. The Cushman passed in front of one of the benches near the entrance, turned left and started to disappear from view.

"Stop there," Foreman said. "Back up a little."

Kiyomi pulled the onscreen slider to the left, causing the motion to reverse, pulling the Cushman back into view.

"Freeze!" Foreman said. "Right there. That's it. The system has a digital zoom, right?"

"Yes," Kiyomi said. She used her mouse to draw a square around the two occupants of the Cushman and blew them up so that their heads filled the entire screen. The images were blurry from pixilation, but the two occupants were clearly Carolyn Batch and Lucy Evans.

"Whew," Foreman said. "I feel like I just identified JFK's killer. We don't even know if this has anything to do with the disappearance of the old woman but it somehow feels big."

Kiyomi brought the original view back on screen. The Cushman sat frozen at the top of the screen.

"Shall we continue?" Kiyomi said. Without waiting for answer, she pressed PLAY. The Cushman drove off screen to the left.

"I'm not sure," Kiyomi said, "but I believe that I encountered Lucy Evans between 8:30 and 8:45. Unfortunately, based on the viewing angles we watched earlier, I do not believe that my conversation with Lucy will show up on any of these cameras."

Kiyomi used the slider bar to skim ahead. Lucy walked into view at 08:41:09 and walked toward the Northern Lights Shopping Avenue. "This must be it," Kiyomi said. At 08:46:11 Lucy walked back into view, headed toward the Welcome Desk and out of view.

"Damn," Foreman said. "Not much to go on."

"No sign of Carolyn Batch, however," Kiyomi said. "I am sure she was not anywhere in view while I was there."

Foreman said. "Skip ahead until they leave."

At 08:53:00 the Cushman, driven by Lucy, without any passengers, came into view heading toward the camera, presumably to the Northern Lights Shopping Avenue.

"Where's Carolyn?" Foreman said.

"Lucy was not driving before," Kiyomi said.

The Cushman departed at the bottom of the screen and reemerged a few seconds later. Lucy drove the Cushman up the right side of the screen, stopped at the top and began backing up in the direction of the lockers and the Welcome Desk on the left, eventually vanishing as it had before.

Kiyomi turned toward Foreman. "Why would Lucy need to back the Cushman up to the lockers or the Welcome Desk?" she said.

Foreman turned his attention back to Kiyomi's computer screen, frowning slightly. "The only times I ever see anyone backing up a Cushman is to park it somewhere, which doesn't seem likely."

"That Cushman has a flatbed on the back of it," Kiyomi said. "People use flatbeds to deliver things, don't they? Or, pick them up."

"What could the two of them be picking up at the Welcome Desk at that hour of the morning?" Foreman said. "What does Carolyn *ever* pick up or drop off herself? She's the boss; she doesn't do physical work like that. She has people do it for her."

"Like Lucy," Kiyomi said.

"I don't think Lucy does that stuff either. She probably calls up an intern or someone in maintenance. I've never followed either Carolyn or Lucy around but I can't imagine them ever carrying anything anywhere."

"Let's check," Kiyomi said. She slid the clip ahead thirty minutes. By 9:30 A.M. a steady flow of people were entering the mall. By 9:55 A.M. the morning attendant arrived to open the Welcome Desk for the day at 9:55 A.M. The Cushman never came back into view.

"Are you thinking what I'm thinking?" Foreman said.

"I am not sure," Kiyomi said. "Carolyn Batch and Lucy Evans drove up to the Welcome Desk in a Cushman sometime after an old woman mysteriously disappeared in the same area. Later on, for reasons we don't know, Lucy, now alone, backed the Cushman up to the Welcome Desk."

"With Carolyn also now mysteriously disappeared," Foreman said. "Except we know she reappeared at some point because she held the big press conference yesterday."

"We are assuming, I believe, that Lucy then loaded something onto the back of the Cushman…." Kiyomi said.

"Aided by Carolyn," Foreman said. "Meaning that whatever it was they were loading had to have been heavy."

"Or perhaps the reason we never saw Carolyn again was that she was aware of the placement of the surveillance cameras in that area and wanted to remain hidden."

"Maybe that, too." Foreman said.

Foreman and Kiyomi sat silently for two minutes, stunned by what they were thinking. Afraid of what it meant.

Foreman squinted his eyes and shook his head, as if trying to make sense of a confusing dream. "Are we saying that the Vice President of MightyMall, along with her assistant, found a dead woman inside the Welcome Desk and, what, decided to load her onto the back of their Cushman and carry her away somewhere?"

Kiyomi looked intently at Foreman. "I can think of no other reason. Can you?"

Foreman was bewildered. "But why? Why something so crazy?"

"We have no way of knowing that without talking with them. Let's look again at what we do know," Kiyomi said. "The only place something as large as a Cushman could go, besides back into the viewing field of one of the cameras, is the service corridor next to the Welcome Desk," Kiyomi said.

"Let's open that video clip for nine o'clock and see where it takes us."

CHAPTER 29

Carolyn closed the Lost Deck door behind her and leaned against it. The three of them—she, Lucy and Dead Dora—were now safely on Lost Deck. No one had seen them come in. No one was yet in the SCP Substation next door.

Carolyn mused that in less than five minutes events would be set in motion that would bring an end to the inconvenient death and discovery of this old woman.

"All right," Carolyn said. She hadn't noticed until that moment how out of breath she was. She took several more breaths before continuing.

"All right," Carolyn repeated. "Here's how it's going to happen. You and I are going to carry old Dora here over to the fence. We'll each take an arm and a leg. That way we should be able to toss her over with a one, two, three heave ho, and Dora falls to her death. Got it so far?"

"Got it," Lucy said.

"We toss her over, then turn immediately—but not too suddenly, we need to look natural, just in case—away from the fence and head for the door. We climb into the Cushman and head back across the shopping avenue to the service door, where you jump out, hold it open and I'll drive into the service corridor."

"The service corridor," Lucy said in a monotone. "Not down the shopping avenue?"

"We went *over* this already," Carolyn said. "You still with me?" She patted Lucy on the cheek. "As soon as the old bag hits the first floor security is going to focus all areas directly above there, with personnel and surveillance cameras. We get spotted around here and both security and the Saint Commercia Police, are gonna want to interview us. *Where were you when it happened? Did you see anyone running away? What did you see?* Lots of questions means lots of chances to slip up with our stories. On the other hand, if we slip back into the service corridor before anyone even knows what floor the woman jumped from, we'll have plenty of time to head down to the fourth floor."

"Where we were doing our regular morning rounds," Lucy said.

"Exactly," Carolyn said, worried that Lucy was beginning to sound like a zombie. "If anyone asks us any questions, today or later, what do you tell them?"

"You and I were doing our morning rounds on the fourth floor when you heard on your walkie-talkie that someone jumped to their death in Gonzoland."

"Don't get ahead of yourself about all the details," Carolyn said. "All you need to remember is that you and I were on the fourth floor. You don't have to make anything else up; we *will* hear something on the walkie-talkie, at some point, and you can just tell people what you actually heard. Don't start making it up now. And don't embellish."

"Okay," Lucy said. "Don't embellish."

"Right," Carolyn said. "I've thought of everything. We'll be as surprised as everyone else. An accident? Oh my! Everyone is going to be running around talking about it, wondering what happened. When you get back to your desk, just go about your work, as you always do. We've got a mall to run, after all. Our security department is trained to handle things like this. If colleagues come by asking what happened, tell them you don't know any more than they do. If someone shares a rumor, pass it along to someone else, as if you believe it to be true. It's natural that people will gossip and conjecture. I'll be calling around to our different departments, trying to find out what happened. Major Power will visit my office to update me on what transpired and what is being done." Carolyn stopped speaking and smiled.

After several seconds of silence, Lucy turned to face Carolyn. "Sorry. What?"

"Oh, nothing," Carolyn said. "I'm just thinking of how I'm going to love ripping a new one for Karl LeVander. Karl, I'll say, how the *hell* did this happen? Where did she fall *from*? You're responsible for the physical integrity of the mall—how did some old lady manage to fall to her death? What do you mean, you don't know? It's your *job* to know."

Lucy continued to stare at Carolyn. She noticed a demonic gleam in Carolyn's eyes. She thought that if she continued to look into those eyes she would lose her soul, fall down the rabbit hole and never return. She jerked back involuntarily.

"What?" Carolyn looked sharply at Lucy.

"Nothing," Lucy said. "Nothing. I got a cramp in my leg, that's all." She reached down to massage her calf muscle, hoping her acting was good enough to fool Carolyn.

CHAPTER 30

Several floors below Lost Deck, sitting at his desk in the maintenance department offices, Eric Lemke was already having second thoughts about his decision to leave the dead woman where he had found her. All legal and personal considerations aside, it just wasn't *right*. A loved one might at this very moment be worried sick, calling area hospitals and the police. Maybe driving around looking for her car. How would he feel if one of *his* parents disappeared without a trace? How would he react if he found out someone had found his dead mother's body and just left it there without notifying the authorities?

Lemke doodled on the notepad in front of him, drawing a series of concentric circles, trying to make the space equal between each ring.

How about an anonymous tip? Lemke thought. A call from his cell phone was out; that could be traced. There were still a few pay phones in the mall at the entrances, but Lemke was fairly sure they were kept under constant video surveillance. A call from a nearby gas station? No way to justify leaving the mall for thirty minutes like that.

Lemke continued to draw, the concentric circles on his notepad growing to encompass half the page. He noticed that they looked like the age circles of some ancient tree, or maybe the opening credits for the original *Twilight Zone.* He was shading in every other circle when his pen ran out of ink. He opened the drawer in his desk to find a replacement when he saw a medium-sized sticky notepad and stared at it.

What about an anonymous note?

Lemke pulled a pencil and the sticky note pad out of his drawer, placed them on his desktop, leaned back in his chair and stared at them.

What if he wrote a brief note in block letters so the police couldn't identify his handwriting—Lemke didn't know if they would bother with a handwriting analysis but it never hurt to be careful—and dropped it casually in a public place? At the Welcome Desk or in a store, even. Keep the information about the body's location nebulous so the police wouldn't connect it to a mall employee. He could carry the note in the palm of his hand, surreptitiously put the note on the counter top and walk away.

Mall security couldn't ignore a note like that, could they? Even if they thought it was a prank they would have to follow up, wouldn't they? Worst case, if they ignored this note, or didn't find the body, he could leave a second note with more details tomorrow.

Meanwhile, Lemke's job would be safe and he and Gail could still visit the grandchildren this weekend.

Lemke spent several minutes crafting just the right message in his head, one vague enough to protect him yet clear enough to lead the authorities to the body.

DEAD WOMAN ON 7TH FLOOR.

Lemke spent a few more minutes considering where to leave his note. He rejected the notion of leaving it randomly in a mall store; too big a chance a bored sales clerk might toss the note without reading it.

Security would be most likely to see the note if he covertly dropped it at a Welcome Desk, one not too near maintenance. After several moments of careful thought, Lemke decided that he had the perfect drop location:

Northern Lights West 1.

CHAPTER 31

The body of Greta Turnblad, whom Carolyn and Lucy continued to refer to as Dead Dora because they had no idea what her real name was, sat awkwardly on the cement floor of the *Gonzoland Observation Deck*, otherwise known as Lost Deck. Rigor mortis continued to keep her legs locked at the knees, and her torso bent at the waist, so that she appeared to be in a sitting position. And with her right arm locked in the upright position, waving off into infinity, she tended to list to the right; without a steadying hand from the living, she kept tipping over.

Carolyn had Lucy stand at the dead woman's right side to keep it stable. "Just stay there and hold her in place," Carolyn said. "Give me a minute to make sure I've thought of everything and we'll get this thing over with and get out of here."

As Lucy held onto Dora's head with her left hand, part of her brain marveled at how easy it had become for her to touch the skin and hair of a corpse. Two days ago she would have been repulsed by the idea of being anywhere near this ... not a person ... this ... piece of *meat* ... something that normally caused people to cry or scream or run away. And here she was, acclimated enough to put her hand on it, no more uncomfortable than she would be keeping a tall pile of books from falling over. No, that wasn't quite right, Lucy decided. It wasn't that she felt no fear; she felt … nothing … as if her brain had been injected with Novocain. When would that wear off? Lucy wondered. She was no saint—hell, she had been planning to blackmail her boss over this thing—but now it was beginning to make her feel, somehow, less than human. What would she be capable of next? She hadn't actually killed the woman, but somehow this felt worse. She had chosen to *ignore* the death. And now the two of them were preparing to mutilate the body. Lucy shuddered at the image of this woman splattering all over the first floor of Gonzoland, like David Letterman dropping a pumpkin from the roof of his building. All in the service of Carolyn Noxon Batch. The body's discovery yesterday would have been inconvenient. Dropping it from Lost Deck today would be opportune; it would make Karl LeVander, Carolyn's chief rival at MightyMall, look bad. Career advancement through corpse relocation.

"Hello? " Carolyn snapped her fingers in front of Lucy's face. "Still with me?"

When Lucy turned to face her boss, Carolyn was taken aback because it was with an expression she hadn't seen before, at least not from Lucy: contempt. Carolyn jerked her head back, as if someone had put smelling salts under her nose.

"Lucy," Carolyn said. "Are you … are you all right?" Carolyn didn't know how to react. *First anger, and now contempt? There's more to you than I thought. Not that it will make any difference to my plan.*

Lucy no longer wanted to be part of Carolyn's plan, but the truth was she could think of no way to back out now. The body was here. She was here. Lucy didn't know how, but she was certain that if she walked away now, Carolyn would pin this all on her, frame her for the death, or at least make her appear responsible in some way. She'd had this nagging feeling in the back of her mind since yesterday when Carolyn had told her to go back to Lost Deck to retrieve her handbag. Carolyn never left anything anywhere by accident. And why send Lucy to get it when a security officer could have retrieved it more quickly? And here they were on Lost Deck to carry out Carolyn's Grand Plan. Coincidence? She didn't think so, but couldn't find the trap.

Lucy just knew that there must be one. That was how it was in the world: rich people and people in positions of authority always got their way, through bribery, manipulation of facts, or by making evidence disappear. In the end, it was always the disgruntled employee who took the fall.

Lucy hated herself for what she was about to do and hated herself for being powerless to do anything else.

Lucy continued looking directly into Carolyn's eyes. "I'm tired. Let's just get it over with."

Lucy bent down beside the dead woman. She took hold of the woman's left arm, the Heil Hitler arm, with her left hand. She placed her right hand underneath the woman's bony knees. She looked up at Carolyn inviting her to get a move on.

"Fine," Carolyn said, regaining her composure. "Let's do it then, shall we?" A couple of minutes more and Lucy could behave any fucking way she wanted. The little tramp's days of employment at MightyMall and her dreams of blackmailing Carolyn were nearly over.

Carolyn crouched next to the corpse. Dora's left side, with her arm locked tight against her ribcage from rigor mortis, was more difficult to lift. That was why she had chosen this side: when you want something done right, you've got to do it yourself. Carolyn didn't want to risk Lucy dropping the body again, mucking up her plans. The rigor mortis continued to bind the woman's left arm to her side. The only way for Carolyn to get a firm hold was to shove her left hand into the woman's armpit, then jam her right hand underneath that. Efficient but awkward.

"One, two, three, *lift,"* Carolyn said. The two of them lifted the body easily this time and began walking over to the fence.

"Remember," Carolyn said as they approached the fence. "Same count as before: I'll say 'one, two, three and *lift*' and then we'll—"

Lucy had stopped listening to her boss once they picked up the body. She no longer wanted a new car. She didn't want anything, at least from her boss. She wanted only to get Dora over the fence as quickly as possible and be done with this entire, hideous experience. She could feel the adrenaline coursing through her body.

That was why when Lucy heard Carolyn say, "lift," she instinctively heaved Dead Dora up with a strength she didn't know she possessed. Carolyn, believing that they had been practicing a run-through for the actual corpse-toss a minute or so later, was unprepared for Lucy's ferocious power. One moment Carolyn was carrying half the weight of a dead body in her hands, the next moment it was miraculously rising, higher and higher, until it was almost above both their heads. The body reached the top of the fence where it perched briefly on top before beginning to tip over the edge. Carolyn, understanding too late what was happening, yelled, "Wait! Wait!" and tried to yank her hands free of the corpse's armpits. Her left hand came out easily enough, but she couldn't dislodge her right hand, the hand on which she wore her precious Cartier. The ring's panther head had snagged on Greta's warm up suit. The more Carolyn pulled and twisted, the more firmly the ring became entangled.

In the final few slow motion moments of Carolyn Noxon Batch's life, or at least the last moments before Carolyn began the seven story fall to her death, her attention was focused less on her personal safety, and almost exclusively on extracting her precious Cartier ring, which Carolyn had no intention of surrendering to this old woman.

Lucy's perspective of events was somewhat different than Carolyn's but in equally slow motion. Initially perplexed that Carolyn hadn't lifted her side of Dead Dora in unison with Lucy, a long list of emotions began flashing through her subconscious mind, like playing cards spewing out of a magician's hand: pride, at easily she had been able to raise Dora's body; embarrassment, that she might have begun her task too soon; dismay, when she saw that Dora's body was pulling Carolyn inexorably toward the fence; indecision: should I help Carolyn or let the bitch fall, wouldn't that be rich? And finally, decisiveness, as she reached over and, while pretending to grab for Carolyn's leg in an effort to save her, instead lifted the leg up, giving it a final nudge over the railing.

Carolyn's final words to Lucy were, "You're fired!" before falling, ass over teakettle, as the British say, her body landing several seconds later on the cold, hard floor of Gonzoland a microsecond behind the body of Greta Turnblad.

"Keep your fucking car," Lucy said, halfway to the door before she heard a sound like a bowling ball landing on concrete, a sound that she assumed, not without pleasure, was Carolyn Noxon Batch's exploding head.

CHAPTER 32

"Here is the clip from the surveillance camera next to the Welcome Desk," Kiyomi said. "If Carolyn and Lucy, or anyone else, came through this service door after nine o'clock yesterday morning, we'll see it here."

Foreman grabbed Kiyomi's list and wrote down the latest file name.

Kiyomi found the proper time and pressed ENTER. At 09:01:18, a Cushman entered the screen from the bottom and headed directly away from the camera.

Kiyomi froze the clip. "That's them entering the service corridor." The Cushman had three passengers. Carolyn Batch was sitting on the edge of the flatbed, facing the camera.

"Must be Lucy driving," Foreman said.

"Yes."

"Then who is," Foreman pointed at the passenger sitting next to Carolyn, " that?"

Foreman and Kiyomi both leaned closer to her computer screen.

"Can you zoom in on the passenger?" Foreman said.

"I will try," Kiyomi said. "But it's so dark in there I don't know what we'll be able to see."

Kiyomi drew a square around the face of the woman sitting next to Carolyn, enlarging it enough to fill the entire screen.

"For all the bragging about this fancy new surveillance system," Foreman said, "it can sure take some pretty low resolution images. Her face is just a big blur now. I wouldn't know that if it was my mother's face."

"It's not very good, is it?" Kiyomi brought the original image back on screen. "That is the missing woman, though, isn't it? She's not wearing her coat anymore but the pants look the same as the woman we saw enter the mall earlier."

"Has to be," Foreman said, scratching the side of his head. "Something odd about the way she's sitting. Can you play the whole sequence again?"

It took less than three seconds for the Cushman to enter the viewing area at the bottom and then disappear at the top.

"Why is the woman looking down like that?" Kiyomi said. "Is she asleep, maybe? Or ill? And do you see that dark spot on her forehead? Did she fall down and injure herself? And look." Kiyomi pointed at the screen, accidentally touching it with her finger before wiping away her fingerprint with the sleeve of her shirt. "Sorry about that. But look: Carolyn has her arm around the woman's shoulder, so maybe she knows her. A friend, perhaps? Or a relative? Is Carolyn trying to comfort her? Are they bringing her to the medical clinic for that injury to her head?"

Foreman tilted his head slightly to the left. "They'd call security if she was sick or injured. Besides, if they had brought the woman to the clinic there'd be some record of it. I checked when I was looking up the day's ambulance visits. Nothing."

"There's another camera fifty feet ahead," Kiyomi said. "Let's check that."

Foreman's eyebrows shot up. "You know exactly how far ahead the next surveillance camera is?"

Kiyomi looked slightly embarrassed. "I'm very thorough in my studies."

"Do you know where all the surveillance cameras are in MightyMall?" Foreman said.

"Not all," Kiyomi said. "Most. Japanese are very good at memorization."

"Amazing!" Foreman said. "A great cook, fun to talk to, beautiful. And a hard drive in your brain."

The voice crackling from the walkie-talkies startled both Foreman and Kiyomi. "General Alert Alpha! General Alert Alpha! Report immediately to the Paul Bunyan statue in Gonzoland. General Alert Alpha! All personnel report immediately to the Paul Bunyan statue in Gonzoland."

Kiyomi leapt to her feet. She picked up the list of video files, folded it, and slid it into her pocket.

"That means both uniformed officers and the X-Team, doesn't it?" Foreman said.

"Correct," Kiyomi said. "General Alert Alpha requires all MightyMall security Personnel to proceed directly to the incident area. X-Team members should remain outside the incident area and await for further instructions." Foreman marveled as Kiyomi easily recited the regulations word-for-word. "Scan onlookers for suspicious behavior and report any irregularities to Officer In Charge or to SAC at once. In the absence of instructions by a senior officer and/or no observation of suspicious onlookers and/or no suspicious behavior after ten minutes, resume regular duties." Kiyomi headed for the door. When Foreman didn't follow she turned back. He was still sitting at her computer.

"You go on ahead," Foreman said. "I'll log off both computers and be up in a minute."

CHAPTER 33

Lucy climbed into the Cushman, put her hands on the steering wheel, and sat motionless for several moments. She didn't consider her options so much as watch them float by, like flotsam on the sea after a shipwreck.

Should she drive away as if nothing had happened? Dash across the food court and disappear into the bowels of the service corridor? Sit here and scream, "Help! Help! Something terrible has happened!" and feign amnesia?

What would Carolyn do in this situation if Lucy had gone over the edge instead? *Poor Lucy*, Carolyn would say, dabbing a crocodile tear. *She was trying to rescue that old woman but lost her balance and was dragged tragically to her death.* Or, more likely, *Lucy went insane and shoved that poor old woman to her death. Should have fired her long ago.*

"Fuck it," Lucy said, stomping on the accelerator pedal.

Time for morning rounds.

Lemke was about one hundred yards from the left turn that would bring him to the Northern Lights West 1 Welcome Desk when he heard the "General Alert Alpha" on his radio. Something about an accident inside Gonzoland. No one outside of security was supposed to respond to such alerts but it was standard policy that everyone working directly for MightyMall—Management, maintenance, housekeeping, operations—be kept up-to-date on what was happening within the building at all times. The broadcasts went to everyone's radio.

Lemke approached an entrance to Gonzoland on his right and unconsciously headed for it. Sure, non-security personnel were supposed to stay away, but he couldn't remember the last time he'd heard a General Alert Alpha, whatever that was. He decided to make a quick detour to Paul Bunyan and sneak a peek at whatever was going on. He could drop off his note after that.

When Lemke arrived at the base of the Paul Bunyan statue there was already a small crowd straining to get a glimpse of what had happened. Some were mall tenants in the building early for one reason or another, a few faces he recognized from the events department … so he wasn't the only curious employee. Several security officers had formed a circle around the station and were facing outward, urging the crowd to stay back. One of the younger officers—Lemke couldn't remember his name—looked pale, shaken up.

"Stay back, please," Lemke heard him say. "There is nothing here for you. Please go on about your business. This is a MightyMall security matter."

Lemke circled around the cluster of gawkers, hoping to find a gap through which he could get a good view of whatever merited a General Alert Alpha. He caught a glimpse of something blue but couldn't discern a shape. Lemke looked around him and spotted the Penny For Your Thoughts Fountain about twenty feet away. He walked over to it and jumped up on its three-foot wall. He saw two or three blue tarps covering a mound a couple of feet high. It was impossible to tell what was underneath. Lemke was about to step down when he noticed something oozing out the left side. Something red.

"Oh my God," he said.

Someone in the crowd must have seen it as well because he heard nervous voices. An elderly man nudged the woman next to him and pointed at the growing pool of blood.

Kiyomi arrived at the base of the Paul Bunyan statue moments after Eric Lemke. Following X-Team protocol she hung back and behaved like an innocent bystander. She recognized all of the uniformed officers on the scene. The few onlookers she could see were obeying instructions to stay back from the line the officers had formed. She noticed one man in blue workpants and denim work shirt climbing up on the Penny For Your Thoughts wall. She couldn't make out the details of the badge he was wearing around his neck but assumed he was from maintenance.

MightyMall security's unwritten but oft-drilled rule about on-site accidents was to keep everything a secret until such as time that Major Power announced otherwise. Witness accounts were sketchy under the best of circumstances; reliability degraded significantly the more time people had to stand around and imagine things they hadn't actually seen. Kiyomi decided the uniformed officers could handle those closest to the scene.

Kiyomi walked over the fountain, looked up at the maintenance gentleman with wide-eyed innocence, and said, "Excuse me. Excuse me, mister. What happened here? Do you know?" No exaggerated foreign accident, this time, just a pretty young woman seeking the latest news from a handsome elderly man.

Lemke stopped looking at the blue mound and jumped down immediately, as if caught looking at dirty magazines. "Ah … well," he said. "Not really." He didn't recognize Kiyomi, just wondered whether he should be discussing the incident with guests.

"Did you see what happened?" Kiyomi said.

"No, I was just in the area." Lemke had regained his composure. "I saw this crowd of people and wondered what was going on."

Kiyomi needed to move him away from the scene so she could turn her attention toward looking for possible witnesses. "Ooh," she said, pointing at Lemke's ID badge, impressed by his authority. "Do you work for MightyMall?"

"Oh, I, uh...." Lemke figured he should get back to his own business before someone from Management spotted him. All he needed was a reprimand today, of all days; Pankow would love to find an excuse to make him cancel his travel plans again. "Excuse me, miss, I need to be getting back to work."

As Lemke headed away, Kiyomi turned to see Foreman standing on the periphery. He caught her eye as she turned, but neither betrayed any recognition of the other; they were both undercover. With her eyes fixed on the crime scene—she would assume it was a crime scene until she heard otherwise—she drifted toward Foreman.

"Hey, toots," Foreman said in a soft voice as he scanned the area. "Come here often?"

Kiyomi suppressed a smile. "Is that one of your tacky pickup lines? No wonder you have no girlfriends."

"That's my best line," Foreman said, palms up. "And how do you know I have no girlfriends?"

"Japanese can tell these things," Kiyomi said, looking prim. "You gave me a one dollar lottery ticket on our first date. Nobody gives a lottery ticket on a first date." She was enjoying the gentle back and forth teasing.

"That was a date?"

"And a five-year-old Japanese girl can use chopsticks better than you."

"Ouch!" Foreman said, laughing involuntarily, then coughing into his hands to cover it up. "See anything?" he said, now serious.

"No," Kiyomi said. "One of the maintenance workers was … how do you say … when someone makes their necks very long in an effort to see something out of view at an accident scene?"

"Rubber necking? Gawking?" Damn, she spoke good English, Foreman thought. And I can't even say hello in any language other than English.

"Yes, that's it. The man was rubbernecking." Kiyomi repeated the word silently, committing it to memory. "But when I spoke to him he didn't seem to know anything."

Kiyomi and Foreman spoke softly, careful not to project their voices to anyone standing nearby. Foreman turned around casually, then to his right, then back to the front. No one was within fifteen feet of them.

"Have you found any witnesses?" Kiyomi said.

"No. I just got here."

One of the security officers guarding the scene turned around and bent down, opening a gap in the wall of officers guarding the scene. Foreman and Kiyomi both saw the same thing: a couple of blue tarps over an area roughly ten feet long by five feet wide. A pool of blood was leaking out the left side.

"A jumper?" Foreman said. "Suicide?"

"It looks like that, doesn't it?" Kiyomi said. "So much blood."

"I've never seen one here," Foreman said. "A suicide, I mean. Have you?"

"No. I've never heard of that happening here."

The security officer was adjusting one of the tarps, pulling it to the left, trying to cover the blood. Kiyomi noticed a human foot wearing a white Nike sneaker protruding from the blue mound.

"*Hora!*" Kiyomi said. Foreman didn't understand the word, but looked quickly at Kiyomi's eyes and followed the invisible line extending from her face to what she was staring at. "Is that...?" she said.

"Let's go see," Foreman said.

"But we're undercover—"

"Hey," Foreman said. "We're mall walkers. We're curious onlookers."

Kiyomi held back, cursing her ingrained Japanese tendency to blindly obey all rules, while simultaneously admiring Foreman's decision, in this case, not bend them. Kiyomi didn't have a "thing" for American men, as she knew some Japanese women did—for her taste, American men tended to be loud and rude, didn't study hard enough, and were, along with American women, too often ignorant and uninterested in the history and current affairs of other cultures—but she did admire the courage Americans had to challenge authority. Japanese were such lemmings.

Foreman stood next to a man he guessed was of Indian or Pakistani descent. "Man," Foreman said shaking his head. "Pretty gruesome, isn't it?"

The Indian/Pakistani gentleman didn't realize at first that Foreman was talking to him. When he did, he turned briefly to look at Foreman, then returned his attention to what was now clearly a body. "It is really quite terrible," the man said, in an accent that reminded Foreman of the Babu Bhatt character on Seinfeld. *How lame is that?* Foreman thought to himself. *I don't even know any Indians or Pakistanis well enough to compare this man's accent to them; I have to use TV caricatures.* "Very, very terrible thing, for someone to end his life in this fashion," the man said.

"Did you see what happened?" Foreman said. He looked more closely at the exposed leg. The officer who had pulled the tarp over the expanding pool of blood hadn't yet noticed the leg poking out the other side. The rest of the officers were still facing outward, away from the body.

"No, sir, I did not," the man said. "By the time I arrived here I saw the officers running around. I was near the elevator and decided to take a look. I own the *Bombay* restaurant on the sixth floor. We serve the Twin Cities' finest Indian cuisine. I was merely heading to work." The man pulled a coupon out of his pocket and handed it to Foreman. "Please visit with your girlfriend there," the man swiveled his head toward Kiyomi, "I will make a wonderful dinner for the two of you. Very nice."

"No," Foreman said, "She's not my—"

"If you come on a Thursday or Friday evening I will prepare a very special meal for you myself." The man snatched the coupon back, scribbled something illegible on it, then returned it to Foreman. "Twenty-five percent off. Give this to the hostess when you come in. She will notify me of your arrival." Foreman liked the way the man rolled his "r"s in "arrival."

Foreman slipped the coupon into his pocket: it was against mall policy to accept special favors from mall tenants while on duty. He wondered idly if Kiyomi liked Indian food.

Returning his attention to the exposed leg and sneaker, Foreman saw that the pink pants leg was a nylon material, like that used in sweat suits. The small patch of exposed skin around the shin was dry and … old looking. He wished their video clips were in color so he could be sure, but—

Which floor had she jumped from? Foreman looked up for a clue. Or fallen from?

"Well, I have to get going," Foreman said.

"Don't forget," the Indian man said. "Come on a Thursday or a Friday night. You will make your beloved very happy. I promise you."

Foreman thanked the man and headed off toward the nearest Gonzoland exit. He caught Kiyomi's attention and tilted his head slightly. When she caught up with him, he said, "Let's be shoppers for a while."

Foreman grabbed Kiyomi's hand. She was surprised, but didn't pull away.

"We're a young couple out for some early morning shopping," Foreman said.

"Very early," Kiyomi said. "The stores don't even open for a couple of hours." Foreman's hand was strong but gentle. She resisted the urge to squeeze it. She didn't want to appear too forward.

"The Indian guy I was talking to called you my 'beloved.' I'm just playing the part."

"I see," Kiyomi said. Then back to business: "So, what did you see?"

Foreman shrugged. "It sure could have been the lady from the tape. But if it is, I can't figure out where she jumped *from* and where she's *been* for the past day. Twenty-four hours is a long time to stay missing inside the mall. And as for how she jumped, or fell or whatever, there's no way she climbed the Plexiglas barriers on each floor—she's too small and, frankly, too old. None of the park rides or monorails are operating at this hour, so she didn't fall off one of them. And besides, no one has ever snuck out of the safety harnesses or forced a monorail door open, have they?"

"I don't think so. And, as you said, how could she evade our patrol officers and video surveillance cameras for twenty-four hours?" Kiyomi said.

Foreman nodded vigorously. "Exactly! The lady I saw on the tape, if it's the same one who jumped, wasn't a hardened criminal, or terrorist. She wouldn't know where to hide. Just doesn't make sense."

Kiyomi said, "Major Power should be in by now. Let's go talk to him."

"Oh, that's right," Foreman said. "I forgot we came in two hours early today." He looked at his watch. "It's almost six-thirty. Let's go see if we can catch him in his office."

Eric Lemke was walking back to his office when he got a call about a burned out light bulb in the management office. He had completely forgotten about his anonymous note until he reached into his pocket for his handkerchief.

"Oh, yeah," Lemke muttered, pulling the note out and looking at it. "Well, this can wait an hour or two." He stuck the note back into his pocket.

With the accelerator pedal pushed all the way to the floor, Lucy's Cushman cruised along at 10mph. No one else was on the floor at that hour so Lucy didn't have to maneuver around anyone or stop suddenly. She focused her attention on an invisible point five feet ahead her. She knew the layout of all the floors by heart, where all the potted trees and benches and display cases and kiosks were. It was an easy obstacle course.

Lucy Evans had completed one full circuit of the seventh floor when she arrived back at the food court. Tim & Kevin's Minnesota Style Pizza caught her eye. The sign said, *Try our Lutefisk with Cream of Wild Rice Pizza Supreme!* She veered over to the public elevator, backed the Cushman in, stepped out of the Cushman, pushed the "6" button and climbed back into her seat.

"Sixth floor," Lucy said as the door closed, her voice like a promotional message playing on an old-style tape recorder with dying batteries. "Don't miss the sensational Mega Monorail Beta. Electronics stores. Furniture showrooms. Nightclubs. Aquariums. Live shows. MightyMall has everything you need."

CHAPTER 34

Major Power's office was on the other side of the mall from the Paul Bunyan statue, and underground. When Foreman and Kiyomi arrived, Power was just stepping out.

"Excellent," Power said. "Full security briefing in the Gym. Two minutes."

"Is this about what happened upstairs, sir?" Foreman said.

"It is."

Foreman wasn't sure how to broach the subject. He knew Power liked to hear things sooner rather than later. On the other hand, Power loved schedules and hated deviations. Foreman wasn't even positive that there was a connection between the body upstairs and what he and Kiyomi had found out.

"Nagata and I have some important information we would like to share with you, sir," Foreman said.

"Can it wait until after the briefing?" Power said.

Foreman considered the question. "Yes, sir, it can."

"Fine. Head to my office as soon as we break here." Power pushed through the security gym door and strode to the front of the room.

Kiyomi counted twenty-two officers besides her, Foreman and Major Power. She and Foreman leaned against the back wall, away from the rest, as was the X-Team custom.

"All right, everybody," Power said, "listen up. For all of you that don't already know, there has been an incident in Gonzoland. At approximately 6:27 A.M. this morning, two women fell to their death, landing near the Paul Bunyan statue.

Foreman and Kiyomi looked at each other. Two?

"We know very little at this time," Power said. "One of the deceased was a woman, between 65 and 80 years of age. No identification on her person."

Power inhaled deeply, once, before continuing. "The other deceased was Carolyn Noxon Batch, Vice President of Business Development at MightyMall."

Officers turned from one colleague to the next:

"What the fuck?"

"No way!"

"Did he just say—?"

"Holy shit!"

"All right, all right," Power said, but the chatter continued unabated. Finally, he said, "AttenTION!" Every officer immediately leapt to his or her feet and stared, silently, straight ahead.

"Better," Power said. "Now, sit down and be quiet."

Foreman and Kiyomi exchanged another look. They dared not speak up, but they knew they were thinking the same thing: Old lady disappears on cart, sitting next to Carolyn Batch. Old lady and Carolyn Batch jump to death together? Not a coincidence.

"Right now we are treating this as an accident. Officers Carlson, Noone and Plumeau have set up a perimeter and are interfacing with the Saint Commercia Police. When the SCP Crime Scene Unit people get here, they'll begin collecting and documenting evidence."

A hand from the third row shot up. "Are we shutting down the mall?"

"Negative," Power said. "MightyMall doors are open now and stores will open at their normal time. Gonzoland will be closed at least until the CSU people are finished. Meanwhile, maintenance folks will be checking rides. Our primary jobs are to protect the integrity of the accident scene, and check each floor for any anomalies like broken Plexiglas walls, open gates: basically, find out how Carolyn Batch and the mystery woman ended up falling, simultaneously, to their deaths. Questions?"

No hands went up.

"Fine," Power said. "Lieutenant Rolvaag here has assignments for everyone. Dismissed." Power pointed his index and middle fingers at Foreman and Kiyomi, then at his office.

Power leaned back in his chair, putting his black military-grade boots, left foot on right, on top of his desk.

"What have you got?" he said.

Foreman said, "I don't know how to say, this—"

"Then just say it, dammit," Power said.

"Yes, sir," Foreman said, and looked down briefly, collecting his thoughts. "First, we may know the identity of woman who died with Carolyn Batch."

"I'm listening." Power's face was impassive.

Foreman told Power about finding the red bag the previous morning and not being able to locate its owner. "I'm sure we'll be able to confirm her identity by looking at her drivers license."

Power punched a button on his phone. "Cindy?"

"Major?"

"Call Officer Engebretsen in Lost and Found and ask her to bring down the red bag that Officer Foreman turned in yesterday. If she's not in yet, run up yourself and get it, will you?"

"Will do."

"Good work," Power said to Foreman. He looked at Kiyomi and said, "You got something for me, too? Or you just along for the ride?"

"No, sir," Kiyomi said, sitting up straighter. "I mean, yes, sir. I may have important information as well." She maintained eye contact with Power every second she spoke. "That is why we are here together. Officer Foreman and I saw the old woman with Carolyn Batch yesterday."

Power dropped his feet to the floor with a loud thud, sat straight up. "You what?"

"Well, not in person, sir, but a video tape of the two of them, Ms. Batch and the woman, riding on the back of a Cushman. Lucy Evans was driving."

Power shifted his gaze to Foreman, like a laser beam into his brain. After several seconds, Power returned his attention to Kiyomi.

"More," Power commanded.

"Actually," Kiyomi said. "I did see Lucy Evans in person." Kiyomi told Power about her encounter with Lucy near the Welcome Desk and all the video clips she and Foreman had reviewed.

Kiyomi spoke steadily for several minutes. Her English was not perfect, but she spoke with an assuredness that many native speakers of English lacked and which Foreman envied as he sat next to her. She finally finished, nodding her head once to indicate she had said all that she had to say.

Power looked down at the hands in his lap, twirling his thumbs. "How did you guys put this together like this?"

"Sir?" Foreman said.

"You found a bag. Nagata had an odd conversation with Lucy Evans. You two weren't investigating anything before this. How did you happen to put two and two together like this?"

"Well, sir," Foreman mumbled. "We, uh, we were talking, and, uh..."

"We were having dinner together," Kiyomi said, chin out, defiantly, looking at a point on the wall behind Major Power. "At my apartment."

"Oh," Power said. "That."

CHAPTER 35

Unseen by most of the public, Karl LeVander, Managing Director of Operations at MightyMall, was Big Man On Campus to everyone except to the prima donnas in marketing, advertising and public relations departments. Listen to them and you'd think they had *invented* MightyMall, that without *them* no one would ever visit, shop or spend money here.

LeVander snorted as he considered the preposterousness of the notion. Without him, there would *be* no MightyMall.

Physically, LeVander *was* big: six foot two and closing in on three hundred pounds. Still in his fifties, his kept his long, prematurely white hair combed straight back. No one in the mall knew much about LeVander's history before he joined MightyMall. Rumor had it that he had been in a biker gang years before and had once gotten in a fight with another biker up in Brainerd at a placed called The North Star Bar. The other guy was six inches taller and a hundred pounds heavier than LeVander. Everybody called him Andre the Giant. LeVander made the mistake of flirting with Andre's girlfriend, which Andre didn't appreciate. LeVander was getting the shit beat out of him when he grabbed a beer bottle, busted it on the edge of the bar counter, and screwed it into Andre's right eye like a light bulb. Andre recovered but lost his eye. Some people said he lived up in the north woods. Others said he got a tattoo of a star around his empty eye socket and was in prison somewhere. Most people chalked the story up to urban legend. All anyone knew for sure was that LeVander had worked for a Green Bay construction company before getting hired away to oversee construction of MightyMall.

LeVander now kept the building running, clean and secure. The way he saw it, no one was going to shop at the mall if his security team didn't keep people safe, if his maintenance crew let the building fall apart, or if housekeeping let the garbage pile up. Hell, nobody'd come at all if leasing didn't fill the place with tenants. Truth was, you could fire all the candy-assed pussies in marketing, advertising and PR and the mall would be just fine. People already knew about the mall, had a good time in Gonzoland and kept coming back. If you build a fun place, keep it clean and safe, people will spend money there. Everybody's happy.

Including the fucking owners.

Smooth talking was good for one thing, though: bullshitting your way to the top. Carolyn Obnoxious Bitch, as he liked to refer to his boss privately, had sure pulled the wool over the eyes of those shithead owners in Dallas, oh yes she sure had: *Put* me *in charge,* she told them. *You can't have those awful* brutes *in operations representing MightyMall. Who'll negotiate with the governor? Who will design the ads? Who but my divine self knows enough to manage the whole Goddam thing?*

Sheeeeeiiiiiiit!

LeVander heard a knock on his door. "Come in," he said.

His security Chief stood in the doorway. "I need a moment of your time, sir."

"Sure, Matt, c'mon in," LeVander said. "Have a seat." LeVander liked Power, liked the way he always called him "Sir."

Power sat on the edge of his chair, back straight. "There has been an accident involving Carolyn Batch," Power said.

I hope the bitch dropped dead, LeVander said.

"She's dead, sir," Power said.

"She's *what*?" LeVander sat bolt upright, his eyes bugging out like the Arnold Schwarzenegger character at the end of Total Recall. "The hell you say!"

"That's correct, sir. It appears she fell, or was pushed, or jumped, from an upper floor; landed in *Gonzo*."

"When?"

"Earlier this morning. Approximately six-thirty."

LeVander almost felt guilty over his whimsical wish of a few moments ago. Almost.

His shook his head to clear his senses, organizing his thoughts. Batch was dead? How wonderful for him!

"How terrible," he said. "Have you notified her family?"

"Yes, sir."

"Dead?" LeVander still couldn't believe it. "How?"

"The only thing we are sure of at this time," Power said, "is that she fell from somewhere high up in the mall. Another thing, sir: there was also a second victim. A Greta Turnblad. She fell at the same time Ms. Batch did."

"Two people at once?" LeVander said. "What is this, some kind of suicide pact?"

"We're still investigating the connection, sir. But we've got some video taken yesterday morning that you might want to take a look at." Power handed LeVander a slip of paper.

"What's this?" LeVander said.

"The file names of several clips from different cameras, different angles, different times. A couple of my officers dug them up. Some show Ms. Turnblad by herself, some are her and Carolyn Batch riding in a Cushman together.

LeVander leaned back in his chair and laced his meaty fingers across his stomach. "Batch was driving this woman around the mall? For … what? … some kind of tour? Are they related or something?"

"We don't think so, sir," Power said. "I spoke with Ms. Batch's mother; she had never heard of Ms. Turnblad. And Batch wasn't driving the Cushman herself; it was her admin, Lucy Evans."

LeVander knew her. "She dead too?"

"No, sir."

LeVander shook his head, searching for answers. "The guys in SAC see anything?"

Power shifted slightly in his chair, phrasing his response carefully. "It was still the nighttime SAC crew when things happened. Just two guys on overnight duty, as you know, since you…since HQ cut our budget last year." Power had to be careful not to blame his boss for the budget cuts. "They spend most of their time looking at the building exterior, parking ramps, entrances, that kind of thing. Not much need to keep an eye on the interior, especially the park, when everything is shut down. I mean, we would if we could … it's the best we could do with what we've got."

"Anything on tape?" MightyMall had recorded all video and still images digitally since 2002. Power understood what LeVander meant.

"We're checking that now," Power said. "Depends where the women fell from."

"How about the Evans girl?" LeVander said. "She involved somehow? Anybody talked to her yet?"

"She got to the office a little after seven," Power said. "As far as we can tell, it all happened before she got here."

"Anybody talk to her yet?"

"No, sir. Not yet. She's just sitting at her desk."

LeVander looked the piece of paper Power had given him.

"Give me a few minutes to look over these video clips, Matt, will you? I'll call you when I've finished. In the meantime, if any of the surveillance cameras turns up anything new, let me know right away."

"Yes, sir." Power rose and headed for the door.

"And let's keep all this pretty close to our vest for now, shall we?" LeVander said. "No need to share our video evidence with the police quite yet; if they ask, tell them you're working on it and will get them whatever information you have as soon as you can."

LeVander found one of the files written on the scrap of paper, then turned to Power while it was loading. "Oh, and let's not tell the SC Police about Lucy Evans for the time being. I'd like to get a better idea of what happened, from our perspective, before we start blabbing everything we know to the police. You know how local cops can be." LeVander turned back to his computer, having already dismissed his security chief.

Power looked hard at LeVander's head for several moments, then said, "Yes, sir," and left the room.

After several minutes of viewing video clips LeVander picked up his phone and punched the extension of his administrative assistant.

"Gail, go on over to the other side in about fifteen minutes and get Lucy Evans." The management offices were physically divided into two sections, one on each side of the mall: departments within operations were on the West Side; marketing, advertising and public relations, were on the East Side. Each referred to the other as "The Other Side."

"No," LeVander said, "don't call her and ask her to come over, I want you to go there escort her back here. You can use my Cushman." LeVander looked at his watch. "You leave in fifteen minutes, have her here by ten." LeVander listened to his Administrative Assistant's response, then said, "I don't care, make up something. Jesus, tell her you're having your period or something and need to borrow some Midol; use your imagination. It'll take you thirty minutes, tops, for Christ's sake."

LeVander hung up, said. "Stupid bitch," and dialed a new number.

CHAPTER 36

"C'mon in, Lucy," LeVander said. "Have a seat. I appreciate your coming over."

Looks like a fucking zombie, LeVander thought. *Looking straight ahead, but not really looking at anything.*

Lucy sat in the chair in front of LeVander's desk, folded her hands in her lap and looked at the wall.

"You okay?" LeVander said. "Can I get you something? Some coffee? Some water?"

"No," Lucy said. "Thank you." She lowered her gaze onto LeVander's face, as if she hadn't noticed him before, looking him straight in the eye.

LeVander smiled back paternally. *Christ. I liked it better when she was looking off into space. She gone psycho or something? She's like a robot.* He held Lucy's stare as long as he could, then looked down and shuffled papers on his desk.

"You *sure* you're okay, Lucy?" LeVander leaned forward. "It must be tough, finding out your boss is dead and all. The shock … I mean …

it must be awful. I know *I'm* upset and I didn't know her near as well as you. We're all upset."

And still the eyes, as if they were boring into the base of LeVander's soul.

He put his hands on his desk, palms down and pressed down. "All right, then. I wanted to talk with you, Lucy, before things get more hectic here. The police will want to talk to you—nothing to worry about, just routine—but I want to learn as much as I can, first, so there are no mix-ups."

Nothing moved on Lucy's face. Her eyes were still focused on him. LeVander didn't notice any muscle twitches, but Lucy's expression had somehow changed. She now looked mildly … amused?"

"Mix-ups," Lucy said.

"Well, you know," LeVander said. "With emotions running high … a huge loss like this … people can become confused, disoriented. Something you think happened at one point, you realize didn't really happen later, after you have time to consider things more calmly."

No reaction from Lucy.

"Several surveillance cameras on the west side shot some interesting footage of you, Carolyn, and Greta Turnblad yesterday morning."

"Greta Turnblad?" Lucy said. Her eyebrows furrowed fractionally.

"Yes. The woman sitting next to Carolyn while you were driving." LeVander opened a viewer on his computer screen and played the clip from the camera inside the service corridor, closest to the Northern Lights West 1 Welcome Desk. He turned the screen around so that Lucy could see.

Lucy leaned forward slightly, raising her eyebrows. She said, "Dora," in a soft voice.

"What's that?" LeVander said. "I couldn't catch that."

Lucy looked away from the screen toward LeVander, leaned back in her seat, and once again relaxed all the muscles in her face.

"I didn't know her name," Lucy said.

"Now *that's* strange," LeVander said. "You drove the two of them around and Carolyn never introduced her?"

Lucy shook her head slightly.

"She's no relation to Carolyn," LeVander said, "so we thought maybe she was your grandmother, a friend of the family maybe. Something like that."

Lucy The Robot remained silent, unmoving.

LeVander cleared his throat and opened up another video file on his computer. "Security also turned up a couple of other strange clips ... bear with me ... they don't seem like much, but I think you'll understand where I'm going with this when we look at all of them." LeVander pressed PLAY on the first clip.

"See, this one here Ms. Turnblad shows entering the mall at around seven, She steps out of the camera's view, then never comes back in. Take my word for it: she didn't go anywhere else in the mall. We checked." LeVander moved his mouse around the screen and opened a second viewer.

"And see *here*," he pointed needlessly at the new viewer, "we've got you and Carolyn driving up to the same Welcome Desk around eight-thirty, parking there a while—see, there you are backing the Cushman up—then ... I'm skipping around here ... a little later we get back to this clip of the three of you. Then a day later ... a few hours ago ... Carolyn and Greta Turnblad are dead."

LeVander sat back in his chair. "I'm sure you can see where I'm going with this," he said. "I'm not accusing you of anything, you understand. I'm just trying to find out what the fuck ... excuse my language ... the three of you were doing together yesterday and what connection, if any, that had to the, you know, the tragic events of this morning."

"She was already dead," Lucy said. *She was dead when Carolyn and I found her. I didn't kill her.*

"We know that," LeVander said. "Several people in the office saw you get to work at seven o'clock this morning, after the accident. Carolyn and Ms. Turnblad died thirty minutes before that. We know you weren't involved in that part anyway."

Maybe she's in shock, LeVander wondered. *We gonna have to pay Workman's Comp on this? Shit.*

He doesn't know, Lucy thought. *How can he not know?*

"Did Carolyn say anything yesterday before you left?" LeVander said. "Anything about continuing the tour the next day? Do you know anything about where the old lady stayed last night? Security says her car was in one of the ramps overnight; did Carolyn maybe put Ms. Turnblad in a hotel for the night…?"

"Ms. Turnblad?" Lucy said.

"The old lady!" LeVander said, raising his voice. "You know? The *dead* one?" He put his two hands on his face, unconsciously combing his beard with his fingers. He opened his eyes and looked up just in time to see Lucy's eyes roll up into her head as she fainted, sliding slowly off her chair and onto the soft nylon carpet.

"Fuck!" LeVander yelled. "Gail! Get in here!"

CHAPTER 37

The paths of Foreman and Kiyomi didn't cross again until the end of the day. Uniformed security officers checked each floor's Plexiglas walls between the shopping avenues and the park looking for cracks, holes, missing attachments—any gap through which two women might have fallen. Several officers grumbled—even if they found something, how could two women accidentally fall through … at the same time? Most of them, especially those with military experience, accepted the task stoically. Yours is not to wonder why, yours is just to keep your mouth shut and do as you're told.

Foreman patrolled floors five and six, Kiyomi floors two and three. The Lieutenant said to leave the investigating to him and the police, and just do their normal job, but that if something jumped out at them, say, like someone walking up and confessing, that they should let him know.

Neither had had any further communication with the Major. At the end of their meeting in the morning when they gave him the video clips, he said not to look at any more surveillance video. He thanked them both for their good work, but said that one of the Lieutenants would take over that part of the investigation.

Foreman caught up with Kiyomi as they were punching out.

"Got time for dinner?" he said.

Kiyomi studied her watch for a moment. "A quick one. I've got plans later."

Foreman tried not to look crestfallen. He'd been hoping to spend more time with Kiyomi tonight. Maybe he was moving too quickly.

"Ooh, I'm sorry." Kiyomi touched his arm. "I got a text from a friend of mine from my home town. I've got to get to the airport by twenty past six. "

"A friend?"

"A *girl* friend, you *aho,"* Kiyomi giggled. When Foreman took an exaggerated breath and drew his right hand over his forehead in that way Kiyomi knew Americans did when they were relieved, she laughed loudly.

"*Homma ni aho ya nah!"* Kiyomi said. Foreman didn't understand her words but she looked like a mother scolding a naughty child. "She's a friend from high school. She's flying in from Osaka tonight. She's spending the weekend here and flying on to the east coast on Sunday night."

"I could chauffeur you both around...." Foreman said.

"I can't," Kiyomi said. "But thank you. We'll be catching up on the latest from Japan and eating Japanese snack food and staying up all night watching Japanese videos. Really. You would just be bored." She looked apologetic.

Foreman knew that nothing Kiyomi could do would bore him, but he didn't want to press his luck. "Fine," he said. "I'll hang out at *Sheik's* all weekend." Kiyomi knew that *Sheik's* was a well-known downtown strip club.

"You had better *not!"* Kiyomi balled her fist and punched Foreman's arm.

Foreman said, "Ow!" though Kiyomi hadn't hit him that hard. He felt good.

"So," Kiyomi said, back to business. "You hear anything?"

"Bits and pieces," he said. "Nothing's broken anywhere. One rumor is that they might have fallen off of Lost Deck. You know how low the safety fence is there."

"Strange," Kiyomi said. "Why would they be up there so early?"

Foreman shrugged. "Maybe one of the surveillance cameras caught something."

"I wish we could have spent more time going through yesterday's footage," Foreman said.

"Me, too." Kiyomi said. She zipped up her coat and put on a hat. "For now, though, I have to get going. Where were you thinking of for dinner?"

"You like pizza?"

"I *love* pizza!"

"Good. There's a place called Fat Lorenzo's just off The Crosstown, over where Route 77 turns into Cedar Avenue. Not too far from the airport."

"Sounds good."

"By the way," Foreman said, "what was that you said a minute ago? Something in Japanese. Sounded like 'ah oh.' Then you said it again with some other words after that."

Kiyomi thought for a moment, then her face brightened as she remembered. "You mean '*aho*.'" I called you a dummy because you thought my friend from Japan was a man."

"I did not—"

"I said, 'You really are a dummy!'" She started to laugh. " Because you *are*."

"Nice," Foreman said. "Real nice."

"Because it's *true!*"

Foreman reached out and grabbed Kiyomi around the waist and tried to tickle her. She shrieked, broke away and ran ahead of him, laughing uncontrollably.

"*Aho,*" she said. "Foreman is a *aho.* Foreman is a *aho.*"

"Go ahead," Foreman yelled. "Have your fun. I'm telling Homeland Security that you're a security threat," and he took off running after her.

MONDAY, NOVEMBER 19TH

CHAPTER 38

Monday morning briefing. 8:05 A.M.

The eight X-Team officers on duty sat in the security gym awaiting the arrival of Major Power and his morning briefing. Everyone was anxious to hear the latest on Carolyn Batch's death. No one had heard of the other woman. Carolyn Batch was a minor celebrity in the Twin Cities. Local news had only the barest of details—names of the deceased and the fact that it took place at MightyMall. Shooting death in South Minneapolis: yawn. Women plummet to their deaths at MightyMall: stop the presses! Absent any hard information, reporters were all over the mall, interviewing guests who were angry that Gonzoland had opened three hours late, upset that MightyMall hadn't done a better job of letting people know about the delay, people asking for park refunds. Inevitably, one TV station dug up crime statistics for MightyMall and compared them to other malls and the national average. Local Sunday talk shows speculated on whether Batch's death was an accident, a stress-related suicide, or even murder by a disgruntled employee. What would happen to *Rodinia*, the huge expansion Batch had announced the previous day, and could her death be related to that somehow?

Calls to Titanic Properties asking for comment went unanswered; Titanic finally issued a bland statement on Sunday night expressing their sorrow over the deaths of Ms. Batch and Ms. Turnblad, assurances that MightyMall was safe, and that they were cooperating with local authorities to determine the cause of this most unfortunate accident.

Mike Foreman had arrived five minutes before eight and found Kiyomi already seated in the front row. He sat down in the open chair to her left.

"Hey," he said.

"Good morning!" Kiyomi said. She was always so bright, so ... *alive.* Foreman could almost feel her presence as a tangible entity, like reflected heat from a renewable energy source.

"How was your weekend? Did your friend arrive okay?" Foreman said.

"She did," Kiyomi said. "After dinner on Friday—thank you for treating me; that was unnecessary but very nice of you—I got to the airport right at twenty past six. The flight had actually arrived early, so by the time I got to the baggage area, Chiyoko was already there."

"Was it her first time here?" Foreman said.

"Yes," Kiyomi said. "She had transited at the airport before but never been outside of the airport. It was fun. I took her to see the Holidazzle Parade downtown. We went to the Minneapolis Institute of Art, the Guthrie Theater. She wanted to see what Minnesota nightclubs are like, so we wandered around the Warehouse District for dinner."

"Meet any cute guys?" Foreman said.

"We *did,*" Kiyomi said. "Two of the most handsome guys you have ever seen took us to dinner, a show at The Orpheum, dancing, and then we invited them back to my apartment for the weekend." Kiyomi turned to her left, tilted her head down slightly, looked up at Foreman and locked her eyes on his, daring him to take seriously what she had said and become jealous.

Foreman held her stare for as long as he could, but couldn't keep a straight face and said, "Liar."

"*So ka nah,*" she said, and looked primly away. She then whipped her face back toward Foreman, flashed her 1000-watt smile again, and said, "How was *Sheik's?*"

"Oh, you know how it is," Foreman leaned back in his chair and pretended to stretch. "There are only so many free lap dances a guy can take before it gets old." He braced himself in case Kiyomi punched his arm. "No, but seriously, I took it pretty easy all weekend. Caught up on some reading. I did some weights at the health club on Saturday, then ran about ten miles on Sunday. I miss riding my bike; it's kind of hard to motivate myself to work out in the cold months. But it felt good."

At 8:05 Foreman looked at his watch; Kiyomi reflexively checked hers. "Where's Major Power?" she said.

"I know," Foreman said. "He's never late for these briefings."

Everyone looked to the left as the gym's side door opened and in walked Karl LeVander, Managing Director of Operations for MightyMall. He walked slowly to the front of the room, looked around as if unsure where to stand, dragged a nearby table to the center, and leaned back against it.

Everyone knew who LeVander was, had seen his face. Few had spoken to him. LeVander was known to do all his communicating through departmental directors and, occasionally, managers. Pass him in the hall if you were of a lower rank and LeVander would ignore you. The few times each year LeVander was forced to interact with regular employees—manning the buffet line, along with other senior executives, once a year at the Team Star Award Ceremony was one such occasion—he liked to recycle the same old jokes and slap everyone on the back like they were old friends. As soon as the event was over, LeVander's mask of conviviality dissolved like wrinkles after a Botox injection.

"Howdy," LeVander huffed, short of breath. Word was that he had been a construction worker in his younger years, quite the physical specimen. Whatever muscle he used to have was now buried beneath a hundred pounds of excess fat that was not easy to carry around.

"I'm sure you all have a whole lot of questions about a whole lot of things and I'll get to those in due time." LeVander took several more deep breaths, plucked a handkerchief out of his back pocket and wiped perspiration from his forehead.

"First, a few announcements," LeVander said. "Effective immediately, Security Chief Matthew Power has been reassigned to a joint venture project that Titanic Properties is developing in China. He flew out of Twin Cities International on Sunday night."

Several officers shouted out questions simultaneously. Major Power leaving the mall was, for some of them, as big and incomprehensible a notion as when Kevin Garnett had left the Timberwolves, or Tori Hunter the Twins. Say it ain't so!

"This is a great opportunity for Matt and I know you will all be as excited as I am for him," LeVander said. "*The Great Mall of China*, as it will be called, will be slightly larger than MightyMall is now. Construction will start a year from now. Power will be directly responsible for creating a security team from scratch and running it until the locals can handle it on their own."

Kiyomi turned to face Foreman, who was staring silently, mouth closed, slight frown on his face, at LeVander.

Foreman raised his hand. "Sir?" he said. "Mr. LeVander? "

"Yes," LeVander said. "Officer…."

"Foreman, sir."

"Ah, Foreman," LeVander said, a look of recognition on his face. "Yes, of course." LeVander hadn't recognized Foreman's face, but he remembered the name from the briefing he got from Power. That girl next to him must be the Nagata girl.

Foreman was sure that he had never spoken to Karl LeVander in his life.

"I think we're all just surprised at how suddenly it happened. I mean," Foreman looked at the faces of the other officers, then back at LeVander, "I'm sure everyone wanted to say goodbye to the Major before he left."

Several of the officers nodded in agreement.

"Yes, well, preparations had been going on for some time," LeVander said. "Power was approached about the position several months ago. He wasn't due to ship out until the end of March, but negotiations with our Chinese partners proceeded more rapidly than planned, moving things ahead by three months. I just got word from HQ myself on Saturday."

"What about his—?"

"Which brings me to my next announcement," LeVander said. "Pending final decision on a permanent replacement for Major Power, Lieutenant Rolvaag will be Acting Chief of Security."

In all the excitement, no one had noticed Lieutenant Rolvaag slip in the back of the room. When LeVander called his name, Rolvaag strode to the front of the room.

"And now that I've answered all of your questions," LeVander said, having answered none of them, "I think I'll turn things over to Lieutenant Rolvaag," and strolled out of the room.

CHAPTER 39

"Okay, everybody, let's quiet down," Lieutenant Rolvaag said. He held up his hands and gently waved everyone to sit back down. "Please."

Rolvaag was small for a MightyMall security officer, five-feet-six, wiry rather than skinny. He had a receding hairline and wore round tortoise-shell glasses that had been out of fashion for years. Rolvaag had been a Social Studies teacher in Richfield for fifteen years before joining security four years ago. What he lacked in physical intimidation he made up for in effective management skills. If you can keep a group of eleventh graders in line, he liked to say, you can manage anyone.

"We're running late, so why don't I answer all your questions before you ask them," Rolvaag said. "First: I don't know any more about Major Power's transfer than you do. I really don't. He called me Saturday night, said he was flying out on Sunday, and asked me to steer the ship until they find a permanent replacement."

"But why—?"

Rolvaag held up a single finger and looked down at the floor, cutting off the question before it went any farther.

"Like I said," Rolvaag said. After waiting through a few seconds of silence for dramatic effect, he continued. "Next: What about the deaths on Friday? What I can tell you is that the two women, Batch and a Greta Turnblad, fell to their deaths from the Lost Deck on seven. One camera on the opposite side of the park, a head-on view, shows two bodies falling over the safety fence. It wasn't set to zoom, so there's almost no detail. We can't identify them but can infer their identities because no one else fell that day. I will also tell you this, though it can't leave this room: it appears that Ms. Turnblad went first and that Batch may have been holding on to her. Speculate all you want from that, but the Saint Commercia Police have not, to my knowledge, come to any conclusions yet. We're continuing to scan video footage, and you know there's a lot of that. I'm working closely with the SC Police."

Rolvaag paused. "That reminds me. Foreman and Nagata: LeVander wants to see you in his office as soon as we break here."

Foreman and Kiyomi felt the eyes of the other officers on their backs. Why would LeVander want to talk to them?

"Finally: I'm surprised he forgot to give you the news himself, but with the death of Carolyn Batch, the owners have promoted Karl LeVander to Vice President of Operations and Business Development. New title. He'll be running both sides of the mall for the foreseeable future."

Rolvaag took off his cap and ran his right hand through his thinning hair. "Okay then," he said. "*Now* I'll take questions."

As Rolvaag had expected, there were none, just blank stares and stunned silence.

"Fine. Then here are your assignments for today." Rolvaag passed around single sheets of paper to each of the X-Team members. "This is a lot to take in all at once, I know. I'd like to show Mr. LeVander that the team that Power created here, the X-Team as well as all the uniformed officers, is so well trained that we can carry on for a while without missing a beat. Let's make him proud."

Rolvaag is talking like Power is dead, not transferred, Foreman thought.

CHAPTER 40

Foreman and Kiyomi sat in front of Karl LeVander's large mahogany desk. Foreman's eyes drifted around the room. A photo of the groundbreaking ceremony with the governor, a United States senator and several local politicians hung on one wall; suspended beneath the photo was a gold-painted shovel.

LeVander's administrative assistant, Gail, had shown them into the office and asked them to have a seat. Mr. LeVander would be along in just a few minutes; he was just wrapping up a videoconference with the owners. Would they like something to drink? Both Foreman and Kiyomi declined.

"What do you think this is about?" Kiyomi said.

"Gotta be about Batch and the Turnblad woman," Foreman said. "Don't you think?"

"I am afraid you may be right," Kiyomi said. "Aren't you worried about Major Power suddenly disappearing like that? I am."

"Does seem kind of weird, yeah."

"He never struck me as the kind of person who would just leave without notifying the team. The whole security team, I mean. An email, at least, to let us know what was going on."

Foreman nodded.

"And doesn't it seem odd that no one yet has talked about—?"

The door clicked open and in walked Karl LeVander.

"Well, then," LeVander said. "My two little detectives." He walked slowly around his large desk, spun his high back chair once around for no apparent reason, and lowered his considerable bulk slowly into the chair.

"Sir?" Foreman said.

LeVander fixed Foreman with a stare meant to frighten mall vendors, unruly tenants and subordinates. Attractive X-Team members from Kobe, Japan occasionally made Foreman nervous. Overweight blowhards did not.

"Major Power filled me in on your little Hardy Boys, Nancy Drew exploits," LeVander said.

Foreman said, "Sir, Officer Nagata and I were following up on leads we had developed. We didn't see the connection at first—an unclaimed handbag, a missing old woman, odd behavior by mall staff—but we found some interesting video evidence that may tie it all together. Part of our job on the X-Team is to connect random bits of information that may not, on the surface, appear to have any connection, and to find patterns."

LeVander had been sitting with both arms flat on the desk in front of him, as if preventing it from rising up and floating away. He lifted his right palm slightly, in a regal demand for silence. "Yes," LeVander said. "I'm fully aware of your former commander's IES Unit: the X-Team, as you kiddies like to call it."

Foreman noted LeVander's second disparaging reference to the X-Team.

LeVander's voice began to rise. "*I'm* the one who approved Power's fucking budget every year. I *know* where the money goes. And I'm the one who you now report to."

Where is this coming from? Foreman wondered.

"Of course, sir," Foreman said, his voice level.

Kiyomi watched the exchange between LeVander and Foreman. Her only interaction with LeVander had been immediately after she was hired. He had started chatting her up one morning after she left the security gym. He introduced himself, welcomed her to "The World's Largest Private Security Force" as he had called it. Where was she from? How did she like America? She was in great shape, he had said while staring directly at her breasts. How much did she weigh? What were her favorite exercises? Then, did she have lots of family here? Boyfriends? LeVander sidled closer to her, closer than he needed to be if all he wanted was to chat. Based on Kiyomi's experience with drunken jocks at the U and stories she had heard from her American roommates, she knew that LeVander was hitting on her. She also surmised that he was trying to intimidate her. Aside from his body odor and foul breath, Kiyomi felt no intimidation; she was confident in her self-defense skills, though she doubted she would need them in a public place. But she did worry about how to best extricate herself from the situation without putting her new job in jeopardy. If the United States was anything like Japan, sexual harassment laws were pretty lame. Fortunately for Kiyomi, one of the other new hires walked by at that moment and Kiyomi quickly suggested that they have lunch together. She excused herself and rushed to join her colleague. Kiyomi had since then occasionally passed LeVander in a hallway but, happily, never sensed any recognition on his face, nor further interest in her. She was sure he hadn't recognized her face when he walked into his office this morning.

Kiyomi heard the tension in LeVander's voice, noticed the vein throbbing between his eyebrows. He was unhappy about something. Power had been satisfied with their report, she was sure. Kiyomi was impressed at how well Foreman was maintaining his calm despite LeVander's hostility.

"So don't go lecturing *me* on *your* job duties, buddy boy," LeVander said. "I *wrote* your fucking job duties."

Foreman didn't believe that was true—Power had written their job descriptions—but saw no point in debating that now.

"Yes, sir," Foreman said. "Of course." He leaned back in his chair slightly. LeVander was marking his territory.

"Those 'leads' you talk about," LeVander said, "Some nonsense about Carolyn Batch's and her secretary's activities the day before the accident." LeVander opened a manila folder on his desk and flipped through several pages. "Last Thursday. Those are *serious* accusations that may have played a part in the mental breakdown of Lucy Evans, right here in my office." LeVander poked his meaty index finger on his desk so hard it sounded like someone knocking at the door.

LeVander's administrative assistant poked her head in the door. "Something, Mr. LeVander?" Gail said.

"No!" LeVander yelled. "Get the hell out of here."

Gail scampered back out and quietly closed the door.

Foreman said, "Breakdown, sir?" He hadn't accused anybody of anything.

"The poor girl fainted dead away," LeVander. "Fell right out of the chair you're sitting in," he waived his chin at Kiyomi. "Had to call the mall clinic."

"Is she all right, sir?" Kiyomi said.

nodded, liking this solution. "Lots of video clips. You probably opened one from the day before. The week before, perhaps."

Foreman said, "I'm sure Major Power will confirm our story. The dates are correct. He may have looked at the files himself. He must know where the list is—"

"I'll follow up with Major Power in good time, " LeVander said. The vein on his forehead was no longer throbbing. The color on his face had returned to its normal pasty pallor. "He's still somewhere between here and his final destination in China." LeVander was back in his comfort zone. "Meanwhile, our investigation into the unfortunate death of a *valued* member of our MightyMall family and an elderly senior citizen will continue, as will our cooperation with the Saint Commercia Police." LeVander beamed at Foreman and Nagata.

Kiyomi knew that she and Foreman were in dangerous waters. Was LeVander planning a cover up? Something more sinister? She and Foreman needed more information. They needed to get out of LeVander's office and compare notes.

While LeVander was looking at Foreman, Kiyomi made a small adjustment to her posture, hunching her shoulders slightly, lifting her eyebrows, conveying through body language a more innocent, wide-eyed, non-threatening, foreign girl, overwhelmed by all these horrible events. "Mr. LeVander? " She raised her left arm hesitantly. "Do, um, za police habu a theory yet?" Kiyomi's English accent deteriorated along with her posture. So obvious, but men always fell for it. "On how Ms. Batch and Ms. Turnblad fell off the observation deck on the seventh floor? We all feel so bery sad about their deaths."

Foreman noticed the change in Kiyomi's demeanor. *She's playing him,* he thought to himself, containing a smile. *She's trying to get him to show his hand.*

"Well, I can't say for sure," LeVander said. "But it seems clear from my review of the video footage of the fall, that Carolyn Batch must have found the old lady on Lost Deck and got tangled up with her when she tried to save her. We don't know how the lady got into the mall so early, or how she managed to get out on Lost Deck; we're investigating that separately. But the way I see it, Carolyn Batch was a hero who just got unlucky while trying to do the right thing." *I have no problem with Carolyn Noxon Batch: Dead Hero. She's out of my hair.*

"*Yappari so,*" Kiyomi said, nodding, serious. "I thought so. She was a great woman. Very, what is the word? Inspiring to Japanese women. In-spi-ra-tion-al!"

"Exactly!" LeVander said. *Inspiring, my ass.* "And the owners think so too. That's why they are especially concerned that we not let anything or anyone besmirch her good name. Not after the good work she did laying the groundwork for the *Rodinia* expansion. If rumors started flying around now that Batch's death was anything but on the up and up, it could complicate things, with the governor, the legislature, the news media."

"So you are asking us to—" Foreman said.

Kiyomi put her hand on top of Foreman's, hoping to silence him. "We must be bery more careful and accurate with the evidence we find." Kiyomi nodded again, showing LeVander how logical his orders were. "Of course. That is very Japanese. Be slow and careful in all things. Yes, yes. I see now."

"Exactly." LeVander smiled at Kiyomi. Nice looking bitch. And young. "You two can best help us all by getting back to your regular job of looking for terrorists. Leave everything else to the professionals."

LeVander stared hard at Foreman. "We clear on that?"

Kiyomi tightened her gripped on Foreman's hand, but he was relaxed now. "Certainly, Mr. LeVander. I've got no problem with that. Sorry for any hassle we caused."

"No problem at all," LeVander said. "We're all one big happy family."

Heading toward the elevator, Kiyomi began to speak but Foreman touched an index finger to his lips and shook his head. He pointed his chin in the direction of the nearest surveillance camera.

"Lunch later?" Foreman said, casually.

"Sure."

"Tim & Kevin's at noon?"

"That's on seven, right?" Kiyomi said. "Ah, I see. That's near Lost Deck. Sure."

They approached the elevator. Kiyomi stepped on but Foreman remained standing outside.

"I'm on one today," Foreman said. "I'll take the stairs."

"See you later," Kiyomi said as the heavy double doors of the service elevator crashed together.

CHAPTER 41

Foreman and Kiyomi stood in front of Tim & Kevin's Minnesota Style Pizza studying the menu.

"Shall we eat here?" Kiyomi said. "The *Lutefisk with Cream of Wild Rice Supreme* sounds good."

Foreman turned to look at Kiyomi. "Have you ever *eaten* Lutefisk?"

"No, but it's fish. Why are you looking at me like that? I like fish."

"You could dispose of weapons-grade plutonium in Lutefisk," Foreman said. "It's cod soaked in lye until it turns into jello."

"You made that up." Kiyomi laughed.

"Not by much." Foreman shivered. "I once had a friend who moved out of state after someone served him Lutefisk. Never came back."

Kiyomi looked back at the menu behind the counter. "How about one of the other toppings?"

"Sure." Foreman read the next item on the menu. "T&K's Hotdish Pizza: Tater Tots, Green Beans, Onions, Ground Beef with Mushroom Soup Sauce on a Lefse Crust."

"Lefse?"

"A kind of Norwegian bread made from potatoes. Popular in Minnesota."

"Hmm."

They got bacon cheeseburgers at Five Guys Burgers next door and sat in the center of the food court. Foreman looked around casually to make sure they were alone.

"Do you think that LeVander is monitoring us now?" Kiyomi asked.

"I don't know what to believe," Foreman said. "But that whole meeting with him this morning was surreal. Missing video footage. Broken surveillance equipment. Batch is a hero."

"Maybe she is," Kiyomi said.

"Maybe," Foreman said. "He just sounded so desperate. Like he knew the story was weak but had to push it anyway."

"Could he be getting pressure from the owners?" Kiyomi said. "In Japan, companies sometimes cover things up, or manufacture new stories, simply because they are embarrassing. Maybe LeVander, or the owners, believes a simple explanation will disappear from headlines faster."

"Did you know that Lucy Evans didn't come in today?" Foreman said. "I asked someone in marketing. She didn't call in. Nobody knows where she is."

"LeVander said something about Lucy fainting," Kiyomi said. "Maybe she's sick. Or went to the hospital."

"Then who is covering for her today?"

Kiyomi picked at a French fry. "Nothing for her to do, with Carolyn Batch dead."

"There must be calls coming in from media, from the public. She wouldn't just not show up without a reason. Wouldn't LeVander notice that? He was the one talking about how upset she was. Wouldn't Human Resources send someone to Lucy's house to check on her?"

The both ate in silence for a few minutes. Foreman finished his bacon cheeseburger, balled up the paper wrapping and shot it, basketball style, at the garbage can about ten feet away.

"He shoots and he *scores!*" Foreman said.

Kiyomi smiled.

"And what about Major Power disappearing like that?" Foreman said. "What was your take on that?"

"It did seem quite sudden," Kiyomi said. "I wish there was a way to contact him."

"I know," Foreman said. "I don't know his email address. Do you?"

Kiyomi shook her head.

"And we can't go asking for that," Foreman said, "without it getting back to LeVander. He made it pretty clear he wants us to back off the whole thing."

"Maybe we should let it go," Kiyomi said. Her face looked apologetic. "The only evidence we had is missing." Kiyomi noticed a flicker of something in Foreman's face. "What?"

"Hmm?" Foreman said. "Oh. Nothing, I was just thinking that you are right."

Kiyomi continued, "The only person who saw that evidence besides us is out of reach."

"And LeVander was throwing out some heavy hints that our jobs are at risk if we don't back off," Foreman said. "I know … it's just not … it sucks, that's all."

"Yes," Kiyomi said. "Indeed it does."

Foreman looked at his watch. "I've gotta get back to work." He loaded their combined cups and plates and cups on the tray and carried it to the garbage can. "You up for dinner tonight?" They had only had one formal date but already he felt comfortable asking out of the blue like this.

"I'd love to," Kiyomi said, "but I'm working a double shift today. Rolvaag radioed me this morning. Henderson can't come in for some reason. Then Tuesday I'm on the overnight shift only, then off Wednesday."

Foreman stopped. "I thought you were always daytime."

"Me, too," Kiyomi said. "Not much need for undercover cops when the mall is closed."

"I've never even heard of X-Team officers working overnight," Foreman said.

Kiyomi smiled resignedly. "Not often. I've never done it before but have heard of it happening. During holidays, sometimes. Or when several uniformed officers get sick at once."

"Really?" Foreman wasn't convinced.

Kiyomi touched Foreman's arm and he had that electric thrill again. "Don't be paranoid. I'm sure it's just a coincidence."

WEDNESDAY, NOVEMBER 21ST

CHAPTER 42

Wednesday morning briefing. 8:20 A.M.

Foreman walked up to Kiyomi as everyone was filing out of the room. "Well, hello there, stranger," Foreman said. "I saw you sneak in the back after things started."

Kiyomi covered her mouth as she yawned. "Excuse me," she said. Her smile looked strained.

"Long night?" Foreman said.

"I … not much sleep."

"Sounds like fun."

"No," Kiyomi said. "I was working late … um … part of last night."

"Wait," Foreman said. "You were supposed to be off today."

"Rolvaag contacted me yesterday afternoon asking me to come in for the graveyard shift." Kiyomi yawned again. "I'm in for this shift this morning, then I can take Thursday off."

Foreman frowned. "But you worked a double shift on Monday. Then graveyard last night and day shift today? I've never heard of that."

Kiyomi put on a brave face. "Oh, you know," she said. "That's life."

Foreman noticed her cheeks trembling. "Hey. Are you all right?"

Kiyomi's eyes began to tear up. "It's nothing." She turned away.

"Here," Foreman put his hand on Kiyomi's back and guided her away from the service elevator. "Let's take the stairs instead. I can use the exercise." He wanted to put his arm around her but their relationship was not public yet and he didn't know what LeVander would do with that information if he found out.

"What floors are you on today?" Foreman said.

"Two and three." Kiyomi's voice was shaky. She dabbed at her eyes.

The two of them climbed two flights of stairs and stopped. The service stairs were dark and rarely cleaned. They were not open to the public. Mall employees preferred the elevators. They were not likely to encounter anyone.

Kiyomi kept averting her eyes when Foreman tried to face her. He finally grabbed her shoulders and gently turned her toward him.

"Tell me," Foreman said.

Kiyomi looked down, shaking her head. "It's nothing. I'm being silly."

"You are one of the most *not* silly people I know," Foreman said. Kiyomi's face began to collapse into itself as she broke down. Foreman put his arms around her, pulling her closer. She buried her face in his chest and started crying more freely, in big racking sobs. The two of them stood there like that for several minutes. Kiyomi's sobs gradually abated, her breathing slowly returning to normal.

"My God," Foreman said. "What happened to you?"

Kiyomi continued to press her face into Foreman's chest. He patted her back gently. She sniffled twice, pulled away, and took a small package of paper tissues with Japanese writing on it from her pocket. She said, "Excuse me," turned away, and blew her nose. She removed a second tissue from the package, dabbed her eyes and took a deep breath.

"I'm okay now," she said after one final sniff. Kiyomi looked up into Foreman's eyes. Foreman had never held Kiyomi before and she realized that he was taller than she had thought, perhaps 30 centimeters taller. Half a foot. And strong.

"I ... it's ..." Kiyomi shook her head.

"It's okay," Foreman said. "Whatever it is. Just tell me."

Foreman looked at Kiyomi, giving her time. She was staring at his chest, but her attention was farther away than that. She nodded occasionally, as if participating in a silent discussion with herself. Finally, she lifted her head and looked Foreman in the eye. Her eyes were red and puffy from crying, but she had regained her composure. She now looked less fragile, angrier.

She took one more large breath and exhaled.

"Karl LeVander," Kiyomi said. "He ... he tried to rape me last night,"

"He *what*?" Foreman's yell echoed off the cinderblock walls of the stairway. More quietly, he said: "He raped you." Not a question this time, his voice ominously quiet.

Kiyomi noticed Foreman clenching his fists. She saw him look down the stairwell. He didn't move, but Kiyomi took hold of his arm anyway, afraid he might run off and do something rash.

"He tried," Kiyomi said. "He was ... unsuccessful."

The steel in Kiyomi's voice brought Foreman's attention back to her. He searched her eyes for confirmation that she was unharmed.

"You're all right?" Foreman said.

"Yes," she said.

"Tell me," Foreman said.

She did.

Kiyomi had been assigned the 10 P.M. to 7 A.M. shift on Tuesday night. Uncommon, as she had told Foreman at lunch on Monday, but not unheard of. The work consisted of quick patrols around each floor. Check entrance doors, gates, look for broken lights or kids hiding out. Around twenty to twelve she got a call from SAC ordering her to the operations offices. The dispatcher said a sensor indicated that one of the doors into the offices was open. That was fairly common: usually a maintenance guy jamming a door open while he wheeled in some equipment. Kiyomi was four floors directly above the operations offices when the call came in; it took her less than five minutes to get there.

Kiyomi had checked the door and found a small piece of cardboard wedged underneath. Kiyomi picked up the piece of cardboard and put it in her pocket. She went inside the operations offices to look around. Lights in the management offices were always on 24/7, so she wasn't worried about anyone hiding there, but it was her job to make sure. That door happened to be next to Karl LeVander's office, which hadn't seemed important at the time. As she was heading back out, LeVander's door opened and out he stepped.

What a surprise seeing you here, he had said. *A most pleasant surprise, however. And since you're here, I'd like to talk more about what you and Officer Foreman think you found last week.*

Kiyomi was immediately uncomfortable: what was he doing here so late and why did they have to talk about anything this late at night? She told LeVander that she had to get back to her patrol.

Nonsense, he had said, *we've got* plenty *of time.*

LeVander had somehow placed himself between Kiyomi and the door to the service hallway.

C'mon in, he had said.

Kiyomi noticed liquor on LeVander's breath.

No, I think I'd better get back, she had said, and started walking in the other direction; there was another exit at the other end of the Operation Offices.

LeVander grabbed Kiyomi's arm and yanked her back.

I insist, he had said, and started pulling her toward his office.

Kiyomi tried to yank her arm away, but LeVander's meaty hands were too strong.

You thought you were pretty smart, you two, didn't you, he had said. *Trying to make the mall look bad, right when it's my turn to take over. Why'd you want to go and do something like that,* he had said. *You're much too pretty to be such a troublemaker, letting Foreman give you bad advice like that. He's not right for you anyway. What you need is a firmer hand.*

Please let go, Mr. LeVander, Kiyomi had said. *You are hurting me.*

I'll bet you like that, don't you? Big strong American knows how to control you.

LeVander kept dragging Kiyomi, relentlessly toward his office. She resisted but was careful to keep both her feet beneath her. Lose her balance now, allow him to get take complete control, and all would be lost. When they were about ten feet away from LeVander's office Kiyomi suddenly went limp. LeVander compensated, putting more of his weight on his right leg. As he turned, Kiyomi kicked sharply at the back of LeVander's right leg, just below the knee. With so much of his weight on his right side, LeVander fell like a stone. Kiyomi jumped out of the way, planted both her feet, and with LeVander's attention now focused on breaking his own fall, yanked her arm with all her might, breaking free of his sweaty grasp.

Foreman waited until he was sure Kiyomi had finished, then said, "What did you do then?"

"I ran out of the office, ran to my car and went home."

Foreman noticed that Kiyomi's breathing was back to normal. Her eyes were a little red.

"I don't suppose you reported him to the police," Foreman said. He had seen LeVander talking to someone when he came in this morning, behaving as if nothing had happened.

"I … no, I didn't," Kiyomi said.

Foreman nodded.

"Do you think less of me?" Kiyomi said, her voice beginning to falter again. "For … you know …"

"No," Foreman said, momentarily confused. "What for? For *him* attacking *you*? My God, no."

"Because sometimes … in Japan …"

"Well, not here!" Foreman said, then realized he had raised his voice. "Not here," he said more softly. "I wish you had gone to the police, though. I'd like to nail the bastard. Send him to jail."

"But how?" Kiyomi said. "I mean, he didn't actually rape me. I stopped him before that, so …" She shrugged. "So there's no evidence. It would be his story against my story. He's the boss. He's the American. I'm just a little foreigner." She shrugged again. "Who would believe me?"

"*I* believe you," Foreman said, looking into Kiyomi's eyes, just a few inches from his.

Kiyomi grabbed a hold of Foreman's shirt and pulled him to her, looking up into his eyes, standing on her toes, and kissed him. Lips closed, she pushed her mouth against his with all her might. She had worked with him only a few months, had dated him only once, but felt she *knew* him, *needed* him. She let go of his shirt and put her hands on either side of his face. The kiss grew into something more. Kiyomi's lips parted and their tongues danced. Foreman put his arms around her, moved his hands up and down, as if searching, wanting to acquaint themselves with as much of Kiyomi's body as they could. He rested them both at the base of her back and pulled her closer. She did the same, pulling Foreman closer, wishing at that moment that there were no clothes between them, feeling wanton but not caring, feeling his hardness, wanting more.

Foreman put his hands on Kiyomi's face, continued kissing her for another minute, then pulled away. "We'd better stop pretty soon or …" His voice sounded hoarse. "Or … we're going to have to get pretty creative." He noticed that a red splotch had formed on one of Kiyomi's cheeks and her neck. He wondered where else she got red splotches when she got excited.

Kiyomi grabbed Foreman's shirt again and buried her forehead in his chest. "I'm so bad," she said, giggling.

"No, you're not," Foreman said. "You're great!"

Kiyomi gently slapped him on the arm. "You'll think all Japanese women are like this."

Foreman took a deep breath and looked back down at Kiyomi. Images of LeVander manhandling her flooded back into his mind, causing his randiness to ebb. "That fucking bastard," Foreman said. He reached out to rub her right arm, wanting to stay connected, to soothe her.

Kiyomi shrugged sharply away.

"Darn," Foreman said. "I'm sorry. I didn't mean to—"

"No, no," Kiyomi said, rubbing the place where Foreman had touched her. "It's not you. It's not that ... it's just my arm. It hurts."

"Is *that* the arm?" Foreman said. "Where LeVander grabbed you? Is it bruised?"

Kiyomi thought for a moment. "I guess it is, yes. I hadn't thought about it. Hadn't really noticed it. I was just so … you know … upset. And then tired."

"Do you mind showing me the bruise?" Foreman said. "Can you roll up your sleeve?"

"Sure." Kiyomi was wearing a U sweatshirt over a T-shirt. She shoved both sleeves as high as they would go.

Foreman inspected Kiyomi's arm carefully, not wanting to hurt her. He found the bruise just above her elbow.

"Can you see anything?" Kiyomi couldn't see anything; the bunched sleeves were blocking her view.

"I can," Foreman said. "Several long, dark blue areas. These have to be from LeVander's fingers. You should really go to the police and show them—"

Kiyomi shook her head sharply. "No, Mike, I won't do that."

"But maybe they can match the bruises to LeVander's hand—"

"No," Kiyomi said. "It's just not ... worth it. Sorry."

"But you don't know—"

Kiyomi touched Foreman's cheek with her hand. "I am grateful for your concern," she said. "I truly am. If he had ... if he were successful ... I would go. But not just with this. I need this job."

Foreman hated Kiyomi's logic, though he believed she was probably right. Even if the markings on her arm matched the size of LeVander's fingers, who's to say Kiyomi hadn't slipped on a wet floor and LeVander was just trying to help her? If only they had some proof.

Proof!

"Follow me. We're taking a detour," Foreman said. He started down the stairs. He almost grabbed Kiyomi's arm but remembered her bruise and her experience of last night, and waved for her to follow instead.

"Follow me."

CHAPTER 43

The Security Action Center was a busier place at 9:30 A.M. than it had been the last time Foreman and Kiyomi were there, the previous Friday at five in the morning. Over a dozen officers sat at scattered terminals, some looking at the big screens in front, others looking into their computer screens. Even with the larger crowd, most of the terminals were empty.

Foreman and Kiyomi jogged down a couple of rows and sat at the first two open terminals they found. Foreman was logging in when they both heard a familiar voice behind them.

"Well, good morning." The large shape of Karl LeVander loomed over them like a malevolent killer whale. "Nice to see two of our wonderful X-Team members hard at work." LeVander's sarcasm was thinly veiled. As he leaned over them both, LeVander put one of his hands on Kiyomi's shoulder. She caught Foreman's attention before he had time to react and made a shake of her head. "Not sure what you two are doing in here so early, but I'm sure it's related to your relentless pursuit of terrorists."

LeVander walked two terminals past Foreman and sat down. "I was just checking up on our surveillance system—those malfunctioning cameras I was telling you about the other day. Until we get a replacement for Major Power I'm kind of pulling double duty overseeing security. Gotta make sure everything works."

LeVander logged onto his terminal. "Bad news, I'm afraid, though," he said. "I've spotted a few more glitches. Now it looks like some of the cameras in the operations offices, or at least the recording mechanisms, are also on the fritz." LeVander turned and looked Kiyomi straight in the eye. "Quite embarrassing, really."

Foreman was gripping his computer mouse so tightly that the shell cracked in his hand.

"Whoa there!" LeVander chuckled good-naturedly. "Easy on the equipment! With budgets the way they are, we can't afford to break our computers. Next thing you know we'll have to start cutting personnel."

Foreman fought to control his breathing. Foreman knew one thing: if LeVander put his hand on Kiyomi again, he would kill him with his bare hands.

LeVander stood suddenly. "Well, some of us have got to work." As he passed their terminals, he said. "Don't stay here playing too long. There's nothing to see."

Both Foreman and Kiyomi watched LeVander lumber out of the SAC.

Kiyomi said, "Do you think…?"

Foreman logged onto his computer, couldn't get it to work, disconnected his mouse, said to Kiyomi, "Can you switch this one with the one at your terminal?" and started looking through the video files related to the camera with the best view of the place in the operations offices where LeVander attacked Kiyomi.

After several minutes, Foreman sat back sharply in his chair. "Damn!"

"Nothing?" Kiyomi said.

"He's deleted every video file for every camera in the operations offices for the past twenty four hours—probably so it'll look like the whole system isn't working."

"Can't they trace that back to him?" Kiyomi said. "Won't they be able to tell that there were files, but now there aren't? And which computer they were deleted from?"

"Maybe...." Foreman said. "Probably, dammit." He put his elbow on the desk and rested his head in his hand. "But he's the Big Boss. The IT department has always reported to him."

"Do you think he deleted all the files himself?" Kiyomi asked.

Foreman shrugged dejectedly. "Who knows? Finding and deleting files isn't that hard, so, yeah, my guess is that he did that himself. Then he doesn't have to worry about anybody else talking."

"So he's won," Kiyomi said. "Again."

"The asshole." Foreman looked at his watch. "Sorry about my language. But we should probably get to work. No sense giving the bastard a legitimate reason to fire us."

Kiyomi remained seated, staring at her own watch.

"What is it?" Foreman said.

Kiyomi closed her eyes and massaged the bridge of her nose with her thumb and index finger. "I was tired."

"You mean you *are* tired," Foreman corrected her English. "Sure you are. You're in the middle of a double shift. You had to fight off a 300 hundred pound mound of pond scum—"

"No," she said, quietly. "I mean … I *meant,"* English became more difficult when she was this tired. "I meant that … I *was* tired, before, and that was why I didn't think of this before."

"Think of what?"

Kiyomi said, "It's Wednesday, isn't it?"

"Sure."

Kiyomi nodded, satisfied. "Good." She switched to massaging her eyebrows, starting in the center and radiating outward.

"Good. LeVander attacked me last night at around eleven-thirty," Kiyomi said. "A little after that."

"Okay."

Kiyomi continued to massage her eyebrows, eyes closed tight. "Maybe eleven-forty-five," she said. "No later than that, I'm sure."

Foreman didn't know where Kiyomi was going with this, but *she* seemed to, so he remained quiet.

"The whole event … his attack … lasted less than five minutes, I think. Maybe less than a minute."

Kiyomi opened her eyes briefly, found one of Foreman's hands and took it in both of hers. She closed her eyes again, squinting slightly.

"That means I was out of the operations office before midnight. I had broken away from LeVander by then. Yes. I'm positive." She nodded once, opened her eyes and blinked a couple of times, and smiled at Foreman, the first real smile he had seen all morning. "Good."

"Why is the time so important?" Foreman said.

"Because," Kiyomi said, her face brightening suddenly, "you handsome American man, it means that Karl LeVander might not get away after all. Maybe."

"Why?" Foreman said. "I mean, how?"

Kiyomi explained that the MightyMall computer server, the central computing system and storage facility for all personal and transactional computers in the mall, was located on the premises. All computer records and files, except for some personal Word and PowerPoint documents people chose to store on their personal computers, were stored on the MightyMall server.

"But LeVander can still erase files from there, can't he?" Foreman said. "He's already done that. We checked. The files are missing. Like the original files of Carolyn Batch and Lucy Evans we viewed last Friday."

"True," Kiyomi said. "But many of the mall's files are so important, and the number of files is so large, that everything on the MightyMall servers gets backed up, copied, daily, to another server, in one giant data dump. That server is located at the Titanic Properties headquarters."

Recognition began to form on Foreman's face. "And that data dump happens at … what time?"

"Midnight," Kiyomi said. "It begins at midnight and takes a couple of hours to complete."

"So," Foreman said, slowly. "Since LeVander attacked you on Tuesday night before midnight, and it's now Wednesday morning…."

Kiyomi nodded. "Unless Karl LeVander ran to SAC, found the right camera and the right video files before midnight," she said, "then the video footage of Karl LeVander attacking me is sitting right now on the Titanic server in Dallas, Texas, and will remain there until midnight tonight."

"Can LeVander access the Titanic server from here?"

Kiyomi shook her head. "I'm sure he can't. The servers down there contain data from dozens, maybe hundreds, of Titanic malls around the world. Credit card transactions, confidential customer data, employee records. Security in Dallas is very, very tight. Almost no one has access to those servers except senior Titanic Properties officers."

"That's good ... I guess," Foreman said. "But if LeVander can't access those files, then how can we? And won't the video files of LeVander attacking you just disappear at midnight anyway when the next data dump updates, adds new files and eliminates old ones?"

Kiyomi nodded, trying to look serious, but looking more like the cat that swallowed the mouse.

"What?" Foreman said. "You know something. Tell me ... you know how to hack into that system."

"No, I don't," Kiyomi said innocently. "I did, however, a couple of years ago, visit Dallas when I first joined MightyMall. They used to—not anymore—send new security hires to Headquarters to see how things were done there. And while I was having lunch there one day, I noticed another Japanese person sitting nearby."

Kiyomi paused, then leaned closer to Foreman, as if confiding something important. "There aren't many Japanese in Dallas. As far as I know, there aren't any other Japanese at Titanic Properties. At least in Dallas."

Foreman grinned. "You are dragging this out on purpose, aren't you?"

"I am," Kiyomi said with a smirk. "So. I noticed this Japanese man having lunch and went over and introduced myself to him—don't worry, he's very nice but he's old and gray and kind of like my grandfather. So, anyway, we had a nice talk and agreed to keep in touch. And we have."

"And he's, what? A big shot at Titanic Properties?" Foreman said.

"Kind of," Kiyomi said. "As head of IT at Titanic Properties, he's in charge of *all* their computers." She shook her head, looking unhappy again.

"What?" Foreman said.

"I just wish I had thought of this before. Last week," Kiyomi said. "Before LeVander erased the Welcome Desk video of Batch, Lucy and the Turnblad woman."

"Don't beat yourself up about that," Foreman said.

"Still … apart from what happened last night, the whole cover-up from last week doesn't make sense. I hope the truth comes out eventually."

"Yeah, well, you never know. Something might turn up," Foreman said. "You have a plan for contacting this friend of yours and getting the data, I assume?"

"I do," Kiyomi said. "But you were right before: we should get back to work."

"Lunch at noon up at Five Guys again?"

"Sure," Kiyomi said. "See you there."

CHAPTER 44

Foreman had his hand in his pockets as he walked in a large circle around the food court, waiting for Kiyomi. He looked at his watch: ten past twelve. Kiyomi was late.

At a quarter past, Foreman dialed Kiyomi's cell. She picked up on the third ring.

"Hi," she said.

"Hi," Foreman said. "Did something come up?"

"Just a second, hold on," Kiyomi said. Foreman could hear background noise, footsteps. He scanned the food court again to see if Kiyomi was walking up behind him.

Foreman heard a door slam shut and then a car engine starting.

"You still there?" Kiyomi said.

"Yeah," Foreman said. "Are you in a car?"

"I am," Kiyomi said. "Sorry, give me a couple of minutes. I'll call you right back." She rang off before Foreman could respond.

Foreman's cell rang five minutes later.

"Hi, sorry," she said. "I'm back."

Foreman had ordered lunch and was sitting alone in front of *Five Guys Hamburgers.*

"What's going on?"

"Well." Kiyomi laughed without humor. "I was just fired from MightyMall."

"What? Are you okay?"

"I'm fine," she said. "Really. Shocked. Angry. But fine."

"Tell me."

"I was doing my normal rounds this morning. At about eleven o'clock SAC ordered me to Human Resources. When I got there, they sent me into Adele's office, you know, the HR Director? She was there, along with Lieutenant Rolvaag. Adele asked me to sit down, smiled, then told me that I was being fired for poor work performance."

"What did Rolvaag say?" Foreman said.

"He didn't say anything," Kiyomi said. "I looked at him once but he was looking down at the table. Adele pulled a page from my personnel file. She said it contained several reports of carelessness, complaints from colleagues, poor people skills, warnings by Major Power—"

"Power never complained about your work performance, did he?" Foreman said.

"I always thought he liked me," Kiyomi said. "Anyway, Adele said that the, uh, 'straw breaking the camel?'"

"The straw that broke the camel's back," Foreman said, helping Kiyomi with her English.

"That's it," Kiyomi said. "She said that the straw that broke the camel's back was when I left MightyMall last night before my shift was over."

Foreman said, "Did you tell them about LeVander trying to rape you?" He already knew the answer.

"I didn't," Kiyomi said, her voice small.

"That's okay," Foreman said. "Then what happened?"

"Rolvaag gave me a cardboard box, escorted me to my locker, watched me collect my things, and then escorted me to my car."

"He was with you when I called you before, wasn't he?" Foreman said.

"Yes."

"And he never said anything?" Foreman said. "No explanation? No support?"

"No," Kiyomi said. "Honestly, I think he was embarrassed. He shook my hand before I got in the car, then turned around and walked away."

"Probably as much of a surprise to him as it was to you," Foreman said. "Nothing he could do. Rolvaag's a stand-up guy."

"You mean a good guy?" Kiyomi said. "Yes, he was always kind to me."

Foreman shook his head in wonder. "Shit." What was MightyMall turning into?

"Yes," Kiyomi said.

"All right," Foreman said. "I'm off at five. Shall we meet?"

"Yes," Kiyomi said. "Come to my apartment after work. I'll make dinner. We still have work to do."

CHAPTER 45

Foreman was cruising the sixth floor when he saw Eric Lemke from maintenance walking through the south entrance by Costco. He noticed that Lemke wasn't wearing his ID badge—he knew Lemke was still employed at MightyMall but it was his job to notice things like that.

"Let me guess," Foreman said. "You forgot your ID badge, so security wouldn't let you through the outer perimeter and into the employee parking lot."

"Fucking things," Lemke said. "I always leave it in my car so I don't forget it. But me and the missus went to Missouri for the weekend and I left it home."

"Oh, yeah," Foreman said. "So you went after all. How was that?" Lemke was a crusty old cuss but Foreman liked him. Because Lemke was not in security, or a member of senior management, he wasn't supposed to know the identity of any of the X-Team members, but he had once seen Foreman assisting a heart attack victim before backing off when the EMTs arrived. They'd been casual friends ever since.

"Well, the weekend was fine," Lemke said.

"But you forgot to put the badge back in the car this morning," Foreman said.

"Fucking things," Lemke said, shaking his head. "So, what's the latest on Carolyn Batch? All I saw was a lot of blue tarps on Friday."

"Oh, that's right," Foreman said. "You've been gone." Foreman didn't know how much to share with Lemke. Probably good to go with the public line, he decided. "Everyone's pretty tightlipped. So far all we know is that it was Batch and one other woman. Looks like they fell off Lost Deck at the same time. Police aren't publicly guessing on a motive or cause yet. People are saying it was an accident, that Batch was trying to help the old lady and just ended up getting pulled over with her."

"Her mother, or something?"

"I don't think so," Foreman said. "Took them a while to identify the other woman because she wasn't carrying any ID. Some mall walker, probably. In pink sweats, no less. Say, remember that lady's handbag I was carrying last Thursday when I ran past you?"

Lemke stopped in his tracks. "Pink sweats?" Lemke looked like he had seen a ghost.

"That's right," Foreman said. "Turns out she owned that red handbag I found last Thursday. The driver's license in the bag had a photo, so they identified her that way. You know her?"

Lemke hesitated, then started walking again. "No, nothing like that," he said.

"What?" Foreman said. "You made a funny face when I mentioned her sweats. How come?"

"No, nothing." Lemke waved his arm, as if shooing away a fly. "I gotta get going."

Foreman watched Lemke hurry down the endless shopping avenue until he disappeared around the bend, like a ship slipping below the horizon.

"Didn't seem like nothing," Foreman muttered to himself.

Foreman had a difficult time maintaining job focus the rest of the afternoon. Kiyomi was attacked. Kiyomi was fired. Batch's death. Deleted video files. A slime-ball rapist now running the mall.

Foreman was hardly looking at anything else as he finished a circuit of six and walked down the escalator to five.

It wasn't so much *what* was on the deleted video files that nagged at Foreman but *why* LeVander had felt the need to delete them. All they showed were Lucy and Carolyn alone and then the two of them carting Ms. Turnblad around. What was so incriminating about that? And why the need to transfer Major Power all the way to China? If Foreman hadn't found that red bag, and Kiyomi hadn't told him of her odd encounter with Lucy by the Welcome Desk, he might not have thought anything was wrong. Odd things happen. But so many ... piling up ... there had to be a connection.

Foreman walked onto the escalator and bumped into a large, bald man wearing a Green Bay Packers team jacket.

"Hey," the man said. "Watch where the fuck you're walking."

"Sorry," Foreman said. The man glared at him.

I don't have time for this, Foreman thought. When they got to the bottom, Foreman saw which way Packers Guy turned, and went the opposite way.

"And Lemke reacting like that," Foreman muttered to himself. A woman standing in front of Lindt Chocolate turned at the sound of Foreman's voice. He ignored her.

Foreman shook his head. "What *was* up with Lemke?"

Lemke's behavior bothered Foreman. The way he reacted when Foreman had mentioned Greta Turnblad. No, that wasn't it. It was when he had mentioned what she was wearing: a pink sweat suit. Why would a pink sweat suit bother Lemke? *Bother wasn't the right word: Lemke looked scared.*

Foreman took out his mall-issued cell phone. The big mobile radios that uniformed officers carried were too conspicuous for undercover work.

Foreman punched the walkie-talkie function. "SAC," the voice said. "Carlson speaking."

"This is Foreman. Can I get a location for Eric Lemke of maintenance?" All the MightyMall mobile radios contained GPS chips, which SAC monitored.

"One second." Then: "Second floor, west. Looks like he's around the kiosk cluster."

"Thanks."

Lemke was kneeling in front of a small kiosk that was promoting Caribbean vacations.

Foreman waited until Lemke was putting away his tools before approaching.

From behind Lemke, Foreman said, "We need to talk."

"About what?" Lemke said, digging around in his toolbox. "Oh." He stood up. "I gotta get going." When he tried to push past, Foreman stepped in front of him.

"Eric," Foreman said. "I think you know something."

"Sorry," Lemke said, avoiding eye contact. "Don't know what you're talking about."

"About pink sweat pants," Foreman said.

Lemke stopped cold, looked around. Shoppers shopped. He pursed his lips together, stuck them out. Shook his head. "Don't mean nothing to me."

Foreman knew that he was onto something. But what? He took a stab in the dark. "You saw."

Lemke pinched his eyes closed, started to breath more rapidly.

Bingo!

"Eric," Foreman pushed harder. "You're not in trouble. Yet."

Lemke's shoulders slumped. "Not here. I'm taking a cigarette break on the parking ramp off the west entrance on the second floor in five minutes. Meet me there." Lemke picked up his heavy toolbox and walked off.

MightyMall was smoke-free, which created hardships for smoking Minnesotans in the winter that smoking Floridians were not likely to encounter. Guests who chose to smoke usually did so outside one of the first floor entrances, where taxi and bus pickups and drop-offs were. And for storekeepers and shoppers who had stuffed their coats in a locker, it was easy to dart outside for a quick puff, then race back in before their noses froze. At three o'clock the second floor exit onto the parking ramp at was relatively people-free. When Foreman arrived, Lemke was already there, the cigarette in his mouth already half smoked.

"Freezing out here," Foreman said. He had no overcoat. The temperature was in the teens; the parking ramp amplified the winds, making it feel colder.

"Just be glad you ain't a smoker," Lemke said. "I'm out here three frickin' times a day."

Foreman said, "Okay then. Eric, we're good friends but this is official business." It wasn't—he wasn't supposed to be working on this case—but Lemke didn't know that. "I need you to tell me everything you know. Now."

Lemke continued puffing his cigarette, back to the mall, gazing out at the sea of cars on the parking ramp.

"Right now, I'm the only one who knows," Foreman said. "But I can't sit on this forever."

"How much do you know?" Lemke said.

"Uh uh." Foreman shook his head. "This is your last chance. Spill everything now or the deal's off." He held his breath.

Lemke's arms were crossed, his hands jammed under his armpits trying to keep warm.

"Aw shit," Lemke said. "It's been bugging me the whole time. The whole frickin' time." Lemke's eyes betrayed his mounting panic. "I almost left a note on Friday but then Batch fell off the Lost Deck and splattered all over Gonzoland and everyone is running around like chickens with their heads cut off and I thought I'll do it later and then I went back to work and then I just forgot about it and then I went home." Out of breath, Lemke looked up at Foreman like a penitent seeking absolution. "Or maybe I pretended to forget about it, I don't know." Lemke's shoulders slumped. "I should've known I'd get caught."

Foreman was hugging himself, rocking back and forth on his heels, trying not to shiver. *A note? Get caught doing what?* He gave Lemke a noncommittal nod.

"I was even going to check on her, when I got in today, really I was. And then, if nobody else found her, I was going to leave that note. Really I was," Lemke said. "Then I ran into you, and found out the body's been found, and then … you know … what was the point?"

Check on her? On who? Found *her?*

Foreman's teeth were chattering. "Sure, I understand," Foreman said, not understanding anything. "I believe you. You were going to check on her." He nodded again, full of compassion.

"How did you find out, anyway?" Lemke said through the side of his mouth not holding his cigarette.

"The pink sweat pants," Hard-boiled Detective Foreman. "You know."

Lemke turned suddenly toward Foreman and frowned. "You don't know shit, do you? You been shittin' me this whole time." He dropped his cigarette and ground it with his work boot. "Aw shit."

Foreman edged between Lemke and the mall entrance. "I don't know *everything*, Eric, but I know *enough*," he said. "And I am freezing to death and tired of dicking around. If you don't fill me in on everything in the next thirty seconds I'm going straight to the police and they'll eventually piece it all together. That's the truth."

Lemke rubbed his hands together. "Then let's at least go stand under the heating elements by the elevator." The temperature was several degrees warmer, but they were still being buffeted by the cold winds.

Lemke told Foreman about finding a dead woman on the seventh floor.

Foreman's mind was spinning from information overload.

"So, she was dead ... you found her dead on Friday morning," Foreman said. "Way over on the catwalk near Haunted Hollow on the seventh floor. And you *didn't* move her body over to Lost Deck?" He looked hard into Lemke's eyes.

"Christ, no," Lemke said. "I swear on my kids. She was dead when I found her and I left her where she was."

Foreman held his stare for a moment longer. *I'm not a mind reader*, he said to himself, *or even a real cop. But Lemke just doesn't look guilty to me.*

"And this was five o'clock," Foreman said. "Friday morning."

"Around there," Lemke said. "I didn't check my watch. But yeah."

Foreman massaged the back of his neck, mostly to warm his hands. "Then how the hell did she get all the way over to the other side of the mall, already dead, and then fall off Lost Deck the same time as Carolyn Batch? Doesn't make any sense."

"I don't know," Lemke said, "and to be honest, I don't really want to know. Anybody hears that I found the body and didn't report it, I'm fucked."

Foreman had come to a decision. "Let's do this: give me your cell number; your personal cell." Lemke dug out a scrap of paper from his pants pocket and jotted down his number.

"I need time to make sense of all this," Foreman said. "But I promise you that, whatever happens, I'll keep your name out of it."

"Thanks, Mike, I appreciate that," Lemke said.

"I might need some more information," Foreman said. " And I might need you to do something for me, so keep your phone on."

"Fine," Lemke said. "Then can we go inside now? I think my toes are frostbitten."

CHAPTER 46

Foreman arrived at Kiyomi's apartment just before six.

Kiyomi opened the door and ran back to her stove. "Sorry to be so rude," she said. "I'm cooking."

"What smells so good?" Foreman said.

"I'm making *gyoza*," Kiyomi said. "Kind of like Chinese pot stickers. You're probably smelling sesame oil. I fry the *gyoza* in that."

As Foreman watched, Kiyomi place a round dinner plate over a frying pan full of perfectly arranged dumplings, put one hand on top of the plate, and flipped the whole thing over.

"*Voila*!" Kiyomi said. "Isn't that what American chefs say? *Voila*?"

"It is," Foreman said. "Maybe French chefs, too."

"I apologize for such a casual dinner tonight," Kiyomi said. "I took a nap and then it was too late to shop."

"This looks great," Foreman said. Kiyomi put the plate of *gyoza* on the dining table, then filled two small bowls with sticky rice and handed one to Foreman.

"I made a green salad, too." Kiyomi took a large bowl with lettuce, chopped carrots, sliced radishes and black olives out of the refrigerator. "I don't want to overdose you on Japanese food."

"You call this a casual dinner?" Foreman said. "Man."

Kiyomi plucked one of the *gyoza* from the cluster, dipped it into a small dish containing a black liquid and popped it into her mouth.

"See?" Kiyomi said. "Now you try."

Conversation over dinner started out innocuously enough—what ingredients were in the *gyoza*? Why do Japanese prefer their rice sticky? How did Kiyomi learn to cook so well?—but they were both anxious to get down to business. Foreman broke first.

"I've got news," Foreman said.

"Tell me." Kiyomi had heard Foreman use that phrase. She liked it.

Foreman told Kiyomi about his conversation with Eric Lemke. She listened silently, her eyes never leaving his.

"So, we don't know how Ms. Turnblad got onto that catwalk," Kiyomi said. "We could probably find out from the nearest surveillance cameras, except that LeVander has probably erased those, too."

"We don't know that for sure," Foreman said. "He probably didn't erase every video file in the mall for that day, just ones for cameras in the area near the Welcome Desk at the West Entrance."

"And we don't have those either," Kiyomi said. "If we only had a copy of that list we made..."

Foreman pushed back from the table and looked at Kiyomi. "About those files..." Foreman walked to Kiyomi's coat closest, took out his wallet. "Remember when we were in SAC looking at them? On Friday morning?"

"Yes."

"Remember the General Alert on Friday? And I told you to go ahead of me while I logged off?"

"Yes...."

"Well," Foreman said, pulling a thumb drive from his wallet. "I didn't log off right away."

Kiyomi's eyebrows arched with comprehension. "You didn't!"

"I did," Foreman said. "I copied several of the files we were looking at before going upstairs." He pointed at the thumb drive. "They're right here."

"Ooh you!" Kiyomi raced around the table, punched Foreman in the arm, then kissed him on the cheek. Even a kiss on the cheek from Kiyomi was electric.

"Why didn't you tell me?"

"Copying video files without signed permission is against mall policy, for one," Foreman said. "If I got in trouble, I didn't want to take you down with me."

"But why copy them in the first place?" Kiyomi said. "Did you already suspect something?"

"No, nothing so dramatic," Foreman said. "I just like to be safe. I lost a term paper in college one time. My hard drive crashed, erasing everything. Now I keep a drive in my wallet." He shrugged. "Seemed like a good time to use it. Just in case."

"Okay," Kiyomi said, back to business. "We know Ms. Turnblad was already dead early Friday morning. Do we know *when* she died?"

"No."

"Did they perform an au-top-sy," Kiyomi knew the word but had trouble pronouncing it, "on the women?"

"I heard that they didn't," Foreman said. "Cause of death was obvious."

"Carolyn Batch's cause of death was obvious. But Ms. Turnblad was already dead. Has anyone—the police—figured that out yet?"

"I don't think so. Or if they have, they're ignoring it."

"How do *you* think she died? Greta Turnblad."

"Heart attack? A stroke?" Foreman shook his head. "Maybe we'll never know. I think LeVander's got everyone in and outside the mall snowed. You think it's time we turned these clips over to the police?"

"I—oh my God!" Kiyomi looked at her watch, then at the clock on the wall. "I never called!"

"Who?"

"My friend in Dallas. Getting fired ... I got home, lay down for a short rest and suddenly I woke up and it was four o'clock. Then I started dinner and forgot all about Dallas. Darn!"

"Too late?"

Kiyomi ran into the kitchen and dialed a number on her cell phone. "I'll try."

Following several seconds of silence, Kiyomi looked over at Foreman and nodded vigorously. "Yes yes, he's— *Ah. Moshi moshi. Yamamoto-san? MightyMall no Nagata desu."*

Kiyomi spoke animatedly for several minutes. Foreman noticed that her voice had a higher pitch than when she spoke English, but he could make nothing of her conversation.

Finally she said, *"Arigato gozaimasu! Matte imasu!"*

"He's going to do it He's going to do it!" Kiyomi said. "He was reluctant at first—Japanese are not fond of breaking rules—but I told him what happened and he readily agreed. He confided that he never felt comfortable around LeVander, but that the owners seemed to like him."

Kiyomi walked toward her bedroom. "C'mon," she said. When Foreman hesitated, she smiled and said, "This is also my workroom. It's okay."

Foreman stood. "How's he getting you the files?"

"He's going to place them directly on my laptop. They are too big to email, so he needs direct access, which I am going to give him. He's emailing me instructions now."

Kiyomi sat at a small desk by her bed and logged on to her computer.

"Have a seat," she said.

Foreman could see no other chairs in the room. He noticed that Kiyomi's bed consisted of a queen-sized mattress, no box springs. He sat on it, barely off the floor, and looked around the room. Framed photos of friends, from college he supposed, next to the bed. A small aquarium on top of her dresser. A poster on the wall of....

"*Journey*?" Foreman said. "You have a poster of the band *Journey*? Aren't they from the 1980s? How have you even heard of them?"

Kiyomi spoke without turning. "The lead singer, Arnel Pineda, when I saw them at the Target Center, was really good." She turned to look at Foreman, smiled, then returned her attention to the laptop. "They've got a new album."

After several minutes, Kiyomi stopped typing and stood up. She looked happy. Relaxed. "All right. Yamamoto-san is my true friend. He now has control of my laptop and says I should leave it on for the next hour. It will take him that long to locate the video files of LeVander attacking me and place copies on my hard drive. He's also going to make his own backup copies just in case."

Kiyomi swiveled her chair around, looked at Foreman and smiled.

"We've got him," Foreman said.

"Thanks to you." She came over and sat next to him on the bed.

"Me?" Foreman said, feeling warm. "You're the one who just got us the files we need to nail his ass."

"*You* cheered me up this morning. *You* remembered the camera near his office—"

"You were tired, in shock from the attack—"

Kiyomi reached over and put her hand over Foreman's mouth. "*You* thought about photographing the bruises on my arm, which is more evidence. I was ready to fall apart. But you saved me."

"You know," Foreman said. "You could probably sue the bastard for a lot of money. The mall, too."

"You think so?"

"Sure. They'll will pay a fortune to keep this out of the press."

"No." Kiyomi closed her eyes, shook her head once and then opened them again. "I've been thinking. If you think we have enough evidence, I'd like to go to the police. I don't want to get rich for something like that; it would feel like dirty money to me. I just want to make sure LeVander can't do that to someone else." She rested her head on Foreman's shoulder. "Does that sound foolish to you?"

"Sounds *great* to me."

"And I don't think I want my old job back at MightyMall."

"I don't blame you." They sat in silence for a several seconds. The aquarium in the corner gurgled. "Do you know what you want to do next?"

"For a job, you mean?"

"Yeah."

Kiyomi shook her head again. "I think I'll take some time. I have some money saved up. Maybe I'll visit my parents. I did like my old job, though. And I know this will sound silly, but I enjoyed everything that happened the past week … except for … you know. I liked wondering about why Lucy was behaving so strangely, and searching for video files and trying to find Greta Turnblad and talking about it all with you." Kiyomi shrugged. "It was fun."

"It *was* fun, wasn't it?"

Kiyomi pulled away, now animated and full of energy. "It *was!* We were like real detectives. And it wasn't about *preventing* something from happening, it was about *finding* things, pieces of a puzzle that *we* had to put together."

Foreman nodded. "You weren't too bad at it either."

"And *you!"* Kiyomi punched him in the arm. "You are smart and honest and hard-working and loyal."

"You can tell all that in one week?"

"I can," Kiyomi said. "And besides, I've known you for several months." Kiyomi nuzzled Foreman's ear. "I've been watching you."

"You have?"

Kiyomi kissed Foreman on the mouth. "You are strong." She kissed him again, lips slightly apart, tongue searching, tentatively.

"And sexy," Foreman said, his voice hoarse. "Don't forget about sexy."

"And sexy," Kiyomi said, kissing his ear. "But for the next hour, until Yamamoto-san sends me those video files, we can do nothing about the future."

Kiyomi stood up, turned out the lights, and returned to bed.

"I thought you Japanese women were supposed to be shy," Foreman said.

"Yes, Kiyomi said, innocently. "I've heard that too."

Slightly over an hour later, Kiyomi climbed quietly out of bed and flipped open her laptop. She read an email and then closed the lid, removing the last source of light in the room.

"Damn," Foreman said. "I was enjoying the silhouette."

"I thought you were asleep." Kiyomi climbed back in bed and insinuated herself against Foreman's body.

"Worn out," he said. "Not asleep." Then, "What were you doing?"

"Checking my email," Kiyomi said. "The files are all there, just as Yamamoto-san promised." She kissed Foreman hard on the mouth. "We've won." She rested her hand on Foreman's stomach, damp with perspiration, admiring his muscle tone.

"Maybe too early to say we've won," Foreman said. "But we sure know a lot of stuff that will interest a lot of people. Not everyone at the mall is going to like what we have. The police will be pretty interested, though."

"What are you going to do? Will you keep working at the mall?"

Foreman stared at the ceiling, relaxed. "For now. Jobs aren't that easy to come by these days and I don't have much money saved up. But I have a feeling … even if the owners don't drum up some excuse for firing me, my days at MightyMall are numbered."

"Numbered," Kiyomi said. "You mean you will leave soon."

"Sooner or later. Yeah."

Kiyomi sat up on one elbow. "Maybe that lottery ticket you bought me was a winner."

Foreman chuckled. "That would be nice." He enjoyed the warmth of Kiyomi's body next to his, her soft skin.

"You think I won?" Kiyomi said.

"Nobody wins those things." Foreman brushed several strands of hair from Kiyomi's eyes. "It was a gag, mostly."

Kiyomi sat up suddenly. "How do I know if I won or not?"

"You haven't checked yet?" Foreman said. "The drawing was last Saturday."

Kiyomi shook her head, now fully alert. "Show me. Show me."

"Thousands of people buy tickets, you know. Your chances are infinitesimal." He was pretty sure she didn't know that word, so was about to explain it—

"It's *my* ticket. Let's play." Foreman couldn't see Kiyomi's face but imagined her lower lip was now sticking out in a playful pout.

"Fine," Foreman said. "You have the ticket?"

"Wait!" Kiyomi lept out of bed and ran to the living room. Even in near darkness, Foreman found it difficult to take his eyes off her.

"I put it on the refrigerator with a magnet," she called.

"Just don't get your hopes up too high," Foreman called back. "If you're lucky you might win a couple dollars."

"Here it is!" Kiyomi ran back into the bedroom, switched on a small lamp and slid back under the covers. "Show me." She handed Foreman the ticket. "What's next?"

Foreman squinted as his eyes adjusted to the light. He found his attention drawn to one of Kiyomi's breasts that the covers had failed to cover.

"My ticket?" Kiyomi said, gently redirecting Foreman's gaze with her hand.

"Sorry." Foreman studied the lottery ticket. "Okay, here's the date of your drawing and here are the numbers for this ticket. You just log on to the website, find the proper date and then see what the winning numbers were."

"How much can I win?" Kiyomi said.

Foreman shrugged. "If all of them match? I don't know. A couple of million dollars, maybe. I think it varies each time. But you can also win something if just a few of the numbers match."

"So I must match these numbers here," Kiyomi said, pointing at her ticket, "with what I find on the website."

"That's right."

"Great!" Kiyomi said, jumping out of bed again. "Let's check." She ran to a dresser, pulled out a T-shirt and boxer shorts, put them on and walked over to her laptop.

"You log on while I go pee," Foreman said. He gave Kiyomi the web address of the Minnesota State lottery and then padded off to the bathroom.

It wasn't until he was inside that he noticed he had developed another erection. "Hey, it's not *my* fault," he muttered to himself. "*She's* the one who looks so good, who is so…" he shook his head searching for the right word, "*alive*." Not wishing to spray all over Kiyomi's bathroom, he decided to pee from a sitting position.

"What was that?" Kiyomi called from the bedroom.

"Nothing," Foreman called back. "Just talking to myself." He imagined running on a treadmill—Foreman hated treadmills but depended on them to keep in shape during the winter—in an effort to make his erection go away.

He heard Kiyomi scream.

"What?" Foreman yelled. He flushed the toilet and ran into the bedroom.

"Usso! Atatteru! Usso! Atatteru! Attateru to omoukedo … Mike! Come here!" Kiyomi was alternately looking at her laptop screen and waving Foreman to come over.

"What happened?" He thought he knew already: Kiyomi had misread the numbers and mistakenly believed she had won something.

"Hora!" Kiyomi said. *"Mite! Hayaku mite!* Look! Look at the screen."

"Okay," Foreman said. "Let's not get too excited here." He crouched down next to Kiyomi's chair and peered at the screen. "Okay, you've got the right date selected. Good." Kiyomi was bouncing up and down on the chair, her hand over her mouth. She moaned liked a gagged hostage.

"Can I see the ticket?" Foreman said.

Kiyomi waved the ticket in front of Foreman's face. He gently snatched it out of her hand and placed it on the desk where they both could see it.

"Okay." He found the ticket numbers. "Now let's compare them with what you've got up on the screen."

Kiyomi froze, unable to move out of fear it would bring bad luck.

"All right," Foreman said, nodding. "Oh, *good*. The first two … no, the first three numbers match." He frowned down at the ticket. "No, wait a second." He looked up at the screen. "This can't be. Let me check again." He held the ticket up to the screen, directly next to the winning numbers displayed on the website.

"No way," he said, shaking his head. "No frickin' *way*!" Foreman turned to Kiyomi. "Ms. Kiyomi Nagata, you've just—"

Kiyomi leapt out of her chair and tackled Foreman before he could finish, causing him to fall backward on the floor, her knees narrowly missing his family jewels.

"Really?" Kiyomi said. "Is it true?"

Smiling up at Kiyomi, he said, "Looks like you've just won $3.2 million."

Kiyomi lay flat on top of Foreman and began showering his face and neck with a barrage of kisses. Foreman gladly bore her weight, happy at the change of fortune of his new … *girlfriend?* After what she had been through, she deserved a break.

The pace of Kiyomi's attack slowed. She brushed her lips lightly back and forth across Foreman's nose, eyes, cheeks. She lifted her head slightly, her face now an inch above his, her hair getting in his eyes.

"No," Kiyomi said. "*We've* won."

CHAPTER 47

One Year Later

On the morning of Tuesday, November 15th at just past seven o'clock, a nice-looking young woman with shoulder-length blond hair tied back in a ponytail strode purposefully down the stairs of the modest bed & breakfast she owned in Gilford, New Hampshire.

A late autumn breeze rustled the few crisp leaves that clung tenaciously to the maple trees in the front yard. It was 40 degrees, unusually warm for this time of year, and the light dusting of snow that had fallen the previous night was now mostly gone.

The young woman used to keep her bangs long to conceal persistent acne, but her complexion had cleared up over the past year and she now rather liked showing her face. She'd also taken to dying her hair a lighter color.

She had purchased the Longmeadow Inn about nine months ago, with part of a generous severance package she'd received from her previous employer. She didn't like talking about it much.

Two of her guests, Josh and Tina Pearce, were sitting in the sunroom, drinking coffee and enjoying the early morning sunshine. The Pearces had been staying a week at a time, two or three times a year since before the young woman had purchased the inn.

"Feel like some waffles?" the young woman said.

"No thanks," Tina, called back over her shoulder. "We're heading over to Kittery today to do some shopping." Kittery, Maine was famous for its outlet malls.

"Well aren't you the brave ones," the young woman said, pouring herself some coffee and joining her guests in the sunroom. "That's a ninety-minute drive in the summer. You sure you want to risk it this time of year? You could get caught in a storm."

"We'll be fine," Gene said. "Weather Channel says no snow for the next several days at least. Good for us, bad for you." He shrugged in apology. There hadn't been any significant snowfall so far this year, which meant the ski resorts weren't open yet, which in turn meant no business for the Longmeadow Inn. The Pearces had been the only guests the previous evening.

"Say, Lucy," Tina said, turning around in her chair. "Why don't you join us—make a day of it! We'll all do some shopping, have some lobster. We'll have you back before nighttime. It'll be fun."

Lucy gazed out at the window, thinking, not for the first time, how much she loved the trees, the mountains, the peace.

"Gosh, Tina, that's awfully nice of you to offer," Lucy said. "The thing is—and I know I'm probably the only person in the world who feels like this—I just don't enjoy the big shopping malls all that much." She took a sip of her coffee and headed back into the kitchen.

"Me neither," Josh said. "My wife doesn't give me much of choice though."

Tina poked Josh in the ribs. "Oh *you*. You're my official chauffeur and number one bag carrier." She leaned over and gave her husband a peck on the cheek, which he gladly accepted.

"Give me a call when you folks you leave Kittery," Lucy said. "I'll have a nice dinner waiting for you when you get back."

In Albany, New York, the grand opening of the new Tim & Kevin's Minnesota Style Pizza on Central Avenue was drawing rave reviews from the local press and long lines from diners eager to sample the restaurant's signature pizza, *Lutefisk with Cream of Wild Rice Supreme.* When asked about the chain's skyrocketing popularity—the Albany location was the company's twelfth to open in six months—co-owner Tim said, "Oh it's the taste for sure, you betcha. That and because of that big Hollywood movie star. She stopped by our first shop while filming her movie, *A Prairie Home Companion: The Next Generation,* and she says our pizza was the best she'd ever eaten. Ya, for sure, that was pretty sweet publicity for us."

The man entered the 6-by-10-foot cell, head down, carrying his prison-issue blankets and sheets and sat down on the bottom bunk and sighed.

After a lengthy court case, the man had been convicted of attempted extortion, assault and criminal sexual misconduct, which his lawyer had negotiated down from attempted rape as part of a plea bargain. The trial had lasted longer than most onlookers expected—the prosecution had video footage of the attack, plus testimony by his victim—what was there to dispute? Rumors ran rampant that a second, unnamed witness, who the media speculated had information pertinent to the deaths of Carolyn Batch and Greta Turnblad, had refused to testify after receiving a huge financial settlement from MightyMall's owners.

The man was found guilty and sentenced to 8 to 12 years in the Minnesota Correctional Facility in Stillwater.

The upper bunk creaked as its occupant rolled, jumped to the floor and padded over to the sink. The man looked at his cellmate's back. A sleeveless T-shirt revealed massive arms covered with tattoos. His clean-shaven head was adorned with an array of blue stars. LeVander figured the guy had to be four or five inches taller than he was and weigh over three hundred pounds.

"Fuckin' giant," LeVander muttered to himself. "All I need."

The Giant splashed water on his face and straightened up, flexing his shoulders.

Might as well get this over with, LeVander thought, visions of being orally and anally violated dancing unwanted through his head. *Maybe I can bribe him to be my fucking bodyguard.* He held out a pack of cigarettes. "Hey. I'm LeVander."

The Giant was still for several seconds, then turned slowly. The first thing LeVander noticed was the eye: a tattoo of a star surrounded a gaping hole where the right eye should have been.

"Karl," the Giant said, in a soft voice. "How nice to see you again."

The meeting in Guanzhou with the American Director of Security at The Great Mall of China project had gone well. Groundbreaking was set for the following day.

"Then you are *satisfied* with personnel we have *supplied* for your security department, Major Powers?" Zhang Wei was tall and slim and looked like a fashion model.

"They're great," Powers said. "Easy to train. They're all in good shape. They do what I tell 'em. Most of them speak pretty good English, which is a help to me." Powers chuckled. "A little stiff, maybe. But great listeners."

"Stiff?" Zhang Wei said. "In what way?"

"Oh, nothing to worry about," Powers said. "It's just that they always stand at attention when I call their names, look straight ahead, never smile." Powers waved his hand. "I can't complain, really. I'd swear, though, that some of them have military experience."

"Excuse me a moment," Zhang Wei said. He turned to his colleague and spoke to him in Chinese for several moments.

Powers noticed that the older gentleman appeared to be upset.

"Fix this!" said Qiao Shi, Assistant Director of Intelligence of The Chinese People's Liberation Army, to his subordinate. "Bring everyone in first thing tomorrow and teach them how to behave less like soldiers and more like civilians. The American will never agree to send anyone to MightyMall for additional training if he knows they are actually engaged in covert activities for the Chinese government."

"I'll take care of it," Zhang Wei said.

Turning back to the American: "My apologies, Major Powers. My boss, Mr. Qiao, wants to *ensure* that our employment agency supplies you with only the most *qualified* candidates for your *security* department. He is concerned that you may be un*happy*."

Powers chuckled. "Please tell him that everyone is fine and that I appreciate the cooperation I've received from your company." Powers had learned to speak more diplomatically since moving to China a year ago.

Zhang Wei spoke again to Qiao Shi, who nodded once sharply.

Powers put out his hand as he stood up. "I am confident that what we achieve here at Great Mall of China will lead to much more interaction between our two countries."

"Indeed," Zhang Wei said, happily. "Indeed."

The four students were clustered around their cadaver, assigned their second year of medical school. They had done enough dissection of animals to overcome their initial squeamishness at cutting into a human body.

They were studying the human brain this rotation. Emily had been assigned the honor of sawing off the top of the skull. The deceased woman, approximately eighty years old, had suffered extensive bone and organ damage from a fall that, the medial students assumed, had been the cause of death. All they knew for sure was that the woman had stated in her will that her body was to be donated to the Selby University Medical School.

They were studying the parietal lobe when Emily discovered something unusual. "Ooh. Guys? Look at this."

She pointed at one section of a blood vessel that looked like a popped inner tube. "That's a burst aneurysm, isn't it?"

No one had noticed Professor Krenz walk up behind them. "Very good," he said. Professor Krenz was gratified to see Emily excelling in her studies despite the loss of her aunt the previous year in a horrific incident at one of the area shopping malls.

"Show off!" One of Emily Batch's lab mates punched her good-naturedly in the arm.

The Grand Opening party for *Kokusai Investigations* was a spectacular success. Over 50 guests had attended; most were friends, some were friends of friends and more than a few were big names that Mike and Kiyomi had invited on a whim. One man was an executive from a large, locally-based food company. A couple of bigwigs came from a medical device maker.

Mike and Kiyomi's modest office—big enough for two desks, a refrigerator and a table for their copier/fax—was unable to accommodate a crowd so they had rented the conference room on the first floor of their office building on York Avenue. Mike had wondered privately if including the Japanese word *kokusai*—meaning "international"—would be too foreign sounding for Minnesotans, but deferred to Kiyomi's intuition. After Karl LeVander's trial had ended, one local TV station had run a follow-up story on the spectacular death of Carolyn Batch a year earlier—Greta Turnblad was hardly mentioned—and a reporter had interviewed both Mike and Kiyomi. The rehashing of their part in LeVander's downfall had naturally raised the question of "What are you both doing now?" which led to "Well, we've just opened a detective agency ..." generating several dozen inquiries from viewers.

The two partners—Mike and Kiyomi both enjoyed using that word—had spent the past thirty minutes throwing away paper plates and plastic cups and wrapping up leftover food. Mike picked up two large garbage bags. "These are the last two. I'll take them out to the dumpsters and see you in the lobby."

"Sounds good," Kiyomi said. "Sounds good" was one of her favorite new expressions, one she had picked up from Mike. "I'll go upstairs and make sure the office is locked and all the lights are off."

Kiyomi scanned her emails, decided none were urgent, and shut down her computer. She grabbed their overcoats—they'd gotten several inches of slushy snow earlier in the day and it was now damp and chilly—and was about to turn off the lights when she noticed a piece of paper in the fax tray. It was a copy of an article from a Japanese newspaper.

Kiyomi was leaning against her desk, still reading the article when Mike walked into their office.

"What have you got there?" Mike said. At 11 P.M. he and Kiyomi were the only ones left in the building. He knew she could handle herself, but worried about her anyway.

Kiyomi looked back down at the piece of paper in her hand and shook her head. "I'm not sure."

Mike sat down in the chair at Kiyomi's desk. He'd been taking Japanese lessons at the U since January–*Hell,* he figured, *if I ever meet her family someday, I'd like to not sound like a complete idiot.* Mike couldn't recognize more than a few words, but was able to confirm that it wasn't Chinese or some other language.

"Ooh, I know that one." Mike said, pointing at one of the *kanji* characters in the headline. "That's 'murder,' isn't it?"

Kiyomi nodded her head absently. Normally she was full of encouragement and congratulations when Mike spoke or wrote something correctly in Japanese—no success was trivial to her.

Kiyomi finally breathed deeply through her nose and turned to look at Mike. "This is very strange."

Mike raised his eyebrows slightly. *What is?*

"This says that the murder of two Japanese men in Minneapolis last month remains unsolved." Kiyomi looked again at the article as she spoke. "They were engineers for a big Japanese construction company involved in the *Rodinia* project, MightyMall's big expansion."

"I haven't read about any Japanese men being murdered," Mike said. "Have you?"

"No," Kiyomi said. "I haven't. And this fax has no identification. Nothing about who sent it. Just blank except for the article itself."

They both jumped as the telephone next to Kiyomi rang. Mike looked at his watch; pretty late for a phone call.

Kiyomi let it ring twice before picking up. "Kokusai Investigations. May I help you?"

The voice on the other line spoke to Kiyomi in Japanese. She was silent, occasionally uttering a clipped, "*Hai"* which meant that she was following what the speaker said. After several minutes, Kiyomi replaced the phone in its cradle.

"What was that all about?" Mike said.

"I'm not sure," Kiyomi said, picking up the fax again, "but we may have our first client."

Manufactured By: RR Donnelley
Momence, IL USA
September, 2010